Rumor
HAS IT

Jill Shalvis

BERKLEY
New York

BERKLEY
An imprint of Penguin Random House LLC
penguinrandomhouse.com

Copyright © 2013 by Jill Shalvis
Excerpt from *Animal Magnetism* copyright © 2011 by Jill Shalvis
Penguin Random House supports copyright. Copyright fuels creativity, encourages
diverse voices, promotes free speech, and creates a vibrant culture. Thank you for buying
an authorized edition of this book and for complying with copyright laws by not
reproducing, scanning, or distributing any part of it in any form without permission.
You are supporting writers and allowing Penguin Random House to continue to
publish books for every reader.

BERKLEY and the BERKLEY & B colophon are registered trademarks of
Penguin Random House LLC.

ISBN: 9780593641644

Berkley mass-market edition / November 2013
Berkley trade paperback edition / April 2024

Printed in the United States of America
1st Printing

Book design by Kristin del Rosario

This is a work of fiction. Names, characters, places, and incidents either are the product
of the author's imagination or are used fictitiously, and any resemblance to actual persons,
living or dead, business establishments, events, or locales is entirely coincidental.

One

K ate Evans would've sold her soul for a stress-free morning, but either her soul wasn't worth much or whoever was in charge of granting wishes was taking a nap. With her phone vibrating from incoming texts—which she was doing her best to ignore—she shoved her car into park and ran across the lot and into the convenience store. "Duct tape?" she called out to Meg, the clerk behind the counter.

Meg had pink and purple tie-dyed hair, had enough piercings to ensure certain drowning if she ever went swimming, and was in the middle of a heated debate on the latest *The Voice* knock-out rounds with another customer. But she stabbed a finger in the direction of aisle three.

Kate snatched a roll of duct tape, some twine, and then, because she was also weak, a rack of chocolate mini donuts for later. Halfway to the checkout, a bin of fruit tugged at her good sense so she grabbed an apple. Dumping everything on the counter, she fumbled through her pockets for cash.

Meg rang her up and bagged her order. "You're not going to murder someone, are you?"

Kate choked out a laugh. "What?"

"Well . . ." Meg took in Kate's appearance. "Librarian outfit. Duct tape. Twine. I know you're the math whiz around here, but it all adds up to a *Criminal Minds* episode to me."

Kate was wearing a cardigan, skirt, leggings, and—because she'd been in a hurry and they'd been by the front door—snow boots. She supposed with her glasses and hair piled up on her head she might resemble the second-grade teacher that she was, and okay, maybe the snow boots in May were a little suspect. "You watch too much TV," Kate said. "It's going to fry your brain."

"You know what fries your brain? Not enough sex." Meg pointed to her phone. "Got that little tidbit right off the Internet on my last break."

"Well, then it must be true," Kate said.

Meg laughed. "That's all I'm saying."

Kate laughed along with her, grabbed her change and her bag, and hurried to the door. She was late. As the grease that ran her family's wheel, she needed to get to her dad's house to help get her little brother, Tommy, ready for school and then to coax the Evil Teen into even going to school. The duct tape run wasn't to facilitate that, or to kill anyone, but to make a camel, of all things, for an afterschool drama project Tommy had forgotten to mention was due today.

Kate stepped outside and got slapped around by the wind. The month of May had burst onto the scene like a PMSing Mother Nature, leaving the beautiful, rugged Bitterroot Mountains, which loomied high overhead, dusted with last week's surprise snow.

Spring in Sunshine, Idaho, was MIA.

Watching her step on the wet, slippery asphalt, she pulled out her once again vibrating phone just to make sure no one was dying. It was a text from her dad and read: Hurry, it's awake.

It being her sister. The other texts were from Ashley herself. She was upset because she couldn't find her cheerleading top, and also, did Kate know that Tommy was talking to his invisible friend in the bathroom again?

Kate sighed and closed her eyes for a brief second, which was all it took for her snow boots to slip. She went down like a sack of cement, her phone flying one way, her bag the other as she hit the ground butt first with teeth-jarring impact.

"Dammit!" She took a second for inventory—no massive injuries. That this was in thanks to not having lost those five pounds of winter brownie blues didn't make her feel any better. The cold seeped through her tights and the sidewalk abraded the bare skin of her palms. Rolling to her hands and knees, she reached for her keys just as a set of denim-clad legs came into her field of vision.

The owner of the legs crouched down, easily balancing on the balls of his feet. A hand appeared, her keys centered in the big palm. Tilting her head up, she froze.

Her polite stranger wore a baseball cap low over his eyes, shadowing most of his face and dark hair, but she'd know those gunmetal gray eyes anywhere. And then there was the rest of him. Six foot two and built for trouble in army camo cargoes, a black sweatshirt, and his usual bad-ass attitude, the one that tended to have men backing off and women checking for drool; there was no mistaking Griffin Reid, the first guy she'd ever fallen for. Of course she'd been ten at the time . . .

"That was a pretty spectacular fall," he said, blocking her from standing up. "Make sure you're okay."

Keep your cool, she told herself. *Don't speak, just nod.* But her mouth didn't get the memo. "No worries, a man's forty-seven percent more likely to die from a fall than a woman." The minute the words escaped, she bit her tongue, but of course it was too late. When she got nervous, she spouted inane science facts.

And Griffin Reid made her very nervous.

"I'm going to ask you again," he said, moving his tall, linebacker body nary an inch as he pinned her in place with nothing more than his steady gaze. "Are you okay?"

Actually, no, she wasn't. Not even close. Her pride was cracked, and quite possibly her butt as well, but that wasn't what had her kneeling there on the ground in stunned shock. "You're . . . home."

He smiled grimly. "I was ordered back by threat of bodily harm if I was late to the wedding."

He was kidding. No one ordered the tough, stoic badass Griffin to do anything, except maybe Uncle Sam since he was some secret army demolitions expert who'd been in Afghanistan for three straight tours. But his sister, Holly, was getting married this weekend. And if there was anyone more bossy or determined than Griffin, it was his baby sister. Only Holly could get her reticent brother halfway around the world for her vows.

Kate had told herself that as Holly's best friend and maid of honor, she would absolutely not drool over Griffin if he showed up. And she would especially not make a fool of herself.

Too late, on both counts.

Again she attempted to get up, but Griffin put a big, tanned, work-roughened hand on her thigh, and she felt herself tingle.

Well, damn. Meg was right—too little sex fried the brain.

Clearly misunderstanding her body's response, Griffin squeezed gently as if trying to soothe, which of course had the opposite effect, making things worse. Embarrassed, she tried to pull free, but still effortlessly holding her, Griffin's steely gray eyes remained steady on hers.

"Take stock first," he said, voice low but commanding. "What hurts? Let me see."

Since the only thing that hurt besides her pride was a part of her anatomy that she considered No Man's Land, hell would freeze over before she'd "let him see." "I'm fine. Really," she added.

Griffin took her hand and easily hoisted her up, studying her in that assessing way of his. Then he started to turn her around, presumably to get a three-hundred-and-sixty degree view, but she stood firm. "Seriously," she said, backing away, "I'm good." And if she weren't, if she'd actually broken her butt, she'd die before admitting it, so it didn't matter. Bending to gather up her belongings, she carefully sucked in her grimace of pain.

"I've got it," Griffin said, and scooped up the duct tape and donuts. He looked like maybe he was going to say something about the donuts, but at the odd vibrating noise behind them, he turned. "Your phone's having a seizure," he said.

Panicked siblings, no doubt. After all, there was a camel to create out of thin air and a cheerleading top to locate, and God only knew what disaster her father was coming up with for breakfast.

Griffin offered the cell phone, and Kate stared down at it thinking how much easier her day would go if it had smashed to pieces when it hit the ground.

"Want me to step on it a few times?" he asked, sounding amused. "Kick it around?"

Startled that he'd read her so easily, she snatched the phone. When her fingers brushed his, an electric current sang up her arms and went straight to her happy spots without passing Go. Ignoring them, she turned to her fallen purse. Of course the contents had scattered. And of course the things that had fallen out were a tampon and condom.

It was how her day was going.

She began cramming things back into the purse, the phone, the donuts, the duct tape, the condom, and the tampon.

The condom fell back out.

"I've got it." Griffin's mouth twitched as he tossed it into her purse for her. "Duct tape and a Trojan," he said. "Big plans for the day?"

"The Trojans built protective walls around their city," she said. "Like condoms. That's where the name Trojan comes from."

His mouth twitched. "Gotta love those Trojans. Do you carry the condom around just to give people a history lesson?"

"No. I—" He was laughing at her. Why was she acting like such an idiot? She was a teacher, a good one, who bossed around seven- and eight-year-olds all day long. She was in charge, and she ran her entire world with happy confidence.

Except for this with Griffin. Except for anything with Griffin.

"Look at you," he said. "Little Katie Evans, all grown up and carrying condoms."

"One," she said. "Only one condom." It was her emergency, wishful-thinking condom. "And I go by Kate now."

He knew damn well she went by Kate and had ever since she'd hit her teens. He just enjoyed saying "Little Katie Evans" like it was all one word, as if she were still that silly girl who'd tattled on him for putting the frogs in the pond at one of his mom's elegant luncheons, getting him grounded for a month.

Or the girl who, along with his nosy sister, Holly, had found his porn stash under his bed at the ranch house and gotten him grounded for two months.

"Kate," he said as if testing it out on his tongue, and she had no business melting at his voice. None. Her only excuse was that she hadn't seen him much in the past few years. There'd been a few short visits, a little Facebook interaction, and the occasional Skype conversation if she happened to be with Holly when he called home. Those had always been with him in uniform on Holly's computer, looking big, bad, and distracted.

He wasn't in uniform now, but she could check off the big, bad, and distracted. The early gray dawn wasn't doing her any favors, but he could look good under any circumstances. Even with his baseball hat, she could see that his dark hair was growing out, emphasizing his stone eyes and hard jaw covered with a five-o'clock shadow. To say that he looked good was like saying the sun might be a tad bit warm on its surface. How she'd forgotten the physical impact he exuded in person was beyond her. He was solid, sexy male to the core.

His gaze took her in as well, her now windblown hair and mud-spattered leggings stuffed into snow boots—she wasn't exactly at her best this morning. When he stepped back to go, embarrassment squeezed deep in her gut. "Yeah," she said, gesturing over her shoulder in the vague direction of her car. "I've gotta go, too—"

But Grif wasn't leaving; he was bending over and picking up some change. "From your purse," he said, and dropped it into her hand.

She looked down at the two quarters and a dime, and then into his face. She'd dreamed of that face. Fantasized about it. "There are 293 ways to make change for a dollar," she said before she could bite her tongue. Dammit. She collected bachelor of science degrees. She was smart. She was good at her job. She was happy.

And ridiculously male challenged . . .

Griffin gave a playful tug on an escaped strand of her hair. "You never disappoint," he said. "Good to see you again."

And then he was gone.

Two

Five minutes later Kate pulled up to her dad's place. One glance in the rearview mirror at her still flushed cheeks and bright eyes told her that she hadn't gotten over her tumble in the parking lot.

Or the run-in with Griffin.

"You're ridiculous," she told her reflection. "You are not still crushing on him."

But she so was.

With a sigh, she reached for the weekly stack of casserole dishes she'd made to get her family through the week without anyone having to actually be in charge. She got out of her car, leaving the keys in it for Ashley, who'd drive it to her private high school just outside of town.

Tommy stood in the doorway waiting. He wore a green hoodie and had a fake bow and arrow set slung over his chest and shoulder.

"Why are you all red in the face?" he asked. "Are you sick?"

She touched her still burning cheeks. The Griffin Reid Effect, she supposed. "It's cold out here this morning."

The seven-year-old accepted this without question. "Did you get the tape?"

"I did," she said. "Tommy—"

"I'm not Tommy. I'm the Green Arrow."

She nodded. "Green Arrow. Yes, I got the tape, Green Arrow."

"I still don't see how duct tape is going to help us make a camel," he said, trailing her into the mudroom.

She refrained from telling him the biggest aid in making a camel for the school play would've been to give her more warning than a panicked five A.M. phone call. Instead she set down the casserole dishes on the bench to shrug out of her sweater as she eyed him. She could tell he'd done as she'd asked and taken a shower, because his dark hair was wet and flattened to his head, emphasizing his huge brown eyes and pale face. "Did you use soap and shampoo?"

He grimaced and turned to presumably rectify the situation, dragging his feet like she'd sent him to the guillotine.

Kate caught him by the back of his sweatshirt. "Tonight'll do," she said, picking back up the casseroles and stepping into the living room.

Evidence of the second-grade boy and the high school–junior girl living here was all over the place. Abandoned shoes were scattered on the floor; sweatshirts and books and various sporting equipment lay on furniture.

Her dad was in the midst of the chaos, sitting on the couch squinting at his laptop. Eddie Evans was rumpled, his glasses perched on top of his head. His khakis were worn and frayed at the edges. His feet were bare. He looked like Harry Potter at age fifty. "Stock's down again," he said, and sighed.

Since he said the same thing every morning, Kate moved into the kitchen. No breakfast. She went straight to the coffeemaker and got that going. Ten minutes later her dad wandered in. "You hid them again," he said.

She handed him a cup of coffee and a plate of scrambled egg whites and wheat toast before going back to wielding the duct tape to create the damn camel. "You know what the doctor said. You can't have them."

His mouth tightened. "I need them."

"Dad, I know it's hard," she said softly, "but you've been so strong. And we need you around here for a long time to come yet."

He shoved his fingers through his hair, which only succeeded in making it stand up on end. "You've got that backward, don't you?"

"Aw. Now you're just kissing up." She hugged him. "You're doing great, you know. The doc said your cholesterol's coming down already, and you've only been off potato chips for a month."

He muttered something about where his cholesterol could shove it, but he sat down to eat his eggs. "What is that?" he asked, gesturing to the lump on the table in front of him.

"A camel." It had taken her two pillows, a brown faux pashmina and a couple of stuffed animals tied together with twine, but she actually had what she thought was a passable camel-shaped lump.

Ashley burst into the kitchen wearing a way-too-short skirt, a skimpy camisole top, and enough makeup to qualify for pole dancing. In direct opposition to this image, she was sweetly carrying Channing Tatum, the bedraggled black-and-white stray kitty she'd recently adopted from the animal center where she volunteered after school. Contradiction, meet thy queen.

Channing took one look at the "camel" and hissed.

"What the hell is that?" Ashley asked of the makeshift prop, looking horrified as she cuddled Channing.

"Don't swear," Kate said. "And it's a camel. And also, you're going out in that outfit over my dead body."

Ashley looked down at herself. "What's wrong with it?"

"First of all, you'll get hypothermia. And second of all, no way in hell."

Ashley narrowed her overdone eyes. "Why do you get to swear and I don't?"

"Because I earned the right with age and wisdom."

"You're twenty-eight," Ashley said, and shrugged. "Yeah, you're right. You're old. Did you find my cheerleading top?"

Kate tossed it to her.

Ashley turned up her nose at the scrambled eggs, though she fed Channing a piece of turkey bacon before thrusting a piece of paper at Kate. "You can sign it or I can forge dad's signature."

"Hey," Eddie said from the table. He pushed his glasses farther up on his nose. "I'm right here."

Kate grabbed the paper from Ashley and skimmed it. Permission slip to . . . skip state testing. "No." Skipping testing was the last thing the too-smart, underachieving, overly dramatic teen needed to do.

"Dad," Ashley said, going for an appeal.

"Whatever Kate says," Eddie said.

"You can't skip testing," Kate said. "Consider it practice for your SATs for college. You want to get the heck out of here and far away from all of us, right? This is step one."

Ashley rolled her eyes so hard that Kate was surprised they didn't roll right out of her head.

Tommy bounced into the room. He took one look at the camel and hugged it close. "It's perfect," he declared. Then he promptly inhaled up every crumb on his plate. He smiled at Kate as he pushed his little black-rimmed glasses farther up on his nose, looking so much like a younger, happier version of their dad that it tightened her throat.

A car horn sounded from out front. Kate glanced at the clock and rushed Tommy and Ashley out the door. Ashley got into Kate's car and turned left, heading toward her high school. Tommy and Kate got into the waiting car, which turned right to head to the elementary school.

Their driver was Ryan Stafford, Kate's second-best friend and the principal of the elementary school.

And her ex.

He must have had a district meeting scheduled because he was in a suit today, complete with tie, which she knew he hated. With his dark blond hair, dark brown eyes, and lingering tan from his last fishing getaway, he looked like Barbie's Ken, the boardroom version. He watched as Kate got herself situated and handed him a to-go mug of coffee.

"What?" she said when he just continued to look at her.

"You know what." He gestured a chin toward the cup she'd handed him. "You're adding me to your little kingdom again."

"My kingdom? You wish. And the coffee's a 'thanks for the ride,' not an 'I don't think you can take care of yourself,'" she said.

Ryan glanced at Tommy in the rearview mirror. "Hey, Green Arrow. Seat belt on, right?"

"Right," Tommy said, and put on his headphones. He was listening to an Avenger's audiobook for what had to be the hundredth time, his lips moving along with the narrator.

Ryan looked at Kate. "Thought you were going to talk to him."

She and Ryan had once dated for four months, during which time they'd decided that if they didn't go back to being just friends, they'd have to kill each other. Since Kate was opposed to wearing an orange jumpsuit, this arrangement had suited her. "I did talk to him," she said. "I told him reading was a good thing."

"How about talking to himself and dressing like superheroes?"

Kate looked at Tommy. He was slouched in the seat, still mouthing along to his book, paying them no mind whatsoever. "He's fine." She took back Ryan's coffee, unscrewed the top on the mug, blew away the escaping steam, and handed it back to him.

"You going to drink it for me, too?" he asked. He laughed. "Just admit it. You can't help yourself."

"Maybe I like taking care of all of you. You ever think of that?"

"Tell me this, then—when was the last time you did something for yourself, something entirely selfish?"

"Ryan, I barely have time to go to the bathroom by myself."

"Exactly," he said.

"Exactly what?"

Now she laughed. Ryan shook his head and kept driving. They passed the lake just before the bridge into town. The water was still and flat in the low light. On the far side was the dam that held back the snowmelt, controlling the volume feeding into the river so that Sunshine didn't flood. Along the very top of the dam was a trail, which Kate sometimes ran on the days that she wanted to be able to fit into her skinny jeans. Up there, at the highest pool was an old fallen Jeffrey Pine. On its side, battered smooth by the elements, it made a perfect bench.

It was her spot.

She went there to think or when she needed a time-out from the rest of the world, which happened a lot.

"You get a date for the wedding yet?" Ryan asked.

No. She'd put that particular task off, and now, with the wedding only two days away, there was only one man who'd made her even think about dating. But tall, dark, and far-too-hot Griffin Reid was way out of her league. In fact, he was so far out of her league, she couldn't even see the league. "Working on it."

Ryan made a sound of annoyance. "You've been saying that for months." He glanced at her over the top of his sunglasses. "Tell me it's not going to be me."

"Hey, I'm not that bad of a date."

He slid her another look. "You going to put out afterward?"

Kate whipped around to look at Tommy, but the kid was still listening intently to his book. "No," she hissed, and smacked him. "You know I'm not going to put out. We didn't . . . suit that way."

"Well, I'm hoping to . . . 'suit' with one of the bridesmaids." He glanced at her again. "You ought to try it."

"Sorry. The bridesmaids don't do it for me."

He smiled.

"Stop picturing it!"

Ryan's smile widened, the big male jerk, and she smacked him again.

"All I'm saying," he said, "is that you should stop treading water and try for some fun. Live a little."

"You think I have no life."

Ryan blew out a sigh. They'd been down this road before. "You know what I think. I think you do everything for everyone except yourself. Look at your track record. You've had exactly one boyfriend in five years, and you're still making him coffee every morning."

"And you're still driving me to work so I can fill you in on the school gossip without you having to actually pay attention in the staff room," Kate said more mildly than she felt. Maybe because she heard the underlying worry in Ryan's voice, and she didn't want anyone to worry about her. She was fine. She was great. "We use each other. And we're both fine with that."

Ryan reached over and pulled out the fancy, thick white envelope with the gold embossing sticking out of her purse. "Fourteen more days."

"Hey," she said, trying to grab it back.

He waved it under her nose. "Treading water, Kate. And the proof's right here. Just like it was at this same time last year. And the year before that."

Again she tried to grab back the envelope.

"Why do you carry the offer around with you when you know damn well you aren't going to go?"

She wanted to go. But . . . "It means a whole year away from here."

"And?"

She blew out a breath.

"It's a dream come true for you," he said quietly.

It was. Being offered a full scholarship to the graduate program for science education at the University of San Diego—a world away from Sunshine, Idaho—was her dream. It would take a year to complete, an entire, glorious, science-filled year. With the degree—and the grant that Ryan promised to get her if she finished—she could bring a new and exciting science program to the county's school district. It was something she'd wanted for a long time. Some women wanted a spa week. Kate wanted to go dissect animals and work with scientists whose work she'd admired for a long time. Yes, it would be great for the school, but the truth was that Kate wanted it for herself.

Badly.

"I was thinking maybe I'd accept and go this time," she said.

"But?" he asked.

"But," she said. "Next year is crucial for Ashley. We have colleges to decide upon . . ."

"Uh-huh," Ryan said. "And last year it was Tommy's health."

"He had pneumonia." Snatching back the envelope, she shoved it in her purse.

And they didn't speak again for the rest of the ride.

Three

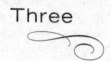

G rif drove through town, attempting to keep the memories at bay. He'd been gone a long time, and the places
he'd been in the military were just about as far from Idaho
as one could get.

He'd once hated Sunshine, but that'd been from a wild
teen's perspective, one who'd grown up chafing at the bit.
To that kid, the small ranching community had felt like iron
bars. Being destined to run his dad's ranching empire had
been a death knell; one Grif had gotten away from by running off and joining the army.

His father still hadn't forgiven him, though their problems had started far before that. With the dubious years of
maturity now on Grif's side, he hoped to change that. But
it wasn't his dad he was thinking about now.

That honor went to Kate, in a prim blouse and cardigan
sweater, a cargo skirt with lots of pockets, and thick tights.
The capper had been her snow boots, untied as if she'd just
shoved them on in a hurry. She was a five-foot-four bomb-
shell with showstopping curves stuffed into an elementary
teacher's wardrobe, and she'd effectively done what noth-

ing else could—she'd taken his mind off the discomfort of
being home. She was a paradox, Little Katie Evans. An
adorably sexy, tousled, slightly repressed hot mess of a
paradox.

And she wanted to be called Kate. Kate was a woman's
name, and she most definitely fit the bill there. She had all
those soft flyaway strawberry blond waves layered around
her face, highlighting mossy green eyes, and the sweetest
mouth known to mankind. He wasn't sure exactly when his
perception of her had changed or when he'd become so
aware of his need to touch. But the sensible attire on that
heart attack inducing bod combined with the one-hundred-
mile-per-hour brain and sweet disposition was sexy as hell.
And irresistible.

Not good, because his sister, Holly, was extremely protective of her best friend. And although Grif had all the
muscle in the family, muscle meant nothing when butting
up against the sheer brick wall of his sister's stubborn will.

Holly wanted him safe and happy, but she absolutely did
not want him within twenty feet of Kate.

Hell no.

And Holly had a way of getting what she wanted, which
was why he was still awake after a red-eye flight and too
many sleepless nights in a row now. She'd wanted to meet
for breakfast, away from the family ranch, presumably to
get a good look at him before anyone else. That was what
nosy sisters did.

He parked at the café where she'd ordered him. As he
walked into the place, scents assaulted him, scents that
were visceral reminders of being home again: coffee,
bacon, and Holly herself as she launched at him. Her loud
squeal of pleasure pierced his still ringing ears as she bur-
rowed in. Ignoring his headache and his unease about being
back, he endured the endless hug.

"Missed you," she whispered in his ear, and squeezed
him half to strangulation.

He held her with one arm, reaching up to resettle his
baseball cap with the other. "Hey, Hol."

"Hey, Hol?" She hauled back and punched him in the arm. "I just said I missed you, you big lug, and all you have to say is 'hey, Hol?' I missed you," she repeated with a devastating wealth of emotion blazing in both her voice and her eyes.

He rubbed his arm. "That's because I'm miss-able."

She made to slug him again, but he caught her hand. "Don't," he said. "And fine, I missed you, too, a little."

"Well, that's more like it," she said, softening. "Let's eat. Dad wanted to come, but he's caught up at Aunt Rena's ranch until later this afternoon."

Uh-huh.

Some of Holly's smile faded at Grif's doubtful expression. "I'm really hoping," she said, "that my number two and three favorite alpha males can share their space without a fight. I want peace for my wedding to my number one favorite alpha." Then she turned and kissed the man at her back. Adam Connelly was big and silent and stoic, and the toughest badass Grif knew. And yet the guy grinned like a sap after that kiss.

Turning her attention back to Grif, Holly tried to pull off his baseball cap, but he dodged her.

"Come on," she complained. "It's been so long since I've seen you."

"Did you forget what I look like?"

"How could I? You look just like Mom . . ." Again she went for the hat, but he simply straightened to his full height so she couldn't reach. "Though you act just like Dad," she said. "I want a look at you."

Grif could've told her she really didn't, but he held his tongue. Best not to give her any ammunition until absolutely necessary. "You can see me just fine."

Adam's dark eyes took in everything Holly was too excited to see. Gently setting aside his fiancée, he stepped in close and gave Grif a very real welcome home hug—minus the usual male backslap.

Somehow Adam knew.

"At least you made it home in time for tonight's bachelor/

bachelorette party," Holly said. "Great timing, you getting that early leave."

Not exactly great timing. And the leave wasn't in her honor at all. Nor was it a leave. He was out, medically discharged, which she didn't need to know about. He'd told no one from home, and he didn't intend to change that any time soon. He didn't want anyone fawning over him, and he sure as hell didn't want anyone to know how badly he'd screwed up or exactly how close he'd come to missing the wedding.

Not to mention the rest of his life.

Out of the military for the first time in his adult life, Grif was home for the wedding and maybe also to make peace with the place that had once been the bane of his existence.

"Have you seen anyone yet?" Holly asked after they were seated and had ordered.

"Kate." The name rolled off Grif's tongue before he could stop himself. She was still on his brain, her and that sweet smile that could slay him dead—which even an IED at ground zero hadn't been able to accomplish.

"Kate?" Holly asked, putting down her coffee. "My Kate?"

"I didn't realize you owned her," Grif said mildly.

Holly was silent for a full beat, staring him down as if she could extract his secrets by osmosis. "No," she finally said in her bossiest sister voice. "No. She's off-limits, Grif."

"Excuse me?" he asked in the tone that would have anyone else running for the hills. Not Holly. Holly had this thing about boundaries. As in she had none.

"Okay," she said. "I know you hate to be told what to do, but don't do Kate. I mean it, Grif."

"He's a big boy, babe," Adam broke in lightly, touching her hand. A gentle warning that she didn't heed.

"She's vulnerable right now," Holly said to Grif.

Yeah, well, he wasn't exactly feeling so steady himself.

"Her mom's gone," Holly said, "and her dad's— Dammit, Grif. You know what her life's like. She's practically raising her siblings on her own, and they're not easy. Tommy thinks he's a superhero, and Ashley does a damn good impression of the Wicked Witch of the West."

"East," Adam said.

"Aw," Holly said. "I love that you know that."

Personally, Grif thought Adam should have to turn in his Man Card for knowing that, but Holly was smiling at him dopily, and then Adam leaned in and she met him halfway for an annoyingly long, hot kiss.

"Great." Grif blew out a breath. "My best friend and my sister swallowing each other's tongues. This is nice. Really. I should have come home sooner."

They kept kissing.

Grif checked his watch.

They kept kissing. "Hey, you're making the kids uncomfortable."

Holly pulled back and grinned. "Jealous?"

"Bored," Grif said.

"Too bad that this week's all about me, then, isn't it?" She sent him a narrow-eyed glance. "Just as soon as I finish warning you off of Kate. I'm serious about this, okay? I've been trying to slowly work her back into the dating pool, but we're starting small. Trust me, she's in no way ready for the likes of you." She looped her arm through his. "Please don't take that as a challenge."

"You think she's too sweet for me," Grif said. "Too good."

"She's not some eighteenth-century virgin, Grif. She's a full-grown woman who, yes, is a really wonderful, giving, warm, good person. She'd give a stranger the shirt off her back. I just don't want that stranger to be you."

Adam snorted, and Grif slid him a look that Adam met evenly. And Grif had to admit, maybe they had a point. Grif liked women.

A lot.

And they tended to like him back.

"All I'm saying," Holly said, "is that sometimes people take advantage of Kate."

"And you think I'd be one of them?"

"Not purposely," she said, "but come on. You know she has a big crush on you. If you so much as look at her, she's spouting science facts. All I'm asking is for you to remember that the women in your world come and go. And she's not one to go."

"I didn't say I was interested in her that way." Having long ago learned the trick to dealing with his sister and her nosiness was a solid distraction, he said, "I bet you're a total bridezilla."

Adam laughed, turning it into a cough when Holly slid her husband-to-be a glance. But suitably distracted, she spent the next hour talking about the imminent wedding.

Grif had zero interest in the material of her dress or the accent color or the difficulty of the seating arrangements, but he had great interest in not talking about himself. Finally, ears still ringing, he left the café and drew in a careful breath.

Since his injury, his sense of smell had been as FUBAR as his head, but just like the café, Sunshine itself also had a distinct scent. Fresh, chilly mountain air. Cedar and pine.

Forgotten hopes and dreams.

He drove to the huge, sprawling old ranch house he'd grown up in and let himself in. He immediately thought of his mom. Though she hadn't lived here in years, the house was a visceral reminder of her, from before the divorce. Long before. Because even well before that she'd been living in New York, separate from Donald Reid. Still, her presence could be felt here, from the pictures of her scattered among others throughout the house, to her touch in the big-but-cozy furniture and other items she'd used to decorate the house. There was a picture of her on the mantel, with a five-year-old Grif on horseback. Holly was right; they were the spitting image of each other with their dark hair, gray eyes, and crooked smiles. It made him ache for her. His head ached, too, rattling his teeth with the pain—the IED blast that kept on giving.

Opening the door to his childhood bedroom, he dropped his bag by the bed and plopped onto the mattress exhausted.

* * *

He came awake badly, as he tended to do these days. Noting the low sun, he sat up. The day had gone by without him, which worked. Heart still pounding, damp with sweat, he stared at four chocolate brown eyes belonging to the two huge golden retrievers sitting bedside, breathing on him. Thing One and Thing Two. They'd started out as his dad's foster dogs last year, but no one ever returned a foster animal, not even the cantankerous Donald Reid. "Hey," he said.

This, apparently, was an invitation to be jumped, and they jostled for space on the bed. Thing One nearly unmanned him. Thing Two licked him from chin to forehead. Both were wild, like kibble-fueled rocket ships made out of pure energy. Laughing, he shoved them both down.

The house was no longer empty. He could hear music, talking, laughing. Head still pounding, Grif forced himself to lie still as he drew in a breath for a count of four, held it for a count of seven, and then let it out for a count of eight. One of his nurses had taught him the trick as a way to calm himself when he first woke up. It never worked, but it was something to do.

Rising, he headed into the adjoining bathroom for a shower. Someone had figured out he was here and had left him fresh towels. He took a long, hot shower and came out feeling slightly more human.

The sounds of a rip-roaring party drove him to the center of the house, a huge living area that had been transformed for Holly and Adam's co-bachelorette/bachelor party. Personally, Grif didn't see the good of a bachelor party if you were going to invite your soon-to-be-wife, but hey, what did he know about such things?

There were at least fifty people spilling out the two sets of double French doors to a large square courtyard. Lights had been strung in the trees, and music was blasting. Laughter and drinks were flowing.

His sister was at the bar wearing a huge tiara and a wide grin, holding a shot glass in each hand. Around her was a pack of women, a few of them wearing smaller versions of the tiaras and equally large grins, also double-fisting shot glasses.

The bridesmaids, he presumed, and cheered up slightly. They came in all shapes and sizes, each glowing as they laughed and talked and tossed back their drinks.

He counted one, two, three tiaras. A fourth was bent over, fiddling with her boot. She wore a white lacy top and a short black skirt with leggings and high-heeled ankle boots. Nice ass. Her shoulders were bare, revealing silky-soft, creamy skin and just a hint of a slinky bra strap running over the top curve.

He loved slinky lingerie. Mostly he loved it on the floor, but they could work on that, and with the evening looking up he headed over there. Just as he got close, Ms. Nice Ass straightened and turned to face him, and he went still.

Kate.

Unlike earlier, her strawberry blond hair was loose and slightly tousled, the shiny waves falling just past her shoulders. She was wearing a shimmery lip gloss that emphasized that sweet, kissable mouth and eyeliner that was smudged just enough to make her look not at all like an elementary teacher but trouble with a capital *T*. When she caught him staring at her, she hesitated, and then smiled.

His own smile was unexpected. And probably idiotic, because although he could take apart damn near anything and put it back together again, he couldn't seem to lust and think at the same time. She had the most amazing eyes, and her smile made him want to do things that were most definitely not on his sister's approved list.

She's vulnerable.

On the best of days a vulnerable woman was a spectacularly stupid idea, and this wasn't even close to the best of days for Grif.

In fact he hadn't even had a passable day in months.

Knowing it, he kept moving. Hell, he very nearly ran. As he headed out of the living room, he let his gaze catch on the big, ornate mirror hanging on the wall.

Another man was already talking to Kate. That was good. That was great.

But the guy looked a little determined as he set his hand on her shoulder, and Kate looked a little . . . relaxed. She'd been drinking.

She's vulnerable . . .

Damn. Stopping, Grif tilted his head back and stared up at the ceiling for an internal debate. Conscience or no conscience, that was the question.

Shit.

Conscience won, and he headed back. The guy looked up from Kate, and Grif slid him a long, hard look. Yeah, that's right, keep touching her, and I'll remove your fingers from your body.

The hand came off Kate.

Good choice. Satisfied, Grif nodded and forced himself to once again walk away, hoping she stayed out of trouble this time because he was out. He didn't tend toward regrets or guilt, but somehow he felt both as he ducked into the blessedly quiet den and headed straight for the small, well-stocked bar on the far wall.

"Showed up at the last minute, I see."

At the gruff, familiar sarcasm Grif turned and faced his father. Donald Reid was sixty-five and starting to look it, and Grif felt a pang for all the years that had passed without much more than a quick bickering session between them.

"You could've called," his dad said. "Let someone know you were coming."

Thing One and Thing Two had entered the room with the older Reid, and they beelined with joy for Grif, who squatted to give belly rubs. "You knew I'd be here," Grif said.

Donald made a derisive noise that instantly made Grif feel fifteen and stupid all over again. "How? You've barely been home except to bury your mother."

That wasn't quite true. Grif tried to make it home whenever he could—but admittedly that hadn't been very often since the two of them tended to circle each other like annoyed bears. And without his mom as a go-between, it had only gotten worse. Grif rose and absently rubbed the scar running along his temple. The long nap had taken care of the headache for now, but it would be back. He was getting used to living with one, along with the ringing ears, light sensitivity, and fatigue. He was lucky these were his only problems, and he knew it. "I'm here now," he said.

His dad looked at him and then nodded curtly. "Holly will be glad for it."

"And you?" Grif asked.

Donald strode to the bar to pour himself two fingers of whiskey.

Thing One and Thing Two leaped to their feet and happily panted along in his wake, hoping he was going for food. Donald smiled and pulled a dog biscuit from his pocket for each, receiving doggie kisses for the effort.

He'd always been a better doggy dad than a real dad. Grif rubbed his temple again, and Donald looked over at him. "What's wrong with you?"

"Nothing."

"Bullshit."

What the hell, Grif thought. "I screwed up and got too close to an IED."

Donald went utterly still for a very long beat. Then he knocked back his drink and slowly set the glass on the bar. And then just as slowly exhaled audibly. "So you nearly bought the farm."

"Turns out, I'm hard to kill."

Donald didn't relax or smile. "You didn't think to call?"

"Did you call me when you had a heart attack?"

"Not the same thing," Donald said tightly.

"No? Why's that, dad?"

"I didn't call you because I didn't want to distract you overseas. You didn't call me because you're stubborn as hell."

Grif smiled thinly. "No idea where I got that . . ."

From inside his dad's pocket came the refrain "I'm A Slave 4 U . . ." He pulled out his phone, and a ridiculous smile crossed his face. "Deanna says to tell you hello."

Deanna was his girlfriend. She was half Donald's age, silly, and highly dramatic. She also loved the old guy just as he was, and had stuck with him longer than anyone else since Grif's mom. Go figure.

His dad thumbed a reply text with surprising dexterity, shoved the phone away, and then got back to business. "What now?" he asked Grif.

"I don't know." Grif shrugged. "I've got some job options to consider."

"Where?"

"DC. Texas. Quantico." Grif might be done with active duty, but he still had skills and knowledge, and any number of alphabet agencies were interested in him.

"So you're in flux," Donald said.

"I'm in flux."

"Which is why you're here. You had a close call, and you had some sort of epiphany. What is it, you need to make peace with your past?"

Grif met his dad's gaze evenly, giving nothing away. "Maybe I'm interested in Idaho."

Donald laughed harshly and set down his drink again. "There was a day when you couldn't wait to get out of here. Hell, the door couldn't have hit you on the ass if it'd tried, you ran that fast. You went far and wide and on your own damn terms."

True story.

"Things would've been easier all around if you'd stuck here in Sunshine," Donald went on, "but you couldn't be bothered to do that, not then. What makes you think you could do it now?"

"I'm not seventeen anymore, dad. And this time I am interested."

"In the ranch?"

"I don't know. Maybe."

Donald laughed harshly. "You think it's easy to run a

ranch? That you can just drop back in after all these years and give it a shot on your own?"

Grif bit back the retort on his tongue, that his dad didn't do it by himself. He ran a huge operation, and he'd always had help. That had never been the issue. Grif tossed back his drink. More than two fingers, which was in direct opposition to what his migraine pills allowed, but there were days when life exceeded allowances, and this was one of them. "You're reading too much into this. I'm back to see my sister get married."

"Wrong. You came back for you," Donald said. And with that possibly very true statement, he left Grif alone in the den.

Four

Needing a moment, Kate moved away from the group at the bar. Treading water . . .

Is that what she was doing? Really?

She dodged through the crowd. She had no idea what she'd hoped to feel tonight. A spark of . . . something. But instead, her happy—already a little tenuous—was slipping.

She'd had two guys come on to her, which in theory should have been a little thrilling, but neither Charlie, a local fifteen years her senior and four times divorced, or Trevan, the father of one of the boys in her class, had interested her.

She was a little worried that nothing could interest her.

And then she'd caught Griffin Reid staring at her, and she'd felt that surge she'd been looking for. Interest? Oh yes. And lust. And excitement.

And more lust.

But it had been short-lived because when he'd realized it was her, he'd stopped short so fast she'd actually looked down at herself to see if she was trailing toilet paper from her boot or if she'd spilled something on herself.

She hadn't. She was wearing big-girl clothes tonight, without so much as a paint stain on her anywhere. And she looked good, too; Charles had said so—six times. Of course he'd said so directly to her breasts, but that might be her fault. They were a little bit on display tonight in her lacy top—something she didn't ever get to wear teaching second graders. After Ryan had thrown her off her game a little bit about her scholarship, she'd needed to mix things up tonight.

Instead she'd actually scared away Grif Reid. That took talent.

With a sigh, she dug into the chips and dip like it was her job. She was pretty certain that the calories in the dip added up to an entire week's worth of points, but she didn't care. Turning off a crush so thoroughly as to have him actually run away trumped point counting. In fact, it made the dip point free.

She'd just stuffed in a big bite when Miranda Brown came up to her side. Miranda was Holly's cousin and one of the bridesmaids. She was taller than Kate, prettier than Kate, and was currently engaged to her college sweetheart, who'd just finished up his residency. She gave Kate a smile. "Someone just suggested we all play some couples games, but Holly vetoed. I think she was worried about you feeling left out."

"I wouldn't have felt left out," Kate said.

Miranda smiled kindly and possibly a little patronizingly. "She said you'd say that, but . . ."

"But what?"

"Nothing." Miranda sipped daintily from her wineglass, her diamond ring nearly blinding Kate when it caught the light. "So when are you going to find your special someone, Kate?"

Yeah, definitely patronizingly. "I have someone on order, actually. He's going to arrive any second."

Miranda blinked. "Is that a joke?"

"Yes."

"Oh." Miranda laughed. "Right. You're . . . funny. Must be all the science degrees. Biology and chem, right?"

And education. And a chance at a master's . . .

"No Mrs. degree yet," Miranda said, and laughed. "Have you tried Match.com?"

More times than Kate wanted to admit out loud.

"Or maybe you're happy being the spinster teacher . . ."

Spinster teacher . . . seriously? Is that how people saw her? She wasn't even thirty yet. "I'm okay with being in between relationships," Kate said. And she'd been "between" relationships for a long time. Men didn't grow on trees in Sunshine, and she'd never been all that good at the serial-dating thing.

"So you don't have a date for the wedding?" Miranda asked.

"I didn't say that." Kate tossed back her second wine and felt her head get a little fuzzy. She was a lightweight, but tonight fuzzy was perfect. She'd be a cheap date.

If she had a date . . . "I have one."

"Who?" Miranda asked. "Anyone I know?"

Good question. Kate searched the room, her gaze landing on Ryan.

With his sixth sense for all things ridiculous, Ryan turned and looked at them. He took in her undoubtedly half-crocked slash panicked expression and, pulling his phone from his pocket, he worked his thumbs for a minute on the screen.

Three seconds later, Kate's phone vibrated. She held up a finger to Miranda—not the finger she wanted to hold up either—and grabbed her phone from her purse.

Hell no am I going to be your date for the wedding.

Dammit, Kate thought.

And stop drinking.

Double dammit.

Miranda's eyes fell on Ryan as well, who was back to flirting with one of the bridesmaids. "Ryan was a good catch for you," she said. "What happened? Did he get a little tired of the whole . . ." She gestured vaguely at Kate. "Sweet act?"

"Sweet act?"

Miranda smiled. "You know what I mean. You're always taking care of everyone and everything." She patted Kate's arm. "I'm sure one of these days you'll figure out how to take care of you and get what you want. In the meantime, at least you have your family. I think you deserve a medal for taking care of your father through his rehab and for how you watch out for your special siblings."

Kate set down her wineglass because she had an urge to accidentally-on-purpose toss the contents in Miranda's smug face.

"And eventually I'm sure you'll find a man who won't dump you."

"Ryan didn't dump me." Kate glanced at Ryan again, who was now giving her the slashing finger across the throat gesture. As in 'don't you dare commit me as your date or I'll kill you.'

Someone on the other side of Kate gasped and whispered, "Is that our principal, making . . . death threats?"

Kate sighed and turned her back on the rat fink bastard. "Ryan didn't dump me," she repeated, but Miranda had moved off.

"And I know what I want," Kate said to no one.

Didn't she? Okay, so yes, maybe eventually she wanted a sparkly diamond. Sue her. But she didn't want it right this minute. Right this minute she wanted to see her dear friend get married. She wanted to see Ashley off to college. She wanted to get all of her second graders through the last three weeks of school. She wanted to bask in having the honor of the pretty white envelope in her purse.

And okay, maybe she also wanted something to assuage this odd . . . ache deep inside. She looked around. Ryan was busy with Meg from the convenience store. Holly had her arms looped around Adam's neck. Her other dear friends Jade and Lilah were dancing with their husbands. In fact, just about everyone was paired off, and for the first time while surrounded by people she'd known forever, Kate felt . . . lonely.

It was natural, she assured herself. With Holly getting married things were changing. Kate was happy for her, so very happy, but apparently she'd let Miranda get into her head a little bit.

Because she didn't feel like a spinster teacher. She felt vibrant and loved and good at her job. And yeah, she took care of people, her people, but she liked doing it. She was good at it. Really good.

And maybe it was true that she hadn't been able to leave town since . . . well, she couldn't remember exactly. Oh, wait! She'd gone to that teaching conference in Coeur d'Alene last year, and it had been good, right up until she'd gotten food poisoning on her second night.

Damn. She was in a rut. But it was a very high-functioning rut, thank you very much. And at least she knew what she wanted for her future. But as for right now? Well, the truth was, her right now was a little bit consumed with others.

Maybe she did need to shake things up.

Ahead of her, way down the hallway, she caught sight of a tall, broad-shouldered guy in a baseball cap vanish into a room.

Griffin.

Before tonight she'd have said that he could shake her up. In fact, he could do whatever he wanted, and she was pretty sure she'd love it. Maybe she'd been wrong about his reaction before. Maybe he'd just been in a hurry. Yeah, surely that was it. Or that's what she wanted to believe, because here was the perfect chance to do something completely for herself, something out of character, something entirely just for her, with no chance of anyone getting hurt.

Griffin himself.

The thought made her heart start to race, like it did when she had a few episodes of *Arrow* to watch in a row. Not quite sure she was equipped to make this decision all on her own, she looked around for someone to check in with, someone who might suggest that this was a bad idea. But one best friend was wearing a big tiara, and the other was moving it like Jagger on the dance floor. Huh. Look at that, no one to talk her out of the insanity. That left only one person to convince.

Griffin himself.

Suddenly and completely determined, she grabbed a bottle of wine and two wineglasses and stepped into the den behind him.

At her entry, he turned, his expression dialed in to big, bad, edgy alpha. He wore a soft-washed henley shirt the exact same color of his gray eyes, and it clung to his broad shoulders and chest. Her heart, already knocking hard against her ribcage, gave a treacherous leap. And that wasn't the only physical reaction either. With a smile, she hoisted the bottle. "Thought I'd do my part to clean up," she said. "Join me?"

He cocked a brow. "You want us to drink the wine just so you can throw away the bottle?"

Okay, her seduction technique needed work. "Not throw away. It's recyclable." And then—big surprise—her brain ran away with her mouth. "But if I did throw it away, it'd take about a million years to decompose." God, she was such a geek. She quickly poured them each a glass and drank to stop herself from talking anymore.

He watched her over his glass. "You okay?"

"Never better."

"How's your ass?"

She choked, then had to swipe her mouth with the back of her hand. Sexy. "Um, what?"

"From when you fell," he said.

"Oh, that." She had a bruise the size of Texas. "It's nothing."

Clearly seeing right through her, he smiled. It was the dangerous smile of a man who could make promises by saying nothing at all, and butterflies fluttered low in her belly. "So how are you?" she asked, desperate for a subject change, one that didn't involve a science fact or her ass. "You having fun?"

"Depends on your definition of fun."

Well, she knew what her definition of fun was, but she wondered about his. In the past his fun had involved fast horses, fast all-terrain vehicles, fast cars, fast women, fast anything. She looked down at her glass. "How did this get empty?"

He took the bottle from her fingers, steadied her glass hand with his, and poured her a refill.

"I probably don't need that," she said.

"It's a right of passage to get drunk at your BFF's bachelorette party," he said. "In fact, you're supposed to have some dramatic moment where you make it all about you. Like life's moving on without you. Everyone's getting married and you're not. That sort of thing. I suggest getting drunk and sleeping with one of the groomsmen. It's practically expected."

She just stared at him, trying to focus past the way he looked in that shirt, which molded to all his hotness. "You think that's what this is?" she asked. "You think I'm jealous of Holly?"

"Are you?"

"No. I love Holly and Adam."

"Good." He toasted her. "Then skip the guilt portion of the evening and move right on to the next portion. You're already drunk . . ."

Actually, that was the funny thing. She wasn't. Relaxed, yes. Drunk, no. But ready to get that something for herself. Setting her glass down, she stepped into him before she lost her courage. "You're a groomsman, right?"

For the first time some of his easy charm slipped. "Uh—"

She slid her hands up his chest and sighed at the feel of his hard-muscled body so close. And he was warm, too, almost hot to the touch.

"Katie—"

"Kate," she reminded him, and went up on tiptoes, for the first time all night thankful for the ridiculously high-heeled boots that had cost her way too much money, because she was now tall enough to press her face to his throat, and oh, sweet baby Jesus, he smelled good. She inhaled deeply.

His hands went to her hips as he let out a breath that warmed her temple. "What are you doing?"

Possibly drooling on you . . . "If you don't know," she said, "then I'm way more out of practice than I thought."

He swore, and she took some gratification in the fact that his voice sounded husky and his hands tightened on her instead of pulling back. Her mouth was still pressed to his throat, which was deliciously rough with at least a day's growth, and when she breathed him in, he exhaled slow and long, so indelibly male. She blamed the sexy sound for what she did next.

She licked him.

He jerked as if she'd taken a bite out of him, and he backed away so fast that he bumped up against the tall bookshelf behind him. "What the hell was that?" he demanded.

"My tongue?"

The look on his face was sheer horror, and she went from pleasantly buzzed to feeling very unsure of herself. And nervous. "The tongue's the sole muscle in your body that's attached at only one end."

"Kate," he said with a single shake of his head.

Oh God. She knew that soft, don't-upset-the-crazy-person tone. Humiliated, she covered her face. "You said to seduce you!"

"No, I didn't."

She dropped her hands from her face. "Yes, you did. You said it was perfectly acceptable for me to seduce a groomsman. Well, here I am, trying to seduce a groomsman. You."

"I didn't mean me!"

"What's wrong with it being you? We're two consenting adults." One of whom was wearing her best panties, too.

"I'm not consenting," he said.

This stopped her in her tracks. "Why not?"

"Why not?" He appeared at a bit of a loss here, which didn't help her ego any.

"Yes, why won't you sleep with me?" Stepping into him again, she poked him in the chest with a finger. "What's so wrong with me that you won't?"

He stared at her like she'd grown a second head. "For one thing, you're drunk."

She was stone-cold sober now, but she cocked her head. "That's never stopped you with other women."

"Don't judge me by my past." But he blew out a breath as he set her away from him and pushed off the bookshelves to prowl the room. "Look, I might be an asshole, but not that big of one."

"And the second thing?"

He turned to face her. "You're Holly's best friend. You're . . . sweet."

Oh no, he did not just say that. "Sweet," she repeated. "You have no idea how tired I am of that word."

"Well you are sweet. Sweet, warm . . . kind."

She drew in a deep breath for calm, which—for the record—didn't help. "You think I'm sweet and warm and kind." She paused. "You realize you've just described a puppy."

His gaze dipped to her low-cut lace top. "You're not a damn puppy, Kate."

"No kidding!" In spite of his heated look, she was really starting to feel insulted now. "And just so you know, I'm not all that sweet either!"

He didn't look convinced.

"I'm not!"

"Tell me one not-sweet thing about you," he said.

"Well . . ." She searched her brain, but for once it was quiet. Then she remembered. "I'm wearing a leopard-print demi-bra." There. Take that.

He stared at her, and then his gaze lowered to her shirt again. Her nipples promptly hardened. The traitors. "And," she said with great attitude, "my panties match." Not that he was going to see them. Ever. "And they're those cheeky cut ones, too."

He groaned. "Killing me," he muttered, pressing the heels of his hands to his eyes before dropping them. "We're not going to talk about sex."

"You're right. We're talking about my undies. And whether or not I'm sweet. Which, FYI, I'm not." She wanted him to feel some of what she was feeling. She wanted him to ache like she did. Even for a moment. So before she lost her nerve, she gripped his shirt in her fists and kissed him. It had made all sorts of sense in her head, but for one single, horrible beat he didn't move. Kate went utterly blank, forgetting how to kiss, but then he let out a very rough, very male sound and took over, fitting his mouth to hers. This caused a wave of desire so strong her knees wobbled, but he caught her up in his arms.

He tasted like wine. He tasted like her secret hopes and dreams. He tasted like the very best thing that had happened to her all week.

All damn month.

Because Griffin knew how to kiss. He was the master of all kissers, and when he started to pull back, she tightened her grip on him in protest.

But he wasn't going anywhere. Instead he spread hot kisses along her jaw and throat, and then he opened his mouth on her heated skin. Her toes curled in response. Clearly it had been way too long since she'd had a social orgasm. Locking her wobbling knees, she tried to live in the moment, tried to soak it all in for the deep dark of the night when she was alone again.

Treading water . . .

He whispered her name, a soft, sexy "Kate." And then his mouth was back on hers.

Trembling with need now, she pushed closer, responding to the raw kiss and wanting so much more. When he broke the connection, it took her a moment, but eventually she realized she was leaning on him and that he was fully supporting her. Her only salvation—he was breathing as raggedly as she was.

"You have to admit," she said. "That wasn't sweet."

He manacled her roaming hands by clamping hard fingers over her wrists. "Kate," he said, voice low and rough with command.

She had no idea why that revved her engine, but it did, and she rubbed her body against his.

Sucking in a harsh breath, he firmly set her away from him, holding her there. His gaze was glued to her mouth. "Christ." He lowered his head and drew in a deep breath.

The hunger was palpable in the room. His. Hers. When he finally opened his eyes again, he looked at her as if he'd never seen her before. His baseball cap was low, covering his expression. Needing to see his eyes, she tried to dislodge it and then found herself pinned to the wall by 180 pounds of muscle.

"Don't," he said.

She stared up at him. "You're not as much fun as I imagined you would be. Which shouldn't surprise me. I have a hard time finding the fun."

He laughed harshly, shook his head, and then, without another word, turned and walked from the room, pulling the door shut behind him.

Stunned, and not quite knowing what exactly had just happened, Kate gave into her wobbling knees and slid down the wall to sit.

She'd kissed him to prove a point, but hell if she could remember what that point was. And somehow in the process she'd been rejected because . . . why exactly? She'd proven she wasn't all that sweet, so it had to be something else. In horror she put a hand in front of her face and checked her breath. Whew. She didn't stink. Oh God, did she kiss badly? No, Ryan would have told her that much.

Whatever the reason, she needed to get over it, stat. She also needed to find her smile and get back to the party, because she was taking this rejection all the way to her grave.

Five

The next morning Kate made her daily stop at her dad's, where it was a wash and repeat of every other morning. Ashley couldn't find her own stuff; Tommy was dressed like . . . "Who are you?" Kate asked him, not sure what the glowing circle on his chest meant.

"Tony Stark," he said, nose in a book.

Channing Tatum scratched at the back door and then came in carrying a still-alive field mouse, which had everyone running around and screaming for a few minutes until said field mouse was caught and exported back outside.

Finally, Kate rushed everyone out the door and slid into Ryan's waiting car, handing him a coffee. "I didn't doctor it up," she warned.

"Why?"

"Because you're mean."

"What? I am not."

She looked at him. "No? So if I said I needed you to be my date to tonight's wedding rehearsal, you'd say . . . ?"

"Hell no."

"And that's why you're drinking black coffee."

"Fair enough," he said, and drank his black coffee without further complaint. "Thirteen days, you know."

"Yes, I know." Thirteen days left to accept at UCSD. She had her acceptance typed up in her e-mail. All she had to do was take it out of the draft folder and hit Send.

But she hadn't.

Because how could she? How could she walk away from her dad for a year? What if he needed her? What if Tommy or Ashley needed her? And her job. Ryan had promised to hold it for her, but he couldn't really guarantee that. It was up to the school district . . .

They drove in silence. Ryan was in his zone, and so was Tommy.

Not Kate. Unless you counted reliving kissing Griffin Reid. Because actually, that had been a hell of a zone . . .

Grif woke up the next morning drenched in sweat, heart pounding out of his chest, and with absolutely no idea where he was. Afghanistan? Germany? Sitting straight up, he took in the room with one glance before sagging back. He was stateside, in Sunshine, at his father's house.

Shoving his fingers through his hair, he let out a long breath. His phone was vibrating across the nightstand, the number unfamiliar though he recognized the DC area code. "Reid," he answered.

"You got your head on straight yet?"

Joe Rodriguez. They'd served together before Joe had gotten out and gone to work for the ATF. "My head's straight," Grif said. "It's the rest of the world that's sideways."

Joe laughed. "Ain't that the truth. Heard you're not going back to Crazy-stan."

Grif knew soldiers whose entire life was caught up in their military career, guys for whom an injury like he'd sustained would have not just been physical.

Grif wasn't one of them. Yes, he'd have stayed in the

military if he hadn't been hurt. But he had been, and he wasn't one to look back with a lot of regrets. "I'm done with all the 'Stans," he confirmed.

"Got something for you then. A job. You interested?"

"Where?"

"In the good ol' US of A, man," Joe said. "The land of free Wi-Fi, Thai takeout, and Fantasy Football. There're a few things uniquely suited to you and your skills here on the East Coast, and a few other places, too. Up to you."

Grif turned his head and looked out the window. He could see the outline of the Bitterroot Mountains. He'd spent a lot of time over the years exploring those peaks— pretty much the only time he'd ever been happy in Sunshine. But he hadn't meant to actually stay here. Had he? Getting away after the wedding would probably be for the best. Having a job would be even better. "I'm interested."

"Good. I'll get back to you soon."

Grif disconnected and lay back, staring at the ceiling for a few minutes, thinking it was sort of nice not to be worried about dying today. He could get used to that.

Then he heard a soft, musical laugh. He knew that laugh, and not just because the sound of it made him hard. It was Kate, and he supposed he knew why he thought he heard her now. After that kiss they'd shared last night, he'd dreamed about her, about being wrapped up in her soft curves, buried deep. And now he was imagining that she was here. Which probably made him crazy.

But then he heard it again. Rolling out of bed, he strode straight to the window.

Reid Ranching was more like an empire these days, but the biggest ranch in the corporation still remained this one. For as far as the eye could see was Reid land. Most of the rugged landscape was outlined by the jagged peaks of the Bitterroot Mountains, formed by glaciers during the Ice Age. At this time of year the huge snowpack was melting, producing a massive water runoff, filling a myriad of streams and rivers carving their way through the valley floor.

Kate stood in the yard surrounded by the majestic view.

Next to her was his dad. They were both talking animatedly and laughing.

His dad was laughing.

It took Grif a moment to realize why he felt so shocked. It was because he couldn't remember the last time he and his dad had laughed together.

Maybe because they'd never laughed together.

And yet Donald was out there playing the part of the charming rancher, laying it on thick, too, and Grif could only stare at the broad, genuine smile on his face. He'd never gotten any of that from the man, ever.

It was Kate's doing. She had a way of bringing the best out of someone. Whatever she was saying had his dad practically bent over with amusement. Then the two of them shook hands, and Donald walked off toward one of the barns.

Kate leaned against the fencing and looked out at the land, hugging herself as if a little chilled. She wore a brightly colored skirt, navy blue tights tucked into boots, and another sweater, this one with a row of teeny-tiny buttons down the front. Her hair had been contained on top of her head, held there by a . . . pencil? Strands were trailing down the sides of her face and throat, all golden red silk against her skin.

She didn't look like any teacher he'd ever had, except maybe in his fantasy life. She'd certainly been his favorite fantasy last night, and everything about her—each smile, each sexy step, hell her every breath—put him in overdrive.

Which meant they had a problem.

Or at least he did.

She turned her head and met Grif's gaze through the window. Seeing him clearly surprised her—unpleasantly so, given the way her eyes widened slightly and then narrowed.

Maybe she was remembering last night, too. He'd honestly believed he could actually resist her—until she'd kissed him. He didn't know what he'd expected, but getting his mouth on hers had knocked his socks off. He'd never made a habit of turning women down, and turning this woman down had been far more difficult than he'd imagined, so he hoped like hell he got some sort of credit for acting like a gentleman.

He sure as hell hadn't walked away in his dreams afterward. Nope, he'd taken her right there in the den against the wall, with her cute little skirt up around her ears and the heels of those sexy boots digging into his ass, and it had been extremely mutually satisfying.

He realized Kate's gaze had fallen south. Grif looked down at himself and remembered—he'd slept in the buff and stood there in the window butt-ass naked.

The sill hit right above his groin so she couldn't see much, though her cheeks were flushed. Still, she didn't play coy or shy and look away. Nope, it was him who moved, and he didn't want to think about why as he yanked on clothes and headed outside.

Kate had moved to the horse pens and was stroking a huge quarter horse named Woodrow. Woodrow was old as dirt, but he still had a thing for the ladies and was leaning heavily on Kate, sniffing out her pockets. This was making her laugh again, that soft, musical laugh that did things to Grif's gut. Stopping with a good ten feet between them, he watched her a minute. Woodrow snotted on her skirt, but she didn't seem to mind. "Hey," he finally said.

"Oh!" She jumped and then turned to face him. She still didn't smile. Which of course was what happened when a beautiful, adorably sexy woman threw herself at you, and you somehow managed to resist her.

Yeah. He was probably going to hate himself for that for a good long time.

She put a hand to her chest, which was rising and falling rapidly like she'd just gone running. "You okay?" he asked.

"Did you know that your right lung takes in more air than your left one?"

"No, I didn't." He was making her nervous again. He searched for something to say to put her at ease, but putting pretty women at ease wasn't exactly his forte. Unless he was trying to get them naked. "Are you hungover?"

"No." She paused. "However, I don't remember anything I said or did last night in the den."

He took in the slight hope in her expression and unbelievably found a laugh.

"It was worth a shot," she said on a sigh. "I guess I hoped that if I pretended not to remember your rejection of my sloppy attempt at seduction then I could tell myself it never happened."

She thought he'd rejected her. He started to tell her that her coming on to him had been the best—and most terrifying—thing that had happened to him in a damn long time. But since he didn't know if he was strong enough to turn her down a second time, he kept his mouth shut.

Kate smoothed an imaginary wrinkle from her skirt and closely examined a speck of lint on her sleeve, and then it was his turn to sigh. Damn, being the good guy sucked. "You need to be more careful," he said. "Just about any other guy there last night would've taken advantage of what you were offering."

She lifted her head at that, staring at him with two high spots of color on her cheeks. "I wasn't offering anything."

They both knew that was a big, fat fib. "Listen," he said. "Guys are dicks. Or at least they think with their dicks. You can't trust them."

"None of them?"

"Not a single one," he said, and meant it.

"I kissed you," she said, as if he needed reminding. "I threw myself at you. And yet you managed to control yourself." She met his gaze evenly. "Either I was totally repugnant to you, or you were one hell of a gentleman."

Shit, he didn't have the brain capacity to spar with her this morning. She was sharp as hell and way too good for the likes of him.

She cocked her head, waiting on his answer, and if it had been any other situation, he might have laughed at her teacher-to-errant-student expression, which she had down. It should've turned him off, but instead he wanted to push her up against the fence railing and show her exactly how not "repugnant" she was.

Which would be an incredibly stupid thing to do. "What are you doing here?" he settled for instead.

"Dropping off some seedlings and then coming back with the kids in an hour."

"Seedlings?"

"We're going to plant them along the creek beds," she said. "It's a living science project that your dad so sweetly agreed to."

Grif nearly laughed. He'd heard his father described in any number of ways, but sweet had never been one of them.

"We'll come back weekly to check in on their progress and report on the growth," Kate said. She stopped talking and frowned up at him.

And then, before he realized what she was up to, she closed the distance between them, went up on tiptoe, and pushed his hair back from his forehead and temple. "Oh, Grif," she said softly, a world of emotion in her voice. "What happened?"

Shit. He'd forgotten to put on his baseball cap, leaving his four-inch scar in plain view. He started to back away from her, but she gripped his arms as she leaned in, pressing her mouth to the scar in a gentle kiss that made his throat feel uncomfortably tight. "What the hell are you doing?" he asked.

"Kissing it better." She settled back down on the balls of her feet and gave him some desperately needed space. "Did it work?"

He had to clear his throat to speak, and he still sounded like he'd just swallowed glass. "You think a kiss can make something all better?"

She met his gaze, her own filled with plenty of emotions, but thankfully pity wasn't one of them. "Yes."

He let out a breath. She was right. A kiss from those lips would make just about anything feel better. He wanted her to do it again and then work her way south, to the other body parts that could use some kisses right about now. He saw the rise and fall of her breasts with each breath she took, and it was fucking with his head more than a little. "So the left lung, huh?"

It took her a moment, and then she looked down at her breasts. Making a sound low in her throat, she crossed her arms over herself. "You turned these down," she reminded him.

He loved that while she looked a little prim and repressed on the outside, on the inside she was anything but. She wasn't shy, and she had no problem stating her mind.

It was sexy as hell.

It wasn't often he allowed regrets, but he was starting to regret that last night hadn't turned into something between them. And it was exactly that way of thinking that could get him into big trouble. *You're stronger than this*, he told himself.

Not today you're not . . .

Not when he was back on his dad's turf, out of his element, and completely off balance. And much as he'd like to blame it all on Kate's fathomless eyes and pinup girl mouth, he couldn't.

"Will you tell me about it?" she asked softly, her gaze back on his scar.

"No."

But because she reacted to that like he'd slapped her, he softened his voice. "I don't like to talk about it."

Her eyes never left his as she pulled a trick from her teacher handbook and said nothing. He was to fill the silence, he knew, and hell if it didn't work. "It's healing," he said. "I'm fine." Well, except for the migraines, sleepless nights, and ringing ears.

She nodded and remained silent, for which he was eternally grateful, though her eyes remained very serious and on his until her cell phone buzzed.

Saved by the bell.

She broke eye contact to look at her phone. "Oh, crap. I'm late. I've gotta go."

He nodded. Going was the right step here. Absolutely the right step. He was going, too.

But then she whirled back around to say something and collided right into him. Her hands slid up his chest searching for purchase, gripping his shirt. He held her upright until she caught her balance, the whole spectacle taking less than two seconds. She let go almost as fast as she'd grabbed him, with a soft laugh and a murmured apology, but the feel of her warm, curvy body up against his imprinted on his brain.

"I . . ." She broke off with a low laugh. "I forgot what I was going to say." She stared up at him.

Asking for trouble, a little voice said as he slowly stepped into her. Stop me, Kate.

She didn't, and between one blink and the next she was in his arms. He lowered his mouth but didn't have to go far because she went up on tiptoe, meeting him halfway. Before last night it had been a damn long time since he'd had human contact, since he'd experienced the scent of a woman engulfing him, the feel of her wrapped around him, the softness of her skin and heat of her soft body . . .

She seemed to need this every bit as much as he did. Hell, she practically crawled up his body, which crumbled his last wall of defense. Raise the white flag; he was going down. When his tongue stroked hers, she moaned, a sound of arousal from deep in her throat that revved his engine. Then she deepened the kiss with a soft sigh, like he was the best thing she'd ever tasted in her life.

And he knew she wasn't going anywhere. In one move he had her backed up against the fence. His hand was heading toward her breast and her knee was sliding up the outside of his thigh when Woodrow stretched his long neck over the rail and pressed his wet nose in between them.

Kate jerked back, removing the hand she'd had on Grif's ass. Fucking horse. He slid Woodrow a look that had glue factory all over it, but the old geezer just snorted and then frisked him.

With a sigh, Grif stroked the old guy's velvety neck, which was all he really wanted, the 'ho, and then trotted off.

The moment broken, Kate backed up a few steps. "I remembered what I was going to say."

"Yeah?"

"I was going to say that I don't plan on accosting any unwilling groomsmen at tonight's rehearsal dinner, so you should be safe." She blushed. "But I can't say that with a straight face now."

"Kate—"

She shook her head. "I really gotta go."

And then she was gone before he could tell her that he wouldn't mind being accosted.

God, he was so screwed up.

Instead of heading straight back to the house, he entered the barn, lured by the long-forgotten scent of hay and horses and leather—distinctly Sunshine smells. They had the years melting away, taking him back to a time when everything he'd done had been trouble or driven by trouble or in the search of trouble, and he'd most definitely found it.

Often.

He'd been a wild teenage boy, unhappy to the marrow, stuck out in the middle of nowhere. He'd consistently dreamed of bigger and better things. More than anything he'd wanted off this ranch and out of Sunshine, and he'd been willing to do whatever it took in order to make that happen. When his mom had separated from his father and gone to New York, she'd left Grif here, telling him that he belonged in Sunshine with his father.

She'd been wrong.

The minute he'd turned eighteen he'd enlisted and gone off to get what he'd been dreaming of. Freedom.

Instead, he'd ended up fighting for it.

The barn door opened behind him, and his father strode in. To his credit, his steps didn't falter when he caught sight of Grif, though they stood there staring at each other in awkward silence.

They didn't look much alike, father and son, though their attitudes matched up like apple and tree. Or so Grif's mom had always said.

"Bored already?" Donald finally asked. "I'm short several hands today if that's the case."

"Sure," Grif said. What the hell. "I'll help."

Donald's brows went up. Clearly he hadn't expected Grif to agree so readily. "There was a time that helping out on this ranch felt like torture to you."

Grif bit back a sigh. "Are we going to bicker like little girls or work?"

"Depends." Donald gestured to Grif's head. "How bad is it?"

Grif rubbed the scar that hadn't yet started to ache today. "I'm fine."

"No doubt in thanks to how thick your skull is." Donald jabbed a hand in the direction of the five horses in their stalls, all watching the exchange between the two men with varying degrees of interest. "I suppose riding is out?"

Two months ago everything had been out: food, exercise, sex . . . everything and anything that had given him that freedom he'd always craved. But he'd recently been cleared for everything—except, of course, his job. Detecting, locating, and defusing anything that might go boom was out entirely. He could do whatever else he damn well wanted, though the thought of riding made his head hurt just thinking about it. "Nothing's out."

Donald just looked at him.

Grif looked right back. Goddammit he didn't want to do this circle and dance. He wanted . . . Well, hell. He didn't actually know.

"How long are you here?" Donald asked.

"As long as I want." He waited for his dad to say he hoped that was for a damn long time, but Donald said nothing.

Instead he pointed to the horses. "Stalls need to be cleaned out."

Grif looked at him. "You want me to shovel shit."

Donald shrugged. "You still think you're too good for shoveling shit? Then don't help."

And then he walked out.

Grif let out a breath. Had he really thought he could make peace here, with him? Because it was looking like he'd have to settle for a truce. So in the name of that truce, he picked up a damn pitchfork. He was still at it an hour later when Kate showed back up at the ranch with twenty second graders.

The mayhem was instant, but it was a controlled mayhem he realized, watching from the barn as Kate handled her class with an ease he couldn't have managed. She answered each of the million questions that came her way with no sign of fatigue or lag in patience, even though a girl named Nina constantly raised her hand to tell on someone. Kate broke up a couple of almost fights, all started by one punk of a kid—Dustin—who was just big enough to make Grif think he'd probably been held back a year.

Kate took the time to love up on Thing One and Thing Two when they bounded over to her, even though Thing Two jumped up and left questionable stains on her clothes. She acted like she'd been given a diamond when some kid named Tucker brought her a shiny rock, even though two others—Mikey and Jase—had just done the same thing. She accepted the gift of a bug when yet another kid brought her one to prove how brave he was.

The fact was, she had a ready laugh and smile for all of them. Any of them. She saw the best in each kid, and she got it. Hell, she saw the best in everyone; he knew that. How or why, he had no idea. Nor did he know how he'd ever been able to resist her.

Six

As she had every few minutes, Kate counted heads to make sure she still had twenty students. Elbows deep in mud, she had them all planting seedlings and recording their efforts.

Well, all of them except one. Tommy had planted his seedlings already and was sitting on a rock, watching the sky for extraterrestrials.

"Aliens like Idaho," he told Kate when she walked over to him. He had his head tilted up, his eyes squinting against the sun. "Because the land is so wide open."

"My dad says aliens don't exist." This from Dustin, who came up next to Kate. "My dad says people who believe in aliens are cuckoo for Coco Puffs."

A couple of the other boys, Tucker and Mikey, snickered at that. Dustin was a year older, and therefore cooler, and also quite charming when he chose to be. The kids gravitated to him, even when he was pushing his weight around.

Except Tommy. He didn't gravitate to anyone. "That's a closed-minded way of thinking," was all he said.

Kate was only ten feet away, and though she wanted to,

she didn't say anything. Tommy hated it when she interfered on his behalf, and it always made things worse anyway. This was his battle.

Dustin frowned. "You're closed-minded."

"Why do you always repeat everything I say?" Tommy asked. "Can't you think of your own stuff to say?"

"I have plenty to say," Dustin said. "I got two homers last night, best in the league so far. I'm going to be like Jeter. Do you even known who Jeter is?"

"Do you even know who Dr. Who is?" Tommy asked.

Dustin stared at him, shook his head. "You're such a dork."

"A dork is a whale's penis."

"Tommy said *penis*," Nina said to Kate.

"We're not supposed to say *penis*," Mikey seconded.

"Everyone stop," Kate said. She looked at Dustin. "That's enough."

Dustin gave Tommy one last look, and then he walked away with the others.

"Whale's penis?" Kate asked Tommy when they were alone. "Really?"

"It's not a dirty word; it's a body part."

Kate squatted in front of her brother and ruffled his hair. "Honey—"

He pushed her hand away. "Don't baby me."

"I'm not."

"You're giving me the sappy eyes," Tommy said. "When you give me the sappy eyes, they treat me different."

"Actually they treat you different because you are different." She sighed at his stubborn expression, which she recognized—from her mirror. "You could try to fit in. You know who Jeter is."

Tommy smiled a little. "But he most definitely doesn't know who Dr. Who is."

Which wasn't her point. She knew he'd been bullied in kindergarten and first grade, before he'd admitted it. It was why he wore the costumes. He liked feeling like a superhero, impervious to weakness. It was wish fulfillment. She had a wish, too, that he could feel safe and secure as himself. "Tommy—"

"Still giving me the sappy eyes." Grabbing his notebook, he clutched it to his chest and moved off in the opposite direction of the others.

Kate let him go, aching for him. She did baby him. She couldn't help it. He was too young to remember their mom, but Kate remembered everything. Belinda Evans had been a teenager when she'd had Kate, but she'd made her marriage work, and years later they'd wanted more kids. Belinda had been a great mom, and she would've found a way to reach Tommy. Kate knew it. She needed to make things right for him. She'd had several meetings with Ryan about whether or not she should be Tommy's teacher this year. He had the smarts to skip a grade and go straight to third but not the social skills, and he was already small for his age.

So in the end, she'd kept him with her. But there were times, like now, when the teacher within her warred with the sister—who really wanted to beat the crap out of Dustin for giving Tommy a hard time.

She parlayed that energy into helping the kids make sure their seedlings were planted correctly. Nina and Tasha got into a little tiff about whose seedlings were cuter but other than that they had no problems, and half an hour later everyone had finished.

"Okay, gang," Kate called out. "It's time to head back to school for lunch."

This was accompanied by the usual protests. Most of the kids didn't want to go back to the classroom; they were happy right there in the dirt. There was only one kid she could think of who might want to go back, and suddenly she realized he wasn't anywhere in sight. Straightening, she turned in a slow circle. "Tommy?"

Nothing.

"Class, has anyone seen Tommy?"

"No," Dustin said, "but Tony Stark's midget double is here somewhere."

A few of the kids laughed, but Kate wasn't amused. "Dustin, if you were missing, you'd want someone to notice."

"No, I wouldn't."

She looked him in the eyes. "I'd notice anyway," she told him. She kept her cool as she walked through her small groups of two and three kids, counting heads.

Nineteen.

Tommy was gone, and he was gone all by himself.

She whipped around to face the creek. It was actually more of a mud zone at the moment and barely running. Nothing was in danger of being swept away, which didn't help ease her sudden fear. "Tommy!"

"Maybe he was abducted by aliens," Dustin said.

Kate yanked off her sunglasses and wool cap, as if that would help her see better. She scoured the clearing and went still at the sound of an engine revving.

A motorcycle came around the bend in the creek, a big dirt bike weaving in and around boulders and stumps and other various forest debris with obvious skill. With the sun behind it, all she could see was that the rider was a man hunched protectively over . . .

"Tommy," she breathed, relieved and then shocked because the driver was . . . Griffin.

Tommy was wearing a helmet, which he tugged off with a huge grin as Griffin pulled the motorcycle to a stop at the edge of the clearing. Tommy hopped off. The face shield slipped down over his eyes, and with a giggle he shoved it back up, having to tilt his head sideways to see Griffin. "That was awesome!"

Griffin held up a fist, and Tommy bumped it with his own, and then they went through some complicated handshake that was entirely new to Kate. "Stay right where you are," she told the kids in her most serious teacher voice before walking over to Tommy and Griffin. "What happened?" she demanded. "Are you okay?"

"Did you see?" Tommy asked. "Did you see me on the bike?"

"Where were you?"

Some of her concern and temper must have been on her face because Tommy's smile faded. "I followed a bird along the creek bed. It was little, Kate. And hurt."

And he'd gotten worried, like he worried about every living thing. There was no use getting mad at him for that; it was who he was to the very marrow. A superhero from the inside out. "Where did it go?"

Tommy looked sheepish at that. "It flew away when I got close."

"The kid was only about twenty-five yards around the bend," Griffin told Kate quietly. "He was within hearing distance of you."

Kate looked at Tommy. "I yelled for you."

Tommy appealed his case. "I had to help the bird, Kate. A thousand birds die every year from smashing into windows."

Kate felt her heart melt. She also felt the weight of Griffin's amused stare at the realization that spouting science facts when frazzled was an Evans hereditary trait.

The other kids had hit their max on behaving and had moved in close, lured by the excitement of the motorcycle and Griffin. Dustin was the leader, of course. "There's no windows out here, super genius," he said to Tommy.

"Dustin," Kate said. "What happens when we insult someone?"

Dustin kicked the ground but stalked off to a rock about ten feet away for his time-out.

Griffin ruffled Tommy's already wildly tousled hair. "Remember what I said about walking off on your own."

"Always have a partner," Tommy said.

Grif nodded once. "And?"

"And no man left behind. Ever."

The other kids were staring in open admiration at the motorcycle and at Tommy, too, awed by his adventure. Kate was busy staring at Griffin. He was still in his well-worn jeans, boots, and a graphic T-shirt that advertised some dive shop in the Caicos Islands. While she appreciated the way the wind plastered the shirt to his broad shoulders and chest, she wondered why he wasn't wearing more layers.

Then she realized Tommy was wearing a large flannel shirt, open and hanging past his knees as he handed the helmet over to Griffin.

"Keep the shirt for now," Griffin told him. "It's cold out here."

"My dad says it's cold enough to freeze the nuts off a brass monkey," Mikey said.

The kids giggled.

"Mikey said *nuts*," Nina said.

Kate held up a hand, the sign for silence. "The saying comes from the Civil War days, when the cannonballs were stacked in a pyramid formation called a brass monkey. When it got extremely cold outside they'd crack and break off. Breaking the nuts off the brass monkey. Get it?"

Tommy grinned. "History's funny."

Dustin snorted derisively from his rock. "Or stupid," he muttered.

Tommy hugged Griffin's shirt to himself. "How will I get this back to you?" he asked Griffin.

Griffin's gaze slid to Kate's. "I'll get it."

"Come to school later," Tommy said. "We're going to have brownies cuz we met our reading goal ahead of schedule." He leaned in and whispered, "It's because of me. I read a book every night."

Someone snickered rudely.

Griffin lifted his head and leveled Dustin with a look that had Dustin zipping his mouth.

"I'll share my brownie with you," Tommy told Griffin. "They're Kate's. She makes the best brownies on the whole planet."

Griffin met Kate's gaze. "Is that right?"

"Yes, and anyway, no man left behind, right?" Tommy asked with an endearing smile, the master of charming any adult in his radius. "Ever. So, you have to come and share my brownie."

Griffin's mouth curved slightly. "Yeah. Sure." Again he

looked at the other kids. "And that no-man-left-behind thing applies to all of you. You're a unit. You take care of each other."

The kids took this in with awe, and when Griffin continued to just stare at them, they all nodded like bobbleheads.

Griffin pulled on the helmet. Kate gave Tommy a long look that said, *We're so not done here*, and moved in closer to Griffin. "Thanks," she said quietly. "For bringing him back. He gets distracted and wanders off."

"He's like you," he said.

She let out a low laugh. "He's a seven-year-old boy. He avoids soap like the plague, watches *The Avengers* on repeat, and sometimes forgets underwear." She paused. "I almost always use soap."

"He'll eventually get into being clean, but as for *The Avengers* and occasionally going commando, he's right on the mark."

At the thought of Griffin being commando under his jeans, she got a little hot. Okay, a lot hot.

He gave her a slow, trouble-filled smile. "He told me that when a male honeybee mates, its testicles explode and the penis is left inside the queen bee."

She gave out a half laugh, half groan. "Okay, so he's a little like me. But to be clear, *penis* is his favorite word, not mine."

"*Penis* is every boy's favorite word." He paused. "Also, I'm eternally grateful not to be a bee." He tugged playfully on a stray strand of hair that had escaped its confines and was in her face. "And also, you smell much nicer than he does." And with that, he got back on the motorcycle and rode off.

Seven

They got back to school in time for lunch with no further problems. Normally Kate took her lunch break with a friend. At least once a week she ate with Holly. Other days she met up with Lilah, Jade, or the new vet, Olivia, when their breaks lined up. Olivia and Kate shared a love of cooking, so they always did a recipe exchange. Other days, Kate stayed at school and ate with Ryan in his office, but today she ran through the cafeteria quickly.

"Hey, honey," Glenna the lunch lady said in her no-nonsense voice. "What'll it be?"

"The Griffin," Kate said, and then clamped a hand over her mouth. The Griffin? Good Lord, even the thought of a Griffin sandwich gave her a hot flash. "The Reuben! I meant the Reuben!"

Glenna cackled. "I'd take a Griffin sandwich."

The afternoon went downhill from there. Mikey and Tasha got sick in the classroom—Mikey managed to do it right on Kate's favorite Toms knockoff boots. Then, two minutes before she had to line the class up for play rehearsal,

Tommy vanished again. But this time she knew it wasn't a bird.

It was the play.

She found him hiding in the closet reading on his e-reader. Relief weakened her knees, and her heart clutched hard at the sight of him. Despite her best efforts, he was skinny as a stick, and his clothes were always just a little too big. Today, like most days, his hair stuck up in tufts, due to his aversion to a brush or comb. And damn, she loved him. She turned back to her class. "If anyone moves from their seat in the next three minutes, we're going to skip recess."

This brought a chorus of promises that no one would move a single inch. Right. Hoping her threat had been enough, Kate crawled into the closet with Tommy. "Hey."

"Hey." He hadn't stopped reading, so she reached out and turned off the e-reader. Finally, he looked at her.

"You know they're not going to stay in their seats," he said. "Recess or not."

"Then we'll have to make this quick, won't we?" She stroked his hair, trying to tame it. Impossible. "You know it's just a rehearsal, right? There's no actual audience yet."

"I don't want to be in the play."

Every kid had a part, and his was as a tree. "You don't have any lines," she said.

"I have to do a stupid tree dance. And it's stupid."

"Everyone's dancing, Tommy. Not just you."

Tommy stared at his dark e-reader screen as if he could still make out the words. "Everyone's mom is supposed to make their costume."

Kate's chest went tight. "You know I'll make your costume," she said softly. Fiercely. "You'll be the best tree that ever danced."

He lifted a scrawny shoulder.

She took in his slightly bowed head and averted eyes, and she knew there was more. "What?"

He shrugged again, and Kate's heart broke a little more. "How about I have Mrs. Garcia put you on the very back edge of the stage, okay? And then, after school, we'll make pancakes." She had no business promising pancakes. Holly's rehearsal dinner was tonight, and as maid of honor, she had a bazillion and one things to do.

"Offstage," Tommy said, negotiating. Clearly, he'd been watching *Pawn Stars* with her dad again. "And chocolate-chip pancakes."

"Onstage." She sighed. "But yeah, I'll cave on the chocolate-chip pancakes."

They shook on the deal.

Griffin walked down the hallway of the elementary school experiencing an odd sense of déjà vu. It had been a whole hell of a lot of years since he'd walked these halls, and mostly back then he'd either been running like hell during an escape or sitting on a bench outside the principal's office.

He had no idea why he was here now.

Except he did. He'd promised Tommy he'd come by for a brownie. And maybe a small part of him wanted to see Kate in her element. He stopped in the doorway to her classroom and took in the scene. She was sitting cross-legged on the floor with the kids, reading to them.

She'd taken off her sweater. Her demure, librarian-approved blouse, skirt, tights, and boots shouldn't have made him hot. The blouse had a little stand-up collar and a row of teeny-tiny buttons down the front. A nightmare to get into in a hurry. Nope, that shirt was made for the slow reveal, and it was really amazing how sexy it was when paired with the reading glasses perched on her nose and the way her hair was twisted in a knot at the base of her neck.

She was every guy's secret teacher-jack-off fantasy. She'd been his just last night.

She was laughing and so were the kids as she picked up a book, opened it to a page, and said a word. She pointed at someone to spell the word, which correlated to the picture on the page of the big book she was holding.

Spelling had been torture for Grif. Sheer torture. He'd

have done anything to get out of it—and often had. Frogs in his pockets let loose at the right moment. Spilling whatever he could get his hands on to garner him an excuse to go to the restroom. Whatever he could think of, he attempted to pull off.

But here no one was attempting escape.

He suspected the reason for the kids' rapt attention was the exact same reason he moved to get closer.

Kate.

She had a way of glowing, of looking so happy to be talking to you, of spreading smiles . . . It was like she was a drug. She met his gaze then, and something came into her smile.

A wariness.

Smart girl.

Tommy turned to see who Kate was looking at. He beamed and scooted over to make some room in the circle for Griffin. A few other parents came in as well, and the kids' circle widened again. It was an ongoing thing, he realized, Kate expanding her circle to accept everyone.

When spelling was over and Kate had excused the kids back to their desks, each of which had a brownie on it, Grif started to head toward the front of the classroom, but Tommy ran over to him. "Griffin!"

"Hey, kid."

"Hey!" Tommy handed over the flannel shirt. "I wore it all day," he said proudly, smiling his gap-toothed smile. "Well, except when I painted. I didn't wanna spill."

Which, given the splotches of green and blue paint smeared on Tommy's cheek, had been a good call.

Tommy held out his right hand for the same fist bump they'd exchanged earlier. Then he held out his left and handed Grif a brownie that was only slightly squished. "I saved this one for you." With one last grin, he turned and ran directly into Dustin.

"Hey, 'tard," Dustin said. "Watch where you're going."

Tommy looked down at the chocolate smeared on his hand and licked his palm.

Grif opened his mouth to say something to the rude punk-ass, but Kate beat him to it.

"That's an unacceptable word, Dustin," she said. "What happens when we use an unacceptable word?"

Dustin huffed out a sigh. "Time-out."

"Then go take one."

As he had earlier, Dustin kicked the ground. No dust rose this time as he walked back to his seat.

Tommy slid Kate a long look but said nothing as he moved back to his seat as well.

Grif leaned in. "Why don't you let that little shit have it?"

She spoke just as quietly. "Because it wouldn't do Tommy any favors to have his teacher—and his sister—defend his manhood."

"Maybe not, but it'd do the bully good to be put in his place."

She glanced at the kids, making sure no one could overhear them. "Bullies usually come from bullies, which means Dustin needs extra kindness at school."

To Grif this seemed like the opposite of what should be done. "You think any of these kids would dare bully Dustin?" he asked her. "He's a lot bigger than they are."

Her gaze held his. "Bullying is learned at home," she said again. "I think that kindness will do more for both boys. Leading by example."

Grif disagreed on all counts, vehemently. But then again, he was a soldier not a second-grade teacher, which was probably a good thing.

Another man entered the classroom, and Grif recognized him as the guy who'd come on to Kate at the bachelor/bachelorette party. The attorney. Trevan Anders. Tall, leanly muscled, and dressed in an expensive suit, he walked across the floor like he owned it.

"Dustin," Anders said, and snapped his fingers. "Let's hit it."

Dustin—Trevan's mini-me—leaped out of his seat.

Kate intercepted, stepping between the father and son to

face Trevan. "Again, Mr. Anders?" she asked quietly. "Can't you schedule Dustin's training for after school?"

"So we're back to Mr. Anders, then?" he asked with a smile that made Grif want to punch him on principle. "What happened to calling me Trevan?"

With cheeks sporting two high spots of color that Grif was pretty sure were from annoyance and not embarrassment, Kate pulled Anders aside. "You're the father of one of my students," she said. "So yes, it's Mr. Anders. As for Dustin leaving class early, it costs him."

"Dustin's coach plays in the minors," Trevan said. "His time is limited. And important."

"So is spelling," Kate said, but Grif knew by the look on Anders's face that he disagreed. "There's a test tomorrow," she went on. "And another only two days after that. He needs to pass these in order to be eligible for our field trips, specifically the upcoming trip to the animal center."

Trevan looked at Dustin. "That's fine. He has to pass them anyway in order to have the grades required by his travel team to play in his upcoming tournament."

Dustin squirmed, and his father's eyes narrowed. "He's in danger of not passing?"

"More class time would help," Kate said. "But I have every confidence in Dustin."

"And I have every confidence in you, Ms. Evans," Trevan said, and snapped his fingers at Dustin. "Come on."

Dustin hesitated. "Dad, I want to get to go to the animal center—"

"Now, Dustin."

"But—"

"You have to the count of three to get moving," Trevan snapped. "Do not make me start counting."

Dustin kicked his desk, shoved Nina who was standing next to him, and came along as ordered.

Kate stopped him and crouched low to meet the boy's eyes. "You have your spelling homework," she said. "After practice, spend some time with it, okay?"

Above her, Anders glanced at his watch.

Asshole, Grif thought.

Kate let them go, but Grif was pretty sure they all knew that Dustin wasn't going to spend much time studying spelling.

After school, Ryan dropped Kate and Tommy off at her dad's house. Kate went inside since she had to make the promised chocolate-chip pancakes, plus Ashley had left three teary messages about some trauma she'd experienced during her day.

The teen was locked in her room, refusing to come out.

Having been an emotional teen herself, Kate knew yelling through the door was a waste of time. She went to the kitchen and pulled a lasagna casserole from the freezer. She wrote out specific instructions on a sticky note, which she placed on the tinfoil. Then she made the chocolate-chip pancakes for a very happy Tommy. Finally, she searched out her dad who was in the living room and had both his laptop and Channing Tatum in his lap vying for space.

"Dinner's on the counter," she told him. "With instructions."

He grimaced. "Ashley told you about last night?"

"She texted to say you burned dinner and set off the fire alarm."

"I don't know what happened."

"I do," Kate said. "You put the casserole in the oven and forgot about it."

He'd forget his own head if it wasn't attached. Once upon a time he'd been a brilliant biologist. He'd studied at Stanford, taught at Berkeley, where he'd met Kate's mom. They'd lived the dream—until Belinda had died in a car accident.

Eddie had been driving, and a part of him had died with her. He'd lost himself and his way. Drowning in guilt, he'd fallen into a depression, and then he had turned to his painkillers to numb his pain while Kate had fought for her family. He was one year sober, and she was proud of him, but he still hadn't stepped fully back into the ring.

He sighed. "I'll be more careful tonight."

She leaned in and kissed his jaw. "Set the timer this time, okay?"

He smiled and pushed his glasses farther up his nose. "I promise." He squeezed her hand. "You should be running your own life, Kate, not mine."

"I don't know what that looks like," she said. "You all are my life. I love you guys. Plus you can't do without me."

"Of course we can." He set the laptop aside and tried to nudge the cat off of him, but Channing Tatum refused to be budged.

"We've talked about this," Eddie said to the cat. "Stop soaking up Ashley's bad 'tude."

The cat hissed and then jumped down, stalking off, tail straight up in the air.

Eddie rose, but then he scratched his head as if forgetting what he wanted to do.

"Dad."

"We're fine, Kate. Get to the rehearsal dinner. We're all good here. Go have a life."

"Sure, go." This was from Ashley, standing in the doorway in all her teenage attitude and glory, and far too little clothing. She looked a lot like Kate, actually, minus about ten pounds of stress ice cream. "Go off and forget us; we'll be fine even though Kyle is a two-timing jerk and Kia is a two-timing bitch and my life is over." By the end of this sentence she was wailing at a decibel that only dogs could hear.

Her dad blinked. "Who's Kyle and Kia?" he asked Kate.

"Her boyfriend and best friend." Kate moved to Ashley.

"Ex-BF. Ex-BFF," Ashley said. She burst into tears and then threw herself into Kate's arms.

Kate looked over her head to her dad, hoping he would step in.

He looked horrified.

Kate sighed and hugged Ashley. "Boys can be jerks, Ash. But Kia dated Kyle first, remember?"

Ashley sniffed and shoved free. "Well, if you're going to be mean . . ."

"Ash—"

"No." She stormed toward her room. "Just go, I don't care. My life isn't as important as a rehearsal dinner."

"Honey, your life is very important to me," Kate said. "But last week you didn't even like Kyle anymore. Remember? Is it possible that you're just getting your period?"

Ashley turned back, her eyes filling again. "Yes! And there's no more Midol! Dad still can't bring himself to buy it. Or tampons. I used to get both from Kia," she sobbed.

Kate emptied out her purse, contributing her stash to the cause, and then she left after being assured by her dad that he wouldn't leave Ashley alone until the Midol kicked in.

Back at her own place, Kate realized she had time to exercise before Holly and Adam's rehearsal dinner.

Dammit.

She changed into her running gear and hit the trail that ran behind her row of townhouses and through a wooded park to the lake and to her tree. Her place.

She started off at a walk but kicked it into gear and ran. She hated running.

Hated.

But it burned calories. Halfway through her torture, she passed the park and then the concession stand, and she slowed. They had fresh popcorn. Damn.

"Got any spare change?"

She looked down at the guy sitting on the park bench. Larry was somewhere between fifty and ancient, and he liked to watch the geese. He'd been here as long as she could remember. Well, except for when the sheriff occasionally rounded him up and dragged him to the homeless shelter. Over the years he'd been placed in the occasional halfway house, but he wasn't good at following the rules, so it rarely lasted long. He wore at least three layers of clothing on his huge frame and took up most of the bench where he always sat, clutching a bottle inside a brown bag.

Kate would absolutely give Larry her spare change—if there were a single hope of him spending it on something other than alcohol. Instead, she did what she usually did. She went to the stand, bought two bags of popcorn, and brought him back one.

He dug in with childlike gusto and a sweet smile. "Thanks, Ms. Evans."

She walked up the hill to the top of the dam, to her favorite place. Her tree. Someone a long time ago had built a makeshift tree house in the tree next to the fallen Jeffrey Pine, but there was a warning posted on it. No climbers allowed.

No problem for Kate; she was afraid of heights. But she'd had to stop bringing Tommy out here because he wasn't, and he always wanted to climb it.

Walking around the trunk of her fallen tree, she sat facing the lake far below and munched on her popcorn.

Some exercise.

She'd run twice as far next time, she promised herself and her jeans.

An hour later, Kate got to the wedding rehearsal. Standing in the doorway of the church, she let out a big long breath and hopefully all of her tension along with it. Tonight was for Holly. Tonight was not for throwing herself at any sexy-as-hell soldiers turned groomsmen.

Absolutely not. Just because he'd refused to take advantage of her last night or because he'd rescued her brother today or because he'd looked so out of his element in her classroom and yet had still managed to be an authority figure to the kids . . .

No. She was not going to soften toward him and try again.

Probably.

Luckily, as the maid of honor, she had a list of wedding duties running through her head and a clipboard to help make sure she didn't forget anything. She'd slapped a little yellow sticky note to the top of the clipboard. It said:

NO ALCOHOL, YOU 'HO.

Things started off smoothly. The music was cued. Each of the bridesmaids took her turn walking down the aisle. When it was Kate's turn, she was pretend-holding flowers and working on getting the right rhythm when she looked up and found Adam, Dell, Brady, and Griffin standing at the top of the aisle in their places, waiting shoulder to shoulder.

Hot guy overload.

Griffin's eyes were on her, dark and serious, and when she stared back, his gaze heated.

Kate tripped over her own feet.

Adam smiled.

Griffin was thinking about smiling, she could tell.

Ignoring him, she took her place at the front of the church next to the other bridesmaids to watch as Holly walked down the aisle toward Adam. Even though it was just the rehearsal, the two of them stared into each other's eyes, completely ignoring the insanity around them.

Kate couldn't help but well up a little. It was beautiful. What they had was beautiful. So much so that it was like she was intruding on a moment of intimacy. Looking away, her gaze again collided with gray steel.

Griffin didn't smile, just held the eye contact until she broke it.

The dinner itself was held at a local restaurant, and a few additional close friends joined the group. This worked for Kate. She needed the anonymity of a crowd tonight. She was at the bar grabbing two pitchers of beer to bring back to the head table for Holly and Adam when she bumped into Ryan, once again making headway with one of the cute bridesmaids. She rolled her eyes at him and turned to leave him to it when she nearly plowed over Griffin.

"Easy," he said, deftly removing the two pitchers from her hands before she could spill down the front of the both of them.

Easy? There was nothing easy when it came to her reaction to him. "Sorry," she said. "I have a propensity for spilling."

He just smiled. "And for fancy words."

She felt herself flush. "I have a word-of-the-day calendar." She paused. "And a fact calendar."

"What's today's fact?"

"An ostrich egg is bigger than its brain."

"Good to know," he said. "How about naughty facts? Got any of those?"

She had to bite her lip before it escaped, but he laughed again, low and sexy as he moved in closer. "You do. Tell me, Kate."

She closed her eyes, but he merely brushed up against her as if he knew the power his body held over hers.

"Your invisibility cloak isn't working," he said. "Spill it."

Dammit. She opened her eyes. "Our earlobes line up with our nipples."

He grinned. "Why, Ms. Evans. You said *nipples*." While she was still blushing—and kicking herself—he brought the pitchers of beer to the head table for her, and letting out a slow, careful breath, Kate absolutely did not watch his ass as he walked away.

"You're drooling," Ryan murmured in her ear as he came up behind her.

Kate swiped at her chin, but he was of course lying. "What are you doing talking to me, where's your conquest?"

"Restroom."

"What are your odds?"

"Better than you accepting your scholarship in the twelve days you have left."

She rolled her eyes and then leaned in to take a sip of his beer.

"Hey," he said, trying to pull away.

"Just a sip," she said, wrapping her fingers around his wrist. "I'm not allowing myself my own alcohol tonight. It doesn't count if it's yours."

"You realize that's stupid," Ryan said, fighting her for his drink. "And stop it— Get your own!"

"I can't. Last night I attempted to seduce a groomsman."

Ryan stopped fighting her and looked up in surprise. "You did? Which one?"

She sighed. "The perfect one."

Ryan made an I-don't-want-to-hear-this grimace.

"And he tasted better than double-fudge ice cream," she said. "Do you know who tastes better than double-fudge ice cream? No one."

"Hey," Ryan said. "I've kissed you. I taste good, right?"

Kate patted his arm. "Can we concentrate here? I have a problem. I want him. Bad. Badder than bad."

Ryan made the face again and then went still.

Kate closed her eyes. "He's right behind me, isn't he?"

"Yep," Griffin said.

Ryan shrugged and took back his drink.

With a wince, Kate glanced over her shoulder. "Um. Hi."

"Would you like your own drink?" he asked with absolutely no mockery in his voice.

Because it was all in his eyes.

"No." Face flaming, she stuck her arm through Ryan's. "I'm good, thanks." Ryan tried to free himself, but Kate held on tight, digging her fingernails into him.

Looking amused, Griffin shrugged and moved to the bar, presumably to order his own drink.

"Shit," Ryan hissed, pulling free to pull up his sleeve and check his arm. "You almost broke skin."

Guilt had her leaning over him to see, but suddenly, Ryan gave her a little push. "Sexy bridesmaid at two o'clock," he said. "Don't touch me."

Out of Kate's peripheral view she could see Griffin leaning against the bar, all easy charm . . . watching her. "Quick, smile at me."

"What? No!"

"You have to," Kate said urgently. "He rejected me last night. I don't want him to think I'm still pining."

"How about crazy? Are you worried about him thinking you're crazy?" Ryan asked.

"Okay, you know what? You're fired as my wingman."

"Thank God," he said fervently. "Now, don't go away mad, just go away."

Eight

Grif was doing his best to be present for Holly and Adam, but the truth was he'd rather have had a root canal without meds than attend a wedding rehearsal. But any idiot, even those who'd completely failed at the love game like himself, could see that his sister and best friend were meant to be together.

He was happy for them. And okay, so he'd not completely failed at the love game. He'd given it a half-ass shot a couple of times. It hadn't worked out, that was all. His life hadn't exactly lent itself to a long-term relationship anyway. Still didn't, since he had no idea what his future held, and at the moment he didn't care too much.

The best that could be said about the wedding rehearsal dinner was that the food was good and his father kept to the other side of the room.

Grif had shoveled horseshit for hours that morning, and he had the pleasantly sore shoulder and arm muscles to prove it. It had felt good to do something after weeks and weeks of forced inactivity. But this, the socializing, was going to kill him. A fiery poker had been stabbing slowly and steadily behind one of his eyeballs for an hour now. He put a finger to it, pressing hard, but it was too late. He'd ignored the signs of the impending migraine, and it had hit him like a fucking freight train.

The last of the day's light slanted in through the restaurant windows, slicing at his brain. The laughter and music around him might as well have been a herd of elephants. Lowering his ever-present baseball cap farther over his eyes, he left their private dining room, walking on shaky legs down the hallway in the opposite direction of the party, needing a quiet place where he could crawl into a ball and wait it out.

He found a small office masquerading as a coatroom, or so he supposed by the layers and layers of jackets and sweaters and other various outer gear on every single available surface. There were a few chairs and a love seat. It would have to do. He was halfway through clearing the love seat when the nausea hit him.

He got lucky that there was a bathroom attached to the office. He was entirely too large for the postage-stamp-size room, but comfort was a distant need behind the waves and waves of pain rolling over him. As always when hit with a massive migraine, he was nearly blinded by it, and he was struck deaf and dumb as well. All he could do was turn off the light, lie on the cold linoleum floor, and pray for a quick finish.

He wasn't lucky enough for that.

It might have been only minutes or an entire year later when he heard someone open the bathroom door. The light came on, which was like being stabbed with lightning bolts. With a groan, Grif squeezed his eyes shut. "Off," he managed.

"Griffin!"

Mercifully, this was followed by the light going off. Next came the wince-inducing click, click, click of Kate's heels, and her soft, warm hand brushing his forehead. "What is it?" she asked. "What's wrong?"

"Shh."

He heard the rustle of her clothing as she crouched at his side. "Are you hurt?" she asked.

Nope. Just sick as a dog, and if she didn't zip it, she was going to see just how sick firsthand. That would suck. So did the fact that he couldn't even open his eyes and see how sexy she looked with that sweater hugging her curves. He couldn't even steal a peek up her skirt—which killed him because this wasn't her usual cargo teacher skirt. Nope, this baby was short, black, and slinky. Reaching out, he clamped a hand over her wrist, halting her from patting his body, trying to find where he was hurt. Or so he assumed. Maybe she was into copping feels of sick guys.

"Griffin." She sounded so worried, which he had to admit was kind of nice. "You're shaking."

Yes, and sweating, too, and utterly incapable of functioning, thank you very much. But he forced his eyes to slit open. "Just a headache."

She stared at him. "It's more than a headache. Is it your . . . injury?" she whispered, saying the word like it was a state secret since she knew he didn't want to talk about it.

Christ, she was sweet. The sweetest person he'd ever known. Holly was right. She was way too sweet for the likes of him. "I'll be okay."

"Griffin, you're flat on your back and so pale your skin's see-through."

"I'm fine."

She made an annoyed sound. "Of course you are. You're a guy. Has this happened before? How do you treat it?"

"Sex."

"What?"

He shouldn't be teasing her when he couldn't even lift his own head, but he couldn't seem to temper himself around her. He wondered if this was what it was like for her when she let loose with those science facts of hers. "Yeah," he said. "Down and dirty, no-holds-barred sex. Cures me every time."

"You're kidding."

Unfortunately, he couldn't have pleased her right now to save his life. And wasn't that just the bitch of it.

"I'm going to get Adam," she said, calm and sure, and started to rise.

He tightened his grip on her wrist. "No, don't. It's his night."

Her hands went to his chest. They were small but strong and sure, and he loved the feel of them on him. Too much. And he began to revise what he might be able to accomplish with a migraine.

"It's his best friend lying on the floor," Kate said. "He'd want to help."

"No."

"Fine." She shifted, and her clothing rustled again. Unable to beat back the curiosity, he slit his eyes open in time to see her shimmying her pencil skirt higher on her thighs. When he shifted to take in the delicious flash of thigh-high stockings, the movement penetrated his skull, giving him a stab of such fierce, icy pain, he gasped with it. Oh Christ. He'd been afraid he was going to die on this bathroom floor, but suddenly he was afraid he wasn't going to die.

Kate had lowered herself to the tile and now gently cradled his head in her lap. "Better?" she murmured, stroking her cool hands on his overheated temples.

Her touch was like heaven, and he heard a moan. His.

"Oh, you poor, stupidly stubborn man," she whispered softly, and gently massaged his scalp and temples until he wanted to whimper with relief.

She didn't push him to talk or try to get him up; she just ran those fingers over him until he was certain he wasn't going to be sick again.

"Okay," he finally managed to say. He was going to get up. "We're even now."

"How's that?"

"You're pretending last night didn't happen, and I'm going to pretend tonight didn't happen." Leaving his eyes closed, he slowly sat up.

She said nothing until he managed to very carefully look at her.

"If you won't let me call anyone for you," she said. "I'm going to help you home."

"I've got it."

"Really? Because you can't even open your eyes all the way, Big Alpha Man. How the hell do you think you can drive?"

"You talk to your students in that tone?"

"When they're acting like little idiots," she said.

If he could have sighed without feeling like his head was going to fall off, he would have. He didn't want to talk about his migraine or why he got them. He just wanted to be in his bed.

She reached for his hand.

"Kate—"

"Shh. Just a little pressure," she said, and began a slow, steady pinch to the skin between his thumb and forefinger. "Acupressure," she said, holding him like that for a long moment before slowly releasing him. "Better?"

He had to think about it. No, his head still wanted to come off his shoulders, but he no longer felt like he was going to throw up. Progress.

"I used to do this for my dad's migraines," she said. "They started after my mom died. At first he had his pain meds, but then he got too attached to them." She paused. "Way too attached. So when he had to learn to go without, I did this to help him."

"Did it work?"

"On the pain, yes. On keeping him off the pills? No."

He knew her father was a recovering addict. Knew also how much of his life Kate had taken over so he didn't lose everything. Grif wondered at the strength of her, giving up her life for her family, something he'd never had to do. His own father hadn't fallen apart when his mom had left. Nor when she'd died. Donald Reid had simply shouldered the grief and gone on. It was what the Reid family did.

Go on.

He rolled to his hands and knees and stilled, taking stock. Before he could stagger to his feet on his own, Kate put a shoulder beneath his armpit and shoved.

She was maybe 120 pounds soaking wet, and yet she managed to get him upright.

"Okay?" she asked very quietly, her arms around him, holding him steady.

He paused, considered throwing up again, but managed to hold it together. What he couldn't do was talk. Thankfully, she got that and steered him to the door.

She took him out the back way of the restaurant, something else he'd have to be grateful for later, because it was taking all his concentration not to whimper like a baby.

Just before she opened the back door, she stopped and fiddled with her purse. Then she was putting something over his eyes.

Sunglasses.

"Come on," she said softly but matter-of-factly. Calm. She led him straight to the ranch truck he'd appropriated from his dad's fleet. He leaned against the side and tried to figure out how to tell her that he probably couldn't drive without killing them both.

That's when he felt her hand in his front pants pocket. Not much shocked him, but her questing fingers came close.

She made a sound of frustration.

An inch to the left, babe, and you'll have all you could ever want . . .

But then she retracted her hand and . . . shoved it into his other front pocket. "There," she said, pilfering his keys right off his person, leaving him hard on top of being in excruciating pain—quite the feat.

"Watch your head," she murmured, and he squinted his eyes open to see that she'd unlocked the truck and wanted him to get into the passenger seat.

And that, according to his reflection in the window, he was wearing neon green sunglasses.

Nice.

With that same calm, matter-of-fact air, Kate got him

seated, and then she leaned over him to fasten his seat belt. Her hair tickled his nose, as did her scent, but he kept his eyes closed.

He must have drifted off because the next thing he knew he was jerking awake when a hand stroked lightly over his arm.

Kate had driven him home. She stood in the open passenger door of the truck, watching him far too carefully for his comfort. He slid out of the vehicle and walked into the ranch house, heading straight down the hall to his bedroom. He kicked off his shoes and stripped in two seconds flat, then stretched out on the bed and closed his eyes, sighing at the blissful silence.

A few seconds later he felt someone come into the room, but he was unable to bring himself to care. He was shivering a little bit, which was par for the course. His body had a hell of a time regulating his own temperature when he got like this.

A blanket was pulled up over him. His head was burning up, but he didn't have the energy to do anything about that either.

A minute later a cold wet washcloth was set against his forehead, and though he hadn't cried in years, he actually nearly lost it then in sheer relief.

"I called Adam," Kate said softly, stroking his hair off his forehead. "Before you get all butt-hurt about that, you have to know I can't leave you alone like this."

"It's his fucking wedding rehearsal, Kate."

"Dinner's over and he's on his way."

He'd have to kill her later because the nausea was back. He couldn't move without throwing up, and he'd sell his soul to the devil himself before doing that in front of her.

Kate was alternately pacing the living room and standing in the doorway to Griffin's bedroom, straining to see his chest rising and falling, when she heard a truck drive up.

Adam, she thought hopefully.

But it wasn't. It was Donald Reid. He looked surprised to see her standing in his house, and she quickly told him about Griffin's migraine.

"Huh," he said, and headed in the opposite direction.

"Wait. Aren't you going to check on him?"

Donald turned back. "Didn't you check on him?"

"Well, yes. Of course."

Donald nodded and kept going. "No worries, his head is hard enough; he'll get past this."

Kate was still standing there in shock when she heard another truck. This time it was Adam. He strode into the house, nodded at her, and went straight down the hall.

Toward Griffin's room, she noted in relief.

Unable to help herself, she followed, staying in the doorway as Adam entered Griffin's room. The two men spoke so quietly that she couldn't hear a damn thing.

A few minutes later, Adam came out and met her in the hallway. He tugged on a strand of her hair. "Looking a little rough, cutie."

"Forget me," she said. "What about Griffin? Is he okay? What's wrong? Has he always gotten migraines like this, or is it from his injury?"

He gave her a second look. "What do you know of his injury?"

"Absolutely zip."

Adam nodded but said nothing.

God save her from alpha men. "Tell me," she said. "I've seen his scar."

And she'd seen a lot more than that earlier when he'd stripped out of his clothes without a thought; there wasn't a self-conscious bone in his body. And now that she'd seen it all—every inch—she could say with certainty that he had absolutely nothing to be self-conscious about, because the promise he made in clothes was absolutely kept without them.

"He was injured in a blast," Adam said. "He sustained a

head trauma, a closed head injury. It left him with ringing ears, headaches, light sensitivity, fatigue . . ."

"And talkative friends."

Both Adam and Kate froze at Griffin's rough, low, irritated voice coming from the bedroom.

"I'm fine," Grif said. "Or I will be. So unless one of you is going to get naked and offer up sex, get the hell out."

"I did offer it up," Kate said. "You weren't interested, remember?"

Adam's brows shot up so fast and far that they vanished under his hairline.

Griffin said nothing, but she could feel his annoyance coming in loud and clear.

"Explain," Adam said.

Griffin said nothing, apparently pleading the Fifth.

And Kate would explain over her own dead body. She shouldn't have said anything at all; she hadn't meant to. But once again her mouth had spoken without permission. "Having sex is three times more effective as a pain reflector than a morphine dose." Dammit! She closed her mouth and then put her hand over it just in case.

A snort came from the direction of the bed but no words.

"Well, I'd offer to take one for the team," Adam said conversationally to Griffin through the open door, "but you're not my type. Now someone talk to me."

More radio silence from Griffin.

Adam slid his back down the wall until he was seated on the floor. "Fine. I'll sit here all night. And then be too tired to bone your sister tomorrow night."

Griffin's silence ramped up a notch.

Kate sighed and sat next to Adam. Time passed.

"You know he's leaving," Adam eventually said. "After the wedding. He's got job offers on the other side of the country."

Kate nodded, pretending she knew and that it didn't matter. But it did matter, if the pang of disappointment was anything to go by, even though logically she never expected him to stick around in Sunshine. "Nothing's going on."

"Why are you still here?" Griffin asked.

"We're not," Adam said.

Griffin swore with impressive skill. "Go home."

"Make me," Adam said lightly.

Either Griffin had nothing to say to that or he'd fallen asleep again.

"He'll be okay," Adam said to Kate.

"How do you know?"

"Because I called in some favors and got his medical history."

"For fuck's sake," Griffin muttered from the bed.

Adam met Kate's gaze. "The problem is that he was at ground zero when the explosion went off."

"Was he alone?" she whispered, horrified.

"No. His unit was with him, at least until a few seconds before when he got a hinky feeling and sent them to safety. He got a medal for that—not that he's said anything about it. Anyway, he's healing up pretty good. Too slow to suit himself, but that's par for the course. He's not exactly a patient guy."

From the bed came a long-suffering sigh, and Adam smiled.

Kate took heart in that. Surely, if Griffin was in any sort of danger, Adam wouldn't be baiting him.

"And this isn't the first time I've sat at his bedside after some stupid move he's made," Adam said.

Kate looked at him. "No?"

"Nope. Fourth of July, twenty years ago. Remember that, Grif?"

Grif didn't respond.

"We stole a box of fireworks from the rec center," Adam told Kate. "We took the haul up to Beaute Point and set out to create us a hell of a show. Except one of the mortars backfired. Landed us both in the hospital. Grif with second-degree burns on his arms and chest, and me with a sprained ankle." Adam smiled fondly at the memory. "Old man Reid was fit to be tied. I think if Grif hadn't been flat on his back, Donald would've beaten the shit out of us both."

"You didn't get the sprained ankle from the explosion," Griffin said from the bed. "You got it from running like hell from the explosion."

Adam grinned and pointed to his head. "No grass growing here." His smile faded as he glanced into the dark room, at the far-too-still figure on the bed. "And you told me to run," he said softly. "You probably saved my life that night."

Griffin didn't answer this.

Long moments went by, and they could hear the steady, deep breathing coming from the bedroom.

"You're a good friend," Kate said quietly.

"He's the good friend," Adam said. "He's not the person who'll call you when you're going through a hard time. He's the person who gets on a plane in the middle of the night when you're going through a hard time, and he won't leave until you're better again."

Kate knew that to be true. Over the years she'd watched as Grif had come through for Holly in every possible way a brother could, being there when their mom died, flying to her when he'd suspected that her first marriage had gone bad in New York. Whatever Holly needed, Grif gave it to her, whether Holly wanted his help or not.

"So," Adam said. "Did you really try to sleep with him last night? Does Holly know?"

"Yes. And no. Not yet." Kate leaned her head back against the wall and closed her eyes. "It was a momentary weakness, and besides, he turned me down flat."

Adam laughed softly. "I bet he's kicking his own ass about now."

"I doubt it." She paused. "Although men do change their minds two to three hundred percent more often than women."

"I'm not going to change my mind," came Griffin's disembodied voice from the bed.

Kate rolled her eyes.

Adam patted her knee. "Go home, cutie. I've got this."

"But you need sleep, too."

"Oh, I'll sleep."

"How?" Kate asked.

He flashed a grin. "Trust me, I've been in worse conditions." And with that, he rose lithely to his feet and walked into Griffin's room, stretching out on the bed next to his oldest friend.

"You've got to be kidding me," she heard Griffin mutter.

"Suck it up, man."

"Jesus. Don't say *suck* while you're in bed with me. Don't even think it."

Confident that if he could joke around like that, then he was probably going to live, Kate left the two of them alone.

Nine

The next day dawned early and bright. Kate got up to run just to make extra-sure her bridesmaid dress fit well. She pulled on her gear, slipped outside into the icy morning air, and hit the trail. She was tempted to run to the ranch just to make sure Griffin wasn't still suffering.

Instead she texted Adam. He okay?

Alive and pissy, came the quick response.

Good enough. She needed to tell Holly that she'd kissed her brother twice in a row now, but that was a conversation best held for after the wedding. She had no intention of hiding anything from her best friend, but it would be selfish to tell her today.

That was her story, and she was sticking to it.

Besides, what if Holly killed Griffin for kissing her? It would rob Adam of a groomsman . . . So really, Kate was doing everyone a favor by keeping it to herself for just a little bit longer. Huffing and puffing, she got to her halfway point. The park concession stand was closed.

No popcorn this early.

And no Larry on the bench. It was too cold for even the

bum. Hoping he was somewhere warm and safe, she forced herself to keep going and hit the hill to climb to the top of the dam. Gasping for breath, she didn't take the time to sit on her tree. She stood looking down at the water for a minute, and when she could draw in air again, she turned around to go back down.

Larry's bench was still empty. Passing it by, she headed into the woods toward home. A minute later she heard footsteps behind her. Startled, she whirled around. "Hello?"

No one was there. She shrugged it off and started at pace again, but after a few steps the hair on the back of her neck stood straight up.

Again she whipped around.

Still no one.

Standing still, breathing wildly, her breath crystallizing in front of her face, she couldn't shake the feeling that someone was watching her. "Anyone there?"

This time the silence felt . . . loaded, like someone was holding his breath. Every single horror flick she'd ever watched came flying back to her, and she did exactly what she would have advised any woman in her situation not to do.

She ran in a blind panic.

She couldn't help it, and it only got worse when she could hear someone running after her. She forced herself to get out of the woods before looking back.

There was no one behind her.

Gasping for breath, she bypassed her townhouse, pulled her keys from her pocket, and slid into her car while hitting Holly's speed-dial.

"Hey," Holly said in a rush before Kate could speak. "I was just going to call you and beg you to come over early. I need ice cream."

They were each other's long-standing ice cream emergency stop. That it was only seven A.M. wouldn't faze either one of them. "Nerves?" Kate asked, hitting her door locks for the tenth time as she drove.

"Just a little," Holly admitted.

"On my way," Kate tried to say confidently, but she must have failed.

"What's wrong?" Holly asked.

"I'll be right there." Kate got to the ranch in record time and was halfway up the walk on still wobbly legs when she heard her name. Turning, she caught sight of Griffin in one of the horse pens. He ducked beneath the railing and strode toward her.

She was an independent, strong woman, she reminded herself. All she needed was the ice cream; that was it. Not the tall, built man in sexy jeans with the assessing gaze.

"What's wrong?" he immediately wanted to know.

"You first," she said. "Your migraine?"

"Gone."

Okay, good. And she walked right into his arms.

They immediately closed around her, which was a relief. She knew that she was in over her head with him, that even though this game they were playing at was temporary, very temporary, she couldn't seem to hold back. Burrowing in closer, she closed her eyes.

"Kate." He pressed his jaw to her hair. "You're trembling. Are you hurt?"

"No. I just needed . . ." This. "Ice cream."

"Ice cream?"

"Holly and I are having ice cream for breakfast."

He pulled back, cupped her face, and lifted her chin to look into her eyes. "Try again."

"I went for a run and got spooked," she said. "No big deal. I'm fine."

"You're not the easily spooked type."

She shrugged.

"Talk to me, Kate."

Maybe it was because his voice was so calm and certain. Authoritative but compassionate. "Someone followed me," she said. It seemed so silly now. "Look, I watched *CSI* last night. FYI? Bad idea. But no worries, ice cream will fix it."

He wasn't buying it.

Neither was Holly, who'd come outside in Hello Kitty pj's holding a quart of ice cream and a big spoon. "Someone stalked you on your run?" she asked. "Where? At your place or . . . at your place?"

"Wait," Griffin said. "What?"

"She has a place at the top of the dam where she goes to think," Holly said. "At the far end of the trail. There's a fallen tree that's been shaped by the elements. Makes a great little hiding spot where you can look down at the water. It's Kate's place."

"It was on the way back," Kate said. "Between the concession stand and my house. In the woods. Forget it; forget me. I'm here; I'm fine. What's with the ice cream emergency on your wedding day?"

"Just having a moment." Holly handed Kate the spoon.

One big bite later Kate felt better already.

"You still give that homeless guy breakfast?" Holly asked, taking the spoon back for herself.

Griffin looked like he was getting another headache. "You feed a homeless guy?"

"Larry's broke," Kate said. "Sometimes I give him food."

Griffin and Holly exchanged a long look.

"He's harmless," Kate said.

"Honey," Holly said, but before she could go on, Griffin cut in.

"Not everyone's as harmless as you think," he said. "I know you want to see the best in everyone, but that's not how the world works."

It was how her world worked. "Larry's always been sweet to me," she said. "He's not the one who ran after me. He weighs like two hundred and eighty pounds. He doesn't move very fast."

"I saw him run like hell at last year's three-legged race in the carnival," Holly said. "The prize was as many hotdogs as you could eat. He took first."

"You need to be armed if you're going to run in the woods by yourself," Grif said.

"Armed?" Kate laughed. "Come on." She gestured at her T-shirt and leggings. "Where would I carry a weapon?"

Griffin's gaze ran over her slowly enough to cause quivering knees.

Holly was dividing a look between them. "Okay," she said. "I'm missing something."

"Yes," Kate said, looping her arm through Holly's. "Your wedding day."

Holly waited until she and Kate were alone in her childhood bedroom to give Kate a look that struck terror in Kate's heart. "What is it?" Kate asked. "What's wrong?"

Holly sank to her bed, which was strewn with the gorgeous white lingerie she would soon put on beneath the gorgeous white wedding dress hanging in the open closet. "I have a secret," she said softly. "And I need a favor."

Kate sat next to her and took her hand. "Anything. You know that. You need a getaway car and driver so you can run away from that horribly ugly man you're about to marry?"

Holly smiled. Adam was tall, built, half Native American, and gorgeous, and everyone knew it. "I don't need a getaway car," she said. "But . . ." She pulled a little white stick from beneath the lingerie. It had two blue lines on it.

Kate stared at it. "You're—"

"Yep. Knocked up," Holly said. "Faulty condom." She grimaced. "Okay, so it was operator error, and I was the operator."

Kate grinned, and Holly let out a small smile. "Yeah?" she whispered, clutching Kate's hand. "It's good, right?"

"It's wonderful!" Kate exclaimed, and hugged her as they both shed a few happy tears.

"Adam knows, right?" Kate asked, reaching for the box of tissues on the nightstand.

"Yeah. He knows." Holly's sweet smile assured Kate

that Adam had taken the surprise news well. "He's going to tell his brothers and Grif today, but no one else for now. I wanted to keep it our own little secret for a little bit longer."

Kate's heart swelled, and she set a hand on Holly's still flat belly. "Wow," she murmured. "We're procreating."

"I know, it's crazy, but . . ." Holly covered Kate's hand with her own. "I'm so happy," she whispered. "I almost feel guilty about it. I just want everyone around me to have this kind of joy inside. I want it for you, Kate."

Kate pulled her hand back with a laugh. She'd just spent the past few years raising her siblings and her father. She wasn't in a hurry for the walk down the aisle, the white picket fence, or the white stick with the two blue lines. "Let's just concentrate on you today."

"Works for me." Holly hugged Kate again, tight. "But you're next."

Kate hugged her back, not sure whether that felt like a comfort or a possible nightmare.

An hour later an impatient Griffin stood at the far side of the top of the dam, studying what he assumed was Kate's "place."

It was beautiful, he could admit. Tucked away, off to the side, he could see her sitting here, looking down at the water, needing a minute away from her busy world.

He backtracked from there, following the route she would have taken earlier, stopping inside the park at the empty bench. He pulled out his phone and called Kel, an old friend and also a local sheriff. "Well?" Griffin asked him.

From the moment Kate and Holly had vanished into the ranch house to do wedding stuff, he, Adam, and Kel had gone looking for Larry, checking out his usual haunts. They'd made good time, even with Adam stopping to tell Grif about Holly being pregnant.

He was going to be an uncle.

"I was just going to call you," Kel said. "We found him.

He was at the animal center. Dell had gone in to feed the horses and found the guy sleeping on the front porch."

Dell was Adam's brother. The two of them, along with a third brother, Brady, ran Belle Haven, the local animal center. "Did you ask him about the park and Kate?"

"Says he can't remember if he was at the park today. But he did ask about the 'cutie-pie second-grade teacher.' His words," he said when Grif got ominously silent. "He can't remember her name."

"He's got a fixation on her?" Grif asked.

"He's got a fixation on pretty, shiny things. We found a bag of screws and buttons and loose change on him."

"You holding him?"

"For what, being a bum?" Kel asked. "No, I'm not holding him. And I don't think he's dangerous."

"You willing to stake Kate's life on it?"

Kel was quiet a moment, and it didn't take a shrink to know that he felt Grif was overreacting.

But Grif never overreacted. He reacted, and he damn well wanted other people to start reacting along with him, especially as it pertained to Kate's safety.

"I called Kate myself," Kel finally said. "She doesn't want to pursue this. And when I mentioned your concern, she said . . ."

"What?" Grif demanded. "She said what?"

Kel hesitated, and when he spoke, Grif got the feeling that he was fighting amusement. "She said that your concern was misguided and misplaced, and that you should mind your own business."

Grif disconnected and headed back to the ranch. He got out of the truck and walked toward the house, still annoyed. He was minding his business. She was his business. And when the fuck he'd decided that, he didn't have a clue. But he wasn't going anywhere until he believed she was safe. And if that meant staying in Sunshine a few days longer, sharing her with her grubby, obnoxious second graders, her siblings, her dad, and hell, the whole damn town since everyone loved her, so be it.

Adam beat him to the front door carrying a wedding banner and a nail gun. "Muttering to yourself is the first sign of mental illness."

Grif flipped him off.

"That's anatomically impossible and politically incorrect."

"I'd mess up that pretty face of yours," Grif said, "but you're getting married today."

Adam smiled. "You're afraid of Holly."

"Hell yeah."

Adam chuckled and rolled out the WELCOME TO THE CONNELLY WEDDING banner. He raised the nail gun and fingered the trigger but nothing happened.

"Shit," Dell said, coming up behind them. "You don't know what you're doing with that thing."

"Sure he does," Grif said. "It's a nail gun, not a condom."

Dell cracked up, and Adam gave Grif a shove. Then they put up the banner, and Dell went to deal with the caterer.

Adam looked at Grif. "You okay?"

Grif let out a low laugh and scrubbed a hand over his face. "Whatever it looks like, yeah."

"We've all got her back, man. You know that. But if it helps, I don't think Larry's dangerous. Nothing's going on."

Grif nodded. Nothing was going on. Nothing at all. Except for whatever the hell he was feeling for Kate. "Don't you have a wedding to get ready for?" he asked. "A pretty-boy tux to put on?"

Adam grinned and hooked an arm around Grif's neck. "What I'm wearing, you're wearing, pretty boy."

The wedding preparations were a whirlwind. Kate worked to make sure that the church and reception were set up just as Holly wanted. After the ceremony, they would all move back to the ranch for pictures and the reception.

Setting up the tables, she caught sight of Adam and Griffin building a gazebo. From across the yard, Griffin met her gaze. He said something to Adam and then came close. He was in jeans and a black sweatshirt with his hood up over his ever-present baseball hat. He pushed the hood off and removed his dark sunglasses.

"Wow," she said. "Almost full disclosure."

His eyes were so very serious. "Adam says Larry was found sleeping at the animal center this morning," he said.

"Oh good." Kate put a hand to her chest. "I was worried about him."

"He asked about the 'cutie-pie' teacher."

Kate smiled. "Aw. Me?"

Griffin pulled something from his pocket and set it into her hand.

Mace.

"I want you to carry this when you run."

She looked down at the small canister and then up into his eyes, which were focused unwaveringly on hers. He was absolutely resolute on this. "I'm okay," she said to him.

"And you'll stay that way. Do you know any self-defense at all?"

"Yes. Jade once taught me how to poke a guy's eyes out with a pen. And I've got the standard kick to the family jewels move."

"Always effective," he agreed. "You'll be careful."

"It's my middle name," she said.

"Thanks for driving me home last night." He pulled her sunglasses from his pocket and handed them over. "These were a big hit with Adam."

Remembering how he'd still managed to look seriously badass even in cheap neon green, she smiled. "You really feeling better?"

"Yes."

She searched his gaze, but he was good at hiding when he wanted to. She could learn a lot from him. At the thought of all that she might learn, she got one of those little tingles that he always seemed to invoke by just standing there. She could only imagine what would happen if they took this thing to bed.

"Kate," he said, his eyes heating as he clearly read her thoughts. "You have to stop looking at me like that."

"Why?"

"I'll take advantage of you," he said, no hesitation.

This caused another tingle. She wouldn't mind him taking that kind of advantage of her . . .

"We're not going there, Kate."

"That's not what your kisses say." And then before he could respond to that, she walked away.

An hour later Kate, Holly, and the other brides-maids met at the church to get ready together. Jade, the most sophisticated of the group, did their makeup. Lilah kept everyone in stitches recounting the trials and tribulations of running the town kennel. As a bonus, Miranda managed to keep most of her snark to herself. When they were all finished, they stood around a huge mirror staring at their reflections.

"Wow," Kate said reverently. "Holly, you look amazing."

Holly's eyes got misty, and she ran a hand along her stomach, a motion Kate knew she was the only one in the room to understand the implication of. "I don't want to forget a minute of this," she whispered.

"I've never seen a more beautiful bride," Miranda said, and mostly redeemed herself in Kate's eyes.

"Never," Kate agreed.

Holly hadn't taken her eyes off herself. "You all need to stop saying nice things. My makeup is too perfect to cry now." She waited a beat. "Okay, don't stop it."

They all gushed some more, shed a few happy tears in spite of their makeup, and then Holly smoothed her dress one last time and smiled. "So, any last-minute advice, girls?"

"Make sure to train him from the get-go," Lilah said. "Toilet seat down."

"And he should sleep in the wet spot at least half the time," Jade said.

"And don't let him contort your body into a position

during sex so that your stomach pooches and your boobs end up in your armpits with your ankles near your ears," Miranda said. "That's just not flattering for anyone."

Everyone stared at her for one awkward beat.

"Um, thank you," Holly finally said. "That's good advice."

Kate's cell rang. It was Ashley. "Dad's lost his keys."

Kate rushed over there to pick them up. Her dad was waiting for her on the porch. "Sorry," he said. "You look beautiful. I hope that sometime soon it might be my turn to walk my little girl down the aisle," he said.

She gave him a hug, and he squeezed her tight as Ashley showed up, wearing a miniskirt and skimpy tank top.

"No," Kate said, pointing to the stairs. "You've got three minutes to add many, many more acres of clothing, or you're going to get left behind."

"When I go off to college, you won't be the boss of me anymore."

"Don't tease me."

Ashley stomped back up the stairs.

Kate looked at her dad.

He shrugged. "She doesn't listen to me."

"She would if you actually said something."

Her father winced in guilt, and Kate felt her own stab of the same emotion. "I know you don't like to upset her, but she's an alien right now. You upset her by breathing, we all do, so you might as well put your foot down and mean it." Then she eyeballed Tommy from head to toe. By some miracle, he appeared to have used both shampoo and a brush. He looked adorable in his khakis and button-down shirt—which was dark brown so as to cover any possible stains because there were surely stains. "Your shoes are on the wrong feet," she said.

Tommy looked down at himself.

Kate waited.

But Tommy just scratched his head. "But I don't have any other feet."

"Fair enough," Kate said. "Let's go."

She drove them to the church, which was full and buzzing with warm vibes, soft music, and the hushed excitement that always came before a wedding.

Kate was in the waiting alcove with Holly and the others when she caught sight of the groomsmen showing guests to their seats. Griffin was one of them. She'd seen him in his army camo. She'd seen him in jeans. She'd seen him in a variety of clothing. But nothing beat seeing him in a tux.

Well, except for when he wore nothing at all . . .

The ceremony was beautiful, from the music to the flowers to the wedding party itself. Kate watched Griffin standing tall at Adam's side, his hair growing out of the military buzz cut, those miss-nothing eyes and that carefully blank face scanning their surroundings.

What was it like, she wondered, to have been so hardened, so honed into a lean, mean fighting machine that you could hide your every emotion?

Or did he just not have emotions?

No, she knew he did. She saw them when he dealt with Holly in an easy, affectionate way. Or when he looked with frustration at his father.

Or when he'd kissed her . . .

Yeah, there'd been a wealth of living, breathing, one hundred percent pure emotion under his surface. He was just entirely too good at keeping it all to himself most of the time.

Adam and Holly had written their own vows. By the time Adam took Holly's hand and looked deep into her eyes as he recited his own words in a firm, steady voice, there wasn't a dry eye in the place.

Except for Griffin. Kate knew he loved his sister, knew he was a good brother, but he was standing there like he was carved out of granite. She stared at him from a view gone blurry with her own tears, longing in a way she didn't understand. What was it about this one man that reached out and grabbed her by the throat? Why him?

The minister said something about the importance of family, and Holly craned her neck and met her brother's gaze.

Griffin flashed her a heart-stopping smile.

The smile got to Kate like nothing else. And she knew right then and there. She was in deep trouble.

The I-do's came, and then the kiss-the-bride part, which Adam appeared to take very seriously given the length of the time it took him to kiss Holly. No one could say that Adam wasn't extremely thorough.

Then the new bride and groom walked back down the aisle, followed by matched sets of bridesmaids and groomsmen. Griffin crooked his elbow and Kate slipped her arm through. He was the hardened soldier again, cool-headed, gorgeous with the strong angle of his jaw, the perfect contours of his cheekbones, the badass testosterone leaking from his every pore, and he represented something she'd never been able to give herself—fun.

The truth was, he flat out stole her breath. He always had, from the first time she'd seen him.

He met her gaze then, and she had to steel her resolve against the unwelcome wave of emotion that welled up inside her. His hand was on hers, and he smelled so fricking amazing, she ached. She ached from head to toe for him.

How stupid was that? She wanted him. Not for comfort or security. Those things were an illusion. She wanted him just for her. She didn't have a chance with him, and yet that didn't seem to matter to her heart. Just once, she thought with yearning.

Okay, maybe twice.

Three times tops.

Ten

The reception started off boisterous and happy, and escalated from there. Kate moved through the room, chatting, helping make sure everything ran smoothly, all while making her plan. How hard could it be to convince a red-blooded male in his sexual prime that one night together was a great idea?

She was smart, she reminded herself. She could do this. Maybe she didn't have a lot of experience, but she had great recall, so she mentally accessed every *Cosmo* article on flirting she'd ever read. And the next time she caught sight of Griffin in his tux, she made subtle—or what she hoped was subtle—eye contact, and making sure her arms were uncrossed, she smiled.

"What are you doing?" Ryan asked, coming up to her side, handing her a flute of champagne.

"What do you mean?"

"You look like you're having a seizure."

She sighed. "I'm trying to flirt."

"That was flirting?"

"Studies say that a woman can increase the likelihood of

a man approaching her if she uncrosses her arms, makes subtle eye contact, and smiles," she said.

"Studies? What studies?"

"*Cosmo.*"

Ryan laughed and looked across the room to see whom she was flirting with. "Mr. Houghton? Your sixty-five-year-old neighbor?"

"No!" She drank down her champagne. "Forget it. What happened to your bridesmaid? You get shut down?"

"Yeah." He stepped closer. "That dress is the exact color of your eyes, did you know that?"

Yes, she knew. It was a happy coincidence, as was the fact that the cut flattered her body. It could have gone either way. She had a closet full of bridesmaid dresses that had gone the wrong way, in fact. And then she realized she wasn't the only one flirting. Ryan was, too, with her. "Hey, you threatened to kill me if I made you be my date tonight," she reminded him. "So you can just take all those bottled-up sexy pheromones and go wave them at some other hot bridesmaid. You lost your chance with this." She waved at herself. "This is for someone else."

Ryan leaned in close enough to murmur in her ear, giving her a little nuzzle first. Which, damn him, he knew was her hot spot. "We could have breakup sex," he whispered hotly.

She slid him a look. "Breakup sex?"

"Yeah." He flashed his winning smile. "The kind of sex you have when you're broken up. To get over each other."

"We were over each other before we were under each other."

He sighed. "This isn't going to happen, is it?"

"Let me spell it out for you," she said. And then she made the same finger across the throat gesture he'd given her the other day.

He sighed again. "You're a little mean when you hold a grudge."

Kate turned and was handed a second flute of champagne by Mr. Nevins, her postal carrier. Mr. Nevins was six foot six and about 140 pounds when soaking wet. A pipe cleaner with eyes. And though he'd been delivering her mail for as long as she could remember, she still didn't know his first name.

"Heard you're looking for a hot date," he said.

Kate slid her gaze to just behind Mr. Nevins. Miranda was watching her. Eyes aglow, she waved at Kate. Kate tossed back her second champagne. "I'm sorry, but I'm not on the market."

"That's okay," he said. "You'd give me a crimp in my neck anyway."

She was then propositioned by Mr. Houghton, who gave her yet another drink and said it looked like maybe she'd been flirting with him earlier.

Kate turned him down gently, but she did accept the drink.

And just like that, the evening got pleasantly blurry. The DJ called the wedding party to the dance floor, and somehow she found herself bumping up against Mr. Tall, Dark, and Annoyingly Gorgeous himself.

"Hey," Griffin said, pulling her into him when she crashed into someone behind her and nearly went down. "You drunk again?"

"Okay," she said, very carefully pointing a finger in his face. "First of all, I wasn't drunk last night. Or the night before." She paused. "But I might be on my way now— entirely by accident, mind you. People keep asking me out, and turning them down requires alcohol."

"Remove your finger from my face."

Instead she waggled it. "Or . . . ?"

He nipped at the tip, and she yelped. Before she could pull it back, he sucked that same tip into his mouth. And just like that, her legs wobbled again. "Damn," she said.

"Tell me about these guys who are asking you out and plying you with alcohol."

She shrugged. "I have options is all."

His eyes narrowed. "Who?"

"Mr. Houghton."

Griffin relaxed. "Houghton's got high blood pressure and some heart problems. You'd probably kill him. Who else?"

"I'm dancing. I can't do two things at once."

"It's not like we're trying to samba," he said.

"Did you know that *samba* means rubbing your belly buttons together?"

"Then by all means," he said. "Let's samba."

"Too late. And BTdubs," she said, poking him in the chest with her finger again. "Lots of people who aren't senior citizens find me hot."

"Everyone finds you hot," he said.

This stopped her temper in its tracks, and she blinked up at him. "Yeah?"

"Hell yeah." He made a sound that might have been a low laugh or some sort of pained groan and pulled her in tighter, resting his cheek on the top of her head.

This was when she realized that they were slow dancing, that he had one big hand at the small of her back, the other wrapped warmly in hers, pressed against his chest.

"Do you?" she whispered. "Find me hot?"

He opened his eyes and met hers. "So hot I'm already burned," he said.

She grinned. "It's the dress."

He let out a low laugh. "I'm pretty sure it's you."

That was just about the nicest thing anyone had said to her lately, and she felt her throat go tight.

His smile faded. "What are you doing?"

It had been a long, emotional three days, she told herself, and swallowed hard. The knot in her throat remained. "Nothing," she said.

"You're not crying."

"No."

He looked vastly relieved at her denial, but then she sniffed. He swore, making her laugh and drop her forehead to his chest. "I'm not." Much. "But I might wipe my nose on you."

"Go for it," he said. "The tux is Adam's. Whatever you want. Anything."

She went still at the possibilities before lifting her face to his. "Anything?"

He paused and then let out another low laugh. "You know, we could use you in the military. One look from those melting green eyes and conflicts would just fall away. Whole armies would line up to give you whatever you want. You're dangerous as hell, you know that?"

She liked that. She liked that a lot. Stupid with lust—and champagne—she smiled, the threat of tears gone. "Did you know that sex is a great way to burn calories?"

He gave her a long look.

"It's true. A real orgasm burns about one hundred and twelve calories."

His brows went up. "A real orgasm? Is there any other kind?"

She bit her lip. "Well, there's the fake kind."

"Why would anyone want the fake kind?"

"Because the fake kind burns three hundred and fifteen calories," she said.

At that, he tossed back his head and laughed.

She stared at him. She couldn't remember ever seeing him laugh like that before, and it melted her all the more. The sight of his smile and genuine amusement . . . she couldn't even put into words how that felt, especially since she'd been the one to make him laugh. He'd thawed. She'd thawed him. "Wow," she murmured.

"What?"

"You don't show what you're feeling very often," she said.

"Do you think that means I don't feel?"

"I think it means that you're pretty guarded and ex-tremely careful." Because she was afraid that sounded crit-ical, she said, "I get that when you're out there, working, it has to be that way to keep you safe. But you're safe here, Griffin."

His gaze touched her features, each one, ending with her eyes. "Am I?" he asked softly.

She opened her mouth, but her breath caught in her

throat because suddenly he'd dipped his head close to hers. So close that their lips nearly touched, and she became extremely aware of how entwined they were and how much body heat they shared. "Griffin," she whispered softly. Hopefully.

His gaze locked on her mouth, and she started to close the distance between them, feeling a slow, sexy dance coming on. But the music stopped.

And then Griffin pulled back. Squeezing her hand, he led her off the dance floor, dropping her off at the head table before walking away.

Watching him go, she let out a low, shaky breath. He was right. He wasn't safe at all.

And neither was she.

Eleven

Yeah, Grif was definitely feeling plenty. Way too much, starting with a bad case of vertigo—compliments of his perforated eardrum. But today's low-level headache wasn't from the blast or the wedding. Nope, that honor went to the odd and opposing sensations of actually enjoying being back in Sunshine and his own inability to figure out how to come to good terms with his family. Specifically his dad.

Grif had been a rebellious, rambunctious, trouble-seeking little punk. He knew that. But he'd hoped to somehow upgrade his image while he was here. Had hoped to make things right. But he was unsure how to do that and even more unsure how to make peace with the man he'd so disappointed.

Leaving the sounds of the merry reception behind, he walked across the yard to the horse pens. Woodrow snickered softly in greeting and walked up to the railing, pushing his head to Grif's chest. Not a loving nudge so much as a "where the hell are the treats?"

Before he could pull out the handful of baby carrots he'd

shoved into his pockets from the buffet table, Woodrow was frisking him, snorting a little. With a low laugh, Grif helped the old guy out, stroking his face as he fed him the carrots. "Miss me?"

"Nah," his dad said from behind him. "He's just happy you brought food."

Grif turned and met his gaze. "It's a wedding, dad. You're supposed to be happy, too."

At the mention of the wedding, the old man softened enough to smile with pride. "She's beautiful, isn't she?"

"Yes." Holly had glowed with happiness, from the inside out. "You managed to raise her in spite of herself," Grif said.

"Yeah," Donald said. "We did.

"Well, I didn't do it by myself," his dad admitted at Grif's surprise on the "we." "You helped me keep her in line, you know you did. Hell, half the time I couldn't manage to even say hello without pissing her off. So yeah. I'm happy. Very happy. And so is she. Are you?"

A loaded speech. A loaded question. The truth was, Griffin had expected to feel caged in by the wide-open spaces and the mountains, by the way everyone in his life had fallen in love and gotten married.

But he didn't.

Instead he felt . . . maybe just the slightest bit envious. "I'm happy to be back," he said carefully, and wouldn't mind hearing the sentiment returned.

Donald turned to look out on the land and leaned on a post. "I thought the place would feel like Mars to you after all this time."

"It's not the land that drew me back."

At that Donald turned his head. "You drink too much already?"

Grif blew out a breath. "Is it so hard to accept that I might not still be that angry kid that left here all those years ago?"

Donald just looked at him for a long beat. "You cleaned the barn."

"You suggested I should."

"Beside the fact that you've never done a damn thing I suggested, we have people who do that."

"I told you," Grif said. "I wanted to help."

Donald stared at him then nodded. The biggest acknowledgement Grif was going to get.

"Donald?" a female voice called out across the yard. "Honey, where are you? I want to dance!"

They both turned at the sound of Deanna.

"Out here," Grif's dad called, his usual gruff voice softening, pleasure crossing his face at the sight of the beautiful, long-haired brunette working her way toward them on her stiletto heels. Deanna wore a skin-tight, siren red dress. Huge diamonds dripping from her ears and neck. She stepped into Donald and gave him a big smacking kiss, leaving a red smudge on his mouth that made him grin like an idiot. "Hey, Grif," she said as she wrapped herself around his dad. "How are you doing?"

"Fine," he said, watching as his dad hugged Deanna into him.

"Good. Cuz I'm stealing your dad. We're going to tear up the dance floor now."

To Grif's surprise, Donald just smiled down at Deanna and allowed himself to be led back to the reception.

Grif followed, the knot in his chest loosened slightly. He'd wanted to come back, and he had. He'd wanted to fit in, and he was trying.

But there was one big distraction. Actually, she was more like a five-foot-four tornado. A five-foot-four sexy-as-hell tornado, who was turning him on with every blush and odd science fact that slipped out of her lush mouth.

He watched that distraction over the next few hours. Mistake number one, because she charmed everyone in her orbit as she enjoyed herself no matter what she was doing, coaxing people onto the dance floor, bringing the older relatives food and drink, playing with the younger guests including her brother . . . Whatever she did, she did with her entire heart and soul.

As someone who hadn't done all that much with his own heart and soul, it drew him in like a moth to the flame.

At midnight Adam and Holly left for their honeymoon among cheers, hugs, and kisses. The party raged on without them. Kate was on the dance floor with Ryan Stafford, the two of them in a conga line. When the music switched to the "Macarena," they kept pace with each other effortlessly like this wasn't their first rodeo.

Which didn't mean Kate was a good dancer. In truth she was awful. But what she lacked in talent, she more than made up for in sheer enthusiasm. She was smiling, eyes flushed, cheeks rosy, her head tossed back, leaning into Ryan as she laughed helplessly at something he said.

She was more than a little tipsy, he realized. And her dancing partner was using the opportunity to be Mr. Handsy.

Grif knew Ryan. He was a good guy but also a serious player. And he was seriously playing Kate at the moment. Not that she seemed to mind. There was clearly still something between them. Sexual tension? Maybe. Whatever it was, it made Grif stop and take a closer look. Yeah, they knew each other well. Were they still sleeping together? He tried to tell himself it absolutely didn't matter if Ryan took her home tonight. Grif had had his shot, and he hadn't taken it. He had no claim on her.

But even as he said it to himself, his feet took him straight toward her. Halfway there he passed his dad talking to Kel. Grif caught the last of Kel's words, " . . . must be pretty proud of your son," and Donald's surprising response.

"Yes. I am."

Grif nearly tripped over his feet. He'd never heard that from the old man before. He thought about stopping and asking his dad to repeat it but kept moving instead, heading straight across the dance floor.

The "Macarena" was in full swing by now. Dell and Brady were leading the whole thing with their wives, which took Grif aback a moment. Brady was just about as badass as they came, but there he was, tux jacket off, sleeves rolled up, moving with some pretty good rhythm. Grif made a promise to himself right then and there. He didn't care if he got stupid with love. He was never going to do the "Macarena."

Ever.

The DJ turned the lights down and encouraged people to let their "inner freak" fly. The dancers went nuts.

Griffin lost sight of Kate for a moment, so he waded onto the dance floor.

Where the hell did she go?

There. He saw a flash of shiny green in a corner, tangling with . . .

Sonofabitch.

It was the father of that little asshole from her class. Trevan Anders.

"Sorry," Kate was saying breathlessly, pushing on Trevan's chest. "I thought you were someone else."

Grif knew exactly who she'd gone looking for in the dark.

Him.

He could only imagine what she'd done to get Trevan's attention.

"It's dark," she said quietly, "And you're both the same height. I'm sorry, I didn't mean to grab you like that—"

Trevan heard her. Griffin knew damn well that the guy heard her, and yet he kept her pinned in the corner. Griffin shoulder-checked him. He'd have liked to shoulder-check him into next week, but this was his best friend and sister's wedding so he kept it light. Accidental.

It was enough to have Trevan shifting back from Kate, and when he saw Griffin standing right there, he backed off.

"Sorry," Kate called after him as he melted away into the crowd. "Oh my God," she muttered, and covered her face. "I grabbed a kid's dad's butt. I'm so going to be fired."

"No, you're not." This from Ryan as he pushed in past Grif, in no way intimidated by Grif the way Trevan had been. "It's a wedding. It's like Vegas—what happens here, stays here."

Kate looked at him hopefully. "You think?"

The music kicked up again, and Ryan pushed her out of the dark corner and to the center of the dance floor, where he leaned in and said something, making her laugh.

Grif watched for a moment, his eyes on Ryan's hands as they slid to Kate's waist. When he lifted his gaze to Ryan's, he found the school principal staring at him as he said something to Kate.

Kate looked up then, too, and her mossy green gaze collided with Grif's. She smiled at him. A big, goofy smile.

Yep. Definitely drunk. Dammit. He waded back through the dancers and stopped in front of her. Mistake number two. "Need to talk to you."

"Okay." But she kept dancing. Or bouncing. Or whatever the hell she thought she was doing. A server walked by, and she snagged a flute of champagne. She toasted him with it. "You're not dancing."

"Over there," he said, gesturing to an empty table.

"Can't dance over there."

"We're going to talk."

She considered that while still moving. She looked at Ryan.

Ryan shook his head. "Bad move," he said.

What the hell. Grif knew he was a damn bad idea, too, but to have Ryan say it just pissed him off. "How many drinks has she had?"

Ryan went brows up to Kate.

She held up four fingers.

Christ. He gave Ryan a long, hard look. "Don't let her drink anymore."

"Let her?" Ryan laughed. "You must be under the impression that Kate allows anyone to make her decisions for her."

Kate grinned and shook her head. "Nope. I make my own decisions. Even the really bad ones." She drilled her pointer finger into Grif's chest. "Which you almost were . . ." She turned to face Ryan and slung her arms around his neck. "I'm so glad you got shot down by your cute bridesmaid," she told him. "Now you can talk to me and share drinks with me and . . ." She waggled her brow. "Have all that breakup sex you wanted to have."

Ryan had the good grace to look slightly ashamed of himself, but before he could speak, Grif pulled her back against him. Spine to his chest, she tipped her head back and stared up at him. "Sorry," she said. "You had your shot. You turned me down, remember?"

"I remember," he said. In truth she was absolutely the worst idea he'd ever had, and yet apparently, that wasn't going to stop him. He pulled her snug to his side.

Ryan straightened as if to say something, and Grif gave him a don't-fuck-with-me look. To Ryan's credit this didn't cow him in the least. He bent at the knees a little to look into Kate's eyes. "Don't forget, your dad took the car and your siblings home. I'm here if you need anything, babe."

Kate smiled at him, a sweet, loving, warm smile. "You're the best almost fiancé I ever had."

"I'm your only almost fiancé," Ryan said, and kissed her on the nose. Then he straightened, gave Grif a don't-fuck-with-me look right back, and walked off the dance floor.

Kate glared at Grif. "You chased away my only shot for tonight. What's with you anyway? You don't want me, so what's the problem with me finding someone else?"

"Christ, Kate, I'm trying to do the right thing here."

"Well, who asked you?" She dropped some of her mad. "I need this, Griffin. I need fun. I need good, naked fun, just for one night."

Yes, genius, Grif asked himself, what was the problem with her finding someone else to do that with? "Sometimes good is overrated," he said.

"I know that," she said. "I actually meant I want to be bad."

He must have looked doubtful because she smacked him. "I can be bad," she said, insulted. "Very, very bad. And you would have liked it, too."

He had absolutely no doubt. "So who the hell were you looking for in the dark?"

She ignored this to study her shoes. Since they were starting to attract attention, he took her hand and pulled her off the dance floor. The tables were just as crowded, and his head was threatening to revolt again, so he led her around the side of the house and then into it, pulling her into the first room they came to.

A bathroom.

Mistake number three. He was really racking them up tonight. But the problem this time was the room was tiny, and he was all pressed up against Kate. Kate with her hair all carefully piled on top of her head except for the few silky strands that had escaped and were lying along the column of her neck. Kate with the expressive eyes and full mouth. Kate with the sweet curves that weren't one hundred percent contained in the silky dress with the intriguing spaghetti straps crisscrossed over one shoulder and her back . . .

But she was half-baked, he reminded himself. No way was he going to be tempted by a half-baked bridesmaid.

Proving it, she slid down the wall until her butt was on the floor, and then she began the tricky process of getting out of her strappy heels. "God," she said on a blissful sigh when she'd freed one foot. "Good God, that feels so good." She lost the other heel, and then she reached up under the hem of her dress and began to wriggle and shimmy. Each move brought the hem of her dress higher. Up over her knee. Mid thigh.

Upper thigh . . .

He caught a flash of something lacy and sheer, and then he realized what she was up to. She was sliding down her nylons.

"Whoever invented nylons was a cruel, cruel person," she said. "And a man to boot." She got back on her feet and looked up at him as she stepped close and then stood right on the tops of his shoes, wrapping her arms around his neck. Now their bodies were lined up, her breasts straining at the front of her dress as she cupped his face.

"Kate," he managed. "What are you doing?"

"The question is," she said with mock seriousness, "what are *you* doing?"

Had he really thought himself safe? Mistake number four, because he was about as safe as a guy who handled explosives for a living.

Oh wait . . .

He put his hands on her hips, hoping to hold her off, but his wires got crossed, and he pulled her in closer instead.

"Mmm," she said, and leaned on him, her cheek to his chest.

He stared down at her dreamy expression and tried to harden his heart. He was good at that. But that wasn't the part of him that hardened. "You're drunk."

"Yes, but only a little."

He closed his eyes. "Look, there's two people here tonight I won't sleep with. My sister and—"

"Don't say me."

"You."

She stared at him then gave him a push. Since he was already up against the sink, he didn't budge.

"What's wrong with me?" she asked. "I looked in the mirror, you know. I didn't see a third eye or anything in my teeth."

"There is absolutely nothing wrong with you," he said. "Not one fucking thing."

"But . . . ?"

"But if I take you, it's going to last all night."

Her eyes went a little glossy. "Still not seeing the problem."

"It's going to be good," he said. "It's going to be so good that we're going to wake up and start all over again. And then you'll want to have breakfast. You'll ask me when we're going to see each other again."

Some of that glossiness vanished, and her eyes narrowed slightly.

"I don't want to hurt you, Kate," he said, desperate for her to understand.

"Uh-huh," she said, not sounding impressed. "Let me

see if I have this right. You don't want to have sex with me because you think I might confuse said sex with love and, as a result, get hurt."

The reference to love threw him, and he hesitated a second too long because she went hands on hips. "You really think that," she said. "Well, how insulting."

"Kate—"

"I'm not stupid, Griffin. Maybe a little inexperienced compared to you, but I know enough to understand that love is earned."

There was that *l*-word again.

She took in his expression and made a sound that managed to perfectly convey what she thought of him. Which was that he wasn't exactly love material anyway.

As he already knew.

"I told you," she said. "All I wanted was a damn adventure. A fun, naked one-night adventure. Why the hell can't I have a damn fun, naked, one-night adventure like everyone else?"

"Kate."

"Am I that undesirable?" she demanded to know. She tipped her head back and let out a big sigh. "Tommy's wearing a cape, and Ashley's going to go postal on her BFF and ex-BF, and my dad's probably going to accidentally burn his house down, so I can't leave them and go to San Diego to dissect a calf, but I really thought I could at least have this."

Was she speaking English?

"I'm Holly's something blue today," she murmured, "and I bet she doesn't even know it." Another heaved sigh as she turned to the window, head tilted up to stare out at the night sky. It was lit by a moon half covered in clouds. "That cloud weighs about two hundred thousand pounds," she said. "Crazy, right?"

No. Crazy was standing in front of him in a bridesmaid dress with her hair now blowing around her face and her pretty eyes all glossy and troubled. Crazy was wanting to shove up her dress and then step between her spread legs and—

"It just really chaps my ass," she said.

Yes, her ass. It was molded in that dress and perfect.

"I wore some great lingerie tonight, too," she went on. "And I mean really great."

This gave him pause.

"Almost slutty even," she said.

Like a dog to a bone. He shifted closer, slid his hand up her back, and wrapped his fingers around the nape of her neck to turn her head to his. "How slutty?"

She shoved past him and headed to the door. "Oh no. Forget it. You missed your opportunity. Again. And you know what? I'm starting to doubt your man-'ho reputation. Because I'm having no luck getting you naked."

He followed the hot, pissed-off, sexy ball of fluff down the hall, deciding not to touch that statement with a ten-foot pole. "I'm driving you home," he said.

"Not necessary." She stepped outside and went still. "Dammit."

Her dad had her car.

Grif came to a stop behind her. "I'll drive you home," he repeated. And he wouldn't be getting out of the car to walk her in.

No possible way.

"This is really annoying," she said. Her hair was a little out of control. Her dress was slipping off one shoulder, revealing a very narrow strap of something indeed pretty great and possibly slutty.

"So screwed," he muttered to himself.

Kate crossed her arms over her chest and lifted her chin. "Nope. Screwing is completely off the table."

Twelve

Fuming, Kate kept her face turned to Grif's truck's passenger-side window. The night was pitch-black as she gave the big, tall, far-too-sexy jerk in the driver's seat her very best silent treatment.

Not that he seemed to notice. Nope, he drove with a quiet, steady calm, deep in his zone, which only served to fuel her temper even more. How did he lock it all away? How did he reveal nothing?

The answer to that slipped into her head, and she sighed. She knew how.

The hard way.

It had been drilled into him young and then further cemented by a life in the military, where feeling too much or allowing emotions to hit the surface could be deadly. It was dark in the interior of his truck, but she didn't need a light to see the scar that ran along his temple and bisected his eyebrow.

Okay. So yeah, he had very good reasons to be stoic and sure of his every move. But she wasn't a war zone. And she wasn't his grumpy father. And she sure as hell wasn't just any silly drunken bridesmaid. She was . . . more.

Or she'd wanted to be.

Grif still hadn't spoken as he drove with single-minded purpose, sitting there in that tux, exuding testosterone with every slow, even exhale. She wished she knew what he was thinking. Maybe she'd know if she could get him out of that tux, strip him down to six feet plus of warm, smooth skin wrapped around hard muscle and sinew and bone . . .

But seriously. Who'd have thought he'd be so hard to get out of his clothes?

"You never answered my question," he said, startling her.

"Which question?"

"Who did you think you were groping in that dark corner on the dance floor?"

Oh yeah. That question.

He slid her a look.

Dammit. He knew. "Ryan," she said.

"Ryan has blond hair."

"Like you said, it was dark."

"Not that dark," he said.

She shrugged.

"You back with him, then?"

"For someone who isn't big on talking or communicating," she said. "You're sure doing a lot of it tonight."

"Yes or no, Kate."

She sighed. "No. I'm not back with Ryan."

"So who'd you think it was?"

Her plan to ignore him was foiled when he slid her another look. It was all but impossible to ignore him when she was in the high beams of that steel gaze. "Fine!" she said. "I thought it was you, okay? But I don't know why, since you're a big, annoying, know-it-all, holier-than-thou alpha!"

"You mistook me for Anders," he said, sounding much more insulted at this than her actual insult. "He's like a foot shorter than me."

"Not a foot. Maybe a few inches."

"And he needs to get to the gym."

"He's fit."

He made a disgruntled sound and pulled into the lot of her townhouse complex, right up to the walkway that led to her place, and left the truck running.

Coward.

As if he read her mind, his mouth twisted a little, and he reached out to cup her jaw. "If I come in, Kate, I'm going to have you naked in three seconds flat."

She started to take offense and then realized it was true. Yeah, he really was a damn coward. But she wasn't. She might be nervous, but that was entirely different from being afraid, because being nervous wouldn't hold her back from taking risks.

Griffin, on the other hand, was afraid of hurting her, and that would hold him back from the risk. But he couldn't hurt her. She wouldn't let him. "Thanks for the ride," she said, which she absolutely didn't mean. She did her best to make a dramatic exit, shoving the skirt of her dress aside, fumbling with the door.

But she couldn't get it open.

It took her an embarrassingly long time to realize this was because it was locked. Glancing at Griffin over her shoulder, she blew a strand of hair out of her face. "When I said I needed fun, this wasn't what I had in mind. Let me out."

"No."

"No?" Had she missed something? "Listen, just because you don't want a piece of this"—she gestured to herself—"doesn't mean that you can—"

"There's a Lexus out front with a guy in it," he said.

She blinked and peered down the street at the car he was looking at. "That's Trevan's Lexus," she said. "He lives two buildings down."

"He's watching you."

"He's listening to music instead of going inside because his kids drive him crazy."

Griffin got out of the car and came around for her, opening her door, walking her toward her townhouse. Not just walking her but clearly escorting her with his hand on her elbow, his sharp eyes scanning the horizon as if he was on guard.

At her door she tugged free. "Okay, I'm here safe and sound and social-orgasm free," she said. "You can go now."

He pinched the bridge of his nose with his thumb and forefinger for a moment, eyes squeezed shut, and she stared up at him, suddenly anxious. "Headache?"

"No," he said. "You're trying my patience."

Oh, for God's sake. She fumbled through her purse for her keys, shoved them into the door, and stepped over the threshold, reaching back to slam it shut.

Preferably on his nose.

Of course he stuck in his big foot in the door, pushed it open, stepped over the threshold, and then shut it.

And bolted it.

She felt a rush of heat that had nothing to do with temper. "You're on the wrong side of the door," she said.

He didn't respond. Fine. She had things to do. He could be his big, silent, mysterious self all on his own. She kicked off her shoes—again. She dropped her purse and headed for the kitchen. She was thinking there were two men in her freezer who wouldn't ever turn her down.

Ben. And Jerry.

Luckily, she had nearly a full quart, and she grabbed a spoon and leaned back against her counter.

Griffin followed her in, and the kitchen instantly shrank. "Talk time," he said.

"Sorry." She dug into the ice cream. "Talking isn't on my agenda tonight."

Griffin watched Kate shovel in shocking amounts of ice cream. He wondered how that was going to mix with the alcohol, but she didn't seem to be tipsy anymore.

She seemed to be pissed off.

He had plenty of experience with pissed-off women. His mom had been the first, and as a wild kid, he'd given her plenty of reasons. Then there'd been his sister and ditto. And then there'd been the women in his life. He'd been really good at pissing them off as well. "Look," he said. "It's not personal."

"It feels personal. We discussed my panties."

This gave him pause because the word panties from her mouth made him hard, and he couldn't think when he was hard. "I'm positive that they're really great," he said carefully. "I'm also positive that you're hot as hell and extremely desirable."

She looked at him. "So . . . you do want me."

"I do," he said. "I want you all the fucking time, but—"

"Oh God," she moaned. "There's a but." She sighed. "Go ahead," she said, waving at him with the wooden spoon. "Give me the line."

"What line?"

"Whatever line you were about to use to explain why we aren't doing it," she said. "Except don't try to attribute it to you being a guy and this just being a sexual itch you can't scratch. Although . . ." She considered him a minute. "Guys do peak at age seventeen, and you're way past that, so maybe you can't scratch it." She licked the spoon, slowly, thoroughly, and completely upended his thought process.

"Did you just imply I'm past my prime?" he asked in disbelief.

She shrugged a pretty shoulder. "Just stating a fact."

"Fact," he repeated. "The fact is that you're my baby sister's best friend, and . . ." And Christ. She was setting down the ice cream, tossing the spoon into the sink, and . . . reaching behind her.

For her zipper.

She struggled a moment, and he stood there riveted on the spot.

"And?" she asked conversationally, finally getting her fingers on her zipper by reaching backward and over her head.

He heard the rasp as it came slowly down. "And," he said. "And . . ." She was undoing him as effectively as she was undoing her dress. She was warm and soft, and she smelled amazing, and he found himself wanting to show her exactly what he felt like in the dark.

But then she turned and looked at him as she let her dress fall, her face politely curious.

The rest of her was in nude lace. A low, barely there bra, panties, and absolutely nothing else. He'd never in his life seen anything more erotically sexy. He had no idea what it was about her that made him want to howl at the moon. Maybe it was the way she had of making the world seem like a safe place—which he knew damn well it wasn't. Or how she laughed at the little things, reminding him that there were still things to laugh at. Or hell, maybe it was simply that she always seemed just on the edge of disaster and still had a smile on her face.

He didn't know, but he wanted to finish unwrapping her and then rewrap her—around him.

"You were saying something?" she asked in that same distant-but-polite tone.

"Yeah . . ." But he had nothing. He'd forgotten what he was going to say. He'd forgotten why he wasn't going to do this. Because she was standing there, bared to him, braver than him, better than him, and she thought she was undesirable. He couldn't let her think that, couldn't bear to let her think that, he thought as he pulled her in against him. The feel of her heated skin, so soft, so smooth, all pressed up to him was heaven. "Kate."

"Mm-hmm?"

"How drunk are you really?"

"Not even a little."

"Swear it."

"Swear."

He stared into her clear eyes.

"Want me to walk a straight line?" she asked. "Sing the alphabet? I can burp it, too, but I need a soda for that."

He fought a smile.

She didn't fight hers at all, just let her lips curve sweetly. "Anything else?" she asked.

"Yeah. One thing." He shifted a little closer so that they were sharing air. "If it had been me you'd found in the dark tonight on that dance floor, you'd have damn well known it."

Her hands clutched his biceps as she nodded. "I have no doubt." She stared at his mouth and licked her lips, and Grif would swear on a stack of Bibles in a court full of his peers that he had no idea how he ended up kissing her like his life depended on it. None. But that's exactly what happened. His hands skimmed up her hot curves, and he heard his own groan escape him as he bent his head to her breasts, which were spilling out the top of her bra.

With a gasp of pleasure, she slid her fingers into his hair, holding him to her.

As if he were going anywhere now. And it wasn't for her either. Even in his lust-induced haze he knew that. This was for him. He needed to be touched by her, needed to feel something with her. Needed to lose himself for this beat in time.

In her.

He nudged the straps of her bra from her shoulders and kissed her breast, letting his tongue slip under the silk and rasp over a nipple before closing his lips and sucking. Her fingers tightened on his hair. She could make him bald; he didn't care.

"Pigs orgasm in thirty minute intervals," she said softly.

His heart squeezed. He was making her nervous. "The real kind or the fake kind?"

She laughed breathlessly. "Pigs can't fake it, I don't think."

"You're beautiful, Kate."

She gave him a shaky smile.

"So damn beautiful." Straightening, he picked her up.

She wrapped her legs around his hips as he backed her to the counter and set her on it.

"Uh-oh," she said. "Are we back to talking?"

"Later," he murmured, and kissed her again. She let him, melting for him, going soft and pliable in his arms.

"The first contraceptive was crocodile dung," she whispered. "The Egyptians used it in 2000 BC."

"You say the sexiest things," he said, and gently sank his teeth into her earlobe.

She shivered and clutched at him. "You're the first man to tell me that. Most would rather I not talk during sex." She grimaced. "And by most, I don't mean there've been lots or anything. There haven't. Two. There've been two."

He went still as she dropped her head to his shoulder. "I swear I'm trying to shut up," she said. "But I have one more thing."

He was still processing the fact that any man would ever ask her not to talk. He loved to hear her talk. And what did she mean there'd only been two . . . Two total? "What?" he asked, still trying to do the math—impossible since all his blood had drained to parts south.

She lifted her head and took his gaze prisoner with her own deep green one. "Do best men carry condoms?" she asked.

"Always."

Her smile was the sweetest, hottest thing he'd ever seen, and his heart squeezed again. She'd been with only two men, and they'd asked her not to talk during sex. She knew that faking an orgasm burned more calories than a real orgasm . . .

Grif had promised himself to keep his hands off of her because she was vulnerable, but he was beginning to suspect he was the vulnerable one here. Vulnerable to her. Because he wanted to gather her in and make things right, show her that talking during sex could be erotic as hell. Teach her that there was no need to fake anything.

Ever.

Before he could say a word, she cupped his face with her hands and pulled him to her. Instead of kissing his lips, she leaned in and kissed the top edge of the scar on his temple.

She followed the length of it with warm little devastating kisses. And she didn't stop there. She kissed his jaw next, working her way slowly, so slowly it was torture, toward his mouth.

And then skipped it and went to the other side of his face. When she got to his ear, he found himself holding his breath.

Not her. She let a soft sigh escape her, and it sent chills skittering down his spine. Not the kind of chills he got right before he was going to get shot at, either, but the really good kind of chills. "Kate, kiss me."

"Hmm?"

"Kiss me, dammit."

She gave him a smile that stopped his heart. "Sorry. I heard you the first time." She bit her lower lip and admitted, "I just like hearing you say it."

And then, before he could grasp the fact that she'd just gotten not only the best of him but had also gotten exactly what she'd wanted, she laid one on him, and it was a kiss for the record books. Nothing of the slightly prim-and-proper second-grade teacher was present as she slid her hands back into his hair and pillaged. There was no other word. She nibbled, licked, sucked, and even bit, and by the time they pulled apart to suck in some desperately needed air, his head was spinning.

"How was that?" she asked, looking a little dazed herself, her eyes dilated.

"Good," he said, "but it's going to get even better. Kate?"

"Yeah?"

"No fake orgasms for three hundred and fifteen calories. Fuck the calories. We're going real, all the way."

She let out a shaky breath and nodded. "Real," she repeated.

Her demi-bra wasn't managing to contain her breasts fully. He could see some nipple, and they were pebbled tight, her breasts rising and falling with her quickened breath. Her legs were still wrapped around his hips. When they'd been kissing, she'd been rocking into him, and the teeny-tiny lace triangle had shifted a bit and molded to her every soft fold.

Her every soft damn fold.

She was a vision, a goddess to be worshipped, and he traced a line along the top of her bra with the pads of his fingers before unhooking it and letting it fall away. Lowering his head, he brushed a kiss across the full curve of a breast.

"Griffin," she whispered, a plea. She steadied herself by gripping him tight, and then tighter still when his thumb skimmed across her nipple. He slid her panties down, and she whispered his name again.

"Tell me," he said.

"More."

"What?"

"More, Griffin. Please more."

He smiled. "I heard you. I just like to hear it." Then he dropped to his knees, because he wanted more, too. He wanted to make her cry out his name.

Instead she splayed a hand between her legs blocking his passage to the homeland. But her fingers, spread over herself, still gave him the most heart-stopping peekaboo hints of what was beneath.

"Twenty-nine percent of Americans have sex on the first date with perfect strangers," she said. "Do you think this applies?"

"We're not strangers."

"No," she said slowly. "You're right."

She was still nervous and anxious to boot. Finally, something he could fix. Leaning in, he kissed one inner thigh and then the other, sucking lightly on her skin until she moaned and spread her legs a little more. He did it again, and she gave him even better access with an appreciative sigh.

"So beautiful," he whispered against her heated flesh, and trailed his tongue over her fingers, getting his first sweet taste of her. "Let me in. Let me have you."

She did, gasping as he explored her every dip and curve and fold.

Moaning his name, she again fisted her fingers in his hair, holding him to her as if she were afraid he'd stop.

He didn't. He took her all the way, loving the way she went wild for him, and when she came, it was with a joyous cry and his name on her lips.

Thirteen

When Kate's world tilted, she opened her eyes. Griffin had risen to his feet, yanked her against him, and headed out of the kitchen, presumably toward her bedroom.

She was still quivering with little aftershocks, but she wasn't so far gone as not to realize that she was completely naked and he was not. It felt a little bit naughty, and she bit his earlobe and then sucked it into her mouth, which made her feel even more naughty.

With a low oath, Griffin stopped right where he was—the living room—and dumped her on the couch, following her down. There'd been a few things on it: a stack of bills, a few magazines, her purse. "Ouch," she said.

"Lift up," he said, and then with one swipe of his arm, everything hit the floor.

They were laughing when they kissed this time, which took away exactly none of the urgency. "Griffin?"

"Yeah?"

"You're overdressed."

He rose and stripped, each movement easy, economical, efficient.

He absolutely stole her breath.

Then he tore open the condom and rolled it on.

Sexiest thing ever.

He came back over the top of her, and being careful with his weight, he slid one of her legs around his waist.

And then, eyes on hers, he slowly pushed inside her. Both of them went still at the exquisite sensation.

He fisted his hands in her hair. "This," he said against her mouth, moving within her and rocking her world. "This is what I needed." His voice was thick and gravelly with desire, and he let out the sexiest male groan of approval she'd ever heard. "You under me, Kate. Me buried deep inside you."

The words were as arousing as his movements—and his movements, good Lord. Reaching up, she kissed and licked whatever she could reach on him, his shoulder, his chest, his throat. His skin was salty, damp, and the taste of him was better than the most decadent of desserts. She couldn't stop whispering his name; she just couldn't.

Rocking into her over and over, he stared into her eyes, his own as hot as liquid steel, and she thought maybe he liked the sound of his name on her tongue.

She did. She loved it, loved this, and she tightened her legs around him, her hands searching for handholds in a crazy, tilting, spinning world.

Then he changed the angle of her hips and went even deeper, making her gasp, making him groan again, and from one breath to the next, she went a little wild, her hips lifting to meet him, her entire body moving with him as he took her to the very edge and held her there. Crying out, she arched against him, lost in him, completely lost in the sweet, hot pleasure.

He was hers.

Hers . . .

At least in that moment he was, and she wanted to remember this, every single second of it, his lips brushing her ear telling her what he was going to do to her next, the weight of him pressing her into the couch, the look in his eyes as he moved inside her . . . "Yes," she said, to all of it, and his hands slid back up her body again, tangling in her hair as he proceeded to take her right out of herself with shocking familiarity. And then a few seconds later, he gripped her hips and pushed into her hard, shuddering in her arms as he followed her over.

Grif opened his eyes knowing two things. One, it was the middle of the night, and two, something was off. He sat up, and Kate murmured a protest in her sleep. "Shh," he said with a light stroke down her back. "Go back to sleep."

And then he slid out of bed and moved down the hall. He'd walked silently through the entire townhouse and was standing in the living room at the glass sliding door when he heard Kate come up behind him.

"Grif?" she asked groggily.

He turned. She'd flipped on a lamp in her bright-as-hell sunshine yellow bedroom, and the light behind her cast her in silhouette. She wore his shirt, some serious bedhead hair, and a confused look.

"What's wrong?" she asked.

When he didn't answer, she frowned and stepped forward. "Are you . . . armed?" She stared down at the knife he'd taken from her butcher block in the kitchen. "You are," she breathed. "You're armed and . . . naked."

Christ. He rubbed a hand over his head. "I heard someone."

Her eyes went big on his. "Here?"

He pointed to her back door. "There's muddy footprints on your patio."

Wrapping her arms around herself, she stepped to his side and looked out the door. "Those are from yesterday. Tommy was over here playing in my garden."

"Those prints are too big for Tommy."

"He was wearing my dad's mud boots."

"Someone followed you here from the woods yesterday, remember?"

She set a hand on his arm, stroking softly. "I just got spooked. It's okay, Grif."

He went still then looked down into her eyes. She thought he was experiencing flashbacks or still adjusting to civilian life. Or hell, maybe she thought he was losing it. "Treading lightly for the crazy person?" he asked quietly.

"No," she said, and kept touching him. "No," she repeated more firmly when he just cocked a brow. "But this is Sunshine," she reminded him.

"The door wasn't locked."

"I must have forgotten."

That's what Kel had told him when he'd called him a moment ago. *It's Sunshine, Grif, go back to bed.*

He was well aware that everyone was thinking he was going over the deep end on this, but he didn't care. He was not losing his mind. Maybe his heart but not his mind. Purposely unlocking his tense jaw, he clicked the lock and gave Kate a pointed look.

She acknowledged it with a nod. "I'll keep it locked," she promised.

He tried to shrug off the adrenaline. He wasn't at war. He was in Idaho. "Always," he said firmly.

"Always," she repeated. "It's very sweet of you to be worried."

Sweet. She thought he was fucking sweet.

"Come back to bed now," she whispered, stroking her hand down his chest.

And now she was humoring him. Perfect.

But then her hand drifted even farther south, and he decided that there was something else he was having a hard time shrugging off.

His need for her.

She was right. Time to go back to bed.

Kate woke up slowly, as always. It took her a moment, but eventually she realized that she was wrapped around a big, hot-as-a-furnace, hard body.

Griffin.

Earlier she'd found him prowling her living room, then standing at the sliding door, arms up, hands braced overhead on the doorjamb.

Sexy as hell.

Tense as hell. And armed.

No longer tense or carrying a knife, he was breathing slowly and evenly, clearly deeply asleep. Taking advantage of this fact, she drank him in. He lay sprawled on his back, all loose-limbed and utterly relaxed. Pride filled her at that because it was her doing. Knowing it, a smile crossed her face, and she had to force herself not to touch. Or stroke.

Or lick.

Yeah, she really wanted to lick, but he looked so peaceful that she didn't want to disturb him. He seemed . . . younger. And completely sated.

She was sated, too. And naked and a little bit sore in spots. Not to mention grinning like an idiot because finally—finally—she'd gotten an adventure.

And oh, what an adventure it had been.

On a normal day Griffin was a force. He was strong inside and out, he was intelligent and tough and dead sexy, and he knew how to get his way in life—and as she'd discovered—also in bed.

She'd gotten everything she wanted out of the night, too, and if she hadn't been wrapped around him like a pretzel, she'd have been floating on air.

Her phone lit up on her nightstand. Moving slowly so as to not wake up Griffin, she reached out and grabbed it. It was a text from Ashley.

WHERE ARE YOU?

Oh crap. She'd completely forgotten. Of course she'd had a few other things on her mind, such as the big, bad, naked Griffin Reid . . .

Don't go there . . .

She shook her head and tried to clear her thoughts. It was her dad's birthday, and this one was special for more than one reason, because it was also an anniversary of sorts.

Her family had planned to meet at the diner at eight, and it was . . . ten after. Slipping out of bed, she grabbed an armful of clothes and tiptoed out to the living room to dress as quietly as she could.

Stuffing her feet into her sneakers, she took a last peek into her bedroom. Griffin was still out like a light, spread out on her bed like a fantasy. Damn. Walking away was the hardest thing she'd ever done. But after a quickly scrawled note that simply said, "I've gotta run," she did just that.

Fourteen

Griffin bolted awake, sitting straight up in the bed, heart pounding, ears ringing. He had a split second of disorientation when he didn't know where he was or why everything was a need-sunglasses-to-look-at-it sunshine yellow. Then he saw the lace panties hanging off the footboard.

Kate.

He was in Kate's bed. But no Kate. He slid a hand over the sheets. Still warm. He rolled over, but he could tell by the stillness of the place that he was alone.

It was a Sunday morning, crack of dawn—or close enough to it—so where the hell was she?

He pulled on his tux pants—all he had—and strode through the townhouse.

Empty, except for her short note.

Why?

The answer to that was painfully clear—he was an idiot. He should have kept his hands—and the rest of him—to himself. He'd known damn well she had a crush on him, forever in fact, and he'd taken unfair advantage.

Holly was going to kill him, and Adam was going to help, and Griffin deserved it.

A little shell-shocked by the events of the past twelve hours, he stood in the empty, quiet living room. The belongings he'd sent flying off the couch last night were still scattered across the floor. The couch itself seemed to stare at him incriminatingly, but all he could remember was the way Kate had wrapped herself around him, rocking up, holding on tight, crying out his name . . .

Christ. He rubbed his hands over his face. It was Sunshine, he decided. It was being home. He'd been prepared to hate it as much as he'd always hated it, but that hadn't happened. The small-town life wasn't stifling him, wasn't sucking the soul out of his body.

And part of it was watching the people in his life go on with theirs. Holly getting married to Adam. His dad with Deanna. Realizing that love and affection had been missing from his life for a damn long time . . .

Also his own doing.

He'd left here on purpose. Run hard and fast. But not Kate. She'd stayed in town for the responsibility, which he admired the hell out of. He admired other things about her as well. Like those warm mossy green eyes. The taste of her. The feel of her satiny skin sliding along his, the sounds she'd made when she'd come.

Sweet, slightly repressed second-grade teacher Kate Evans wasn't so sweet and repressed after all . . .

Someone rang the bell. Thinking she'd somehow gotten locked out, he buttoned and zipped his pants and tugged open the door to a tiny little girl in pigtails and a pink and white dress.

"Hi!" she said at a decibel level that made him wince, and she thrust out a book with the picture of a puppy on it.

He stared down the book.

"Read," she demanded.

"Uh . . ."

"Kate. Read."

Ah, now he got it. "Kate reads the book to you?" he asked.

She nodded and waited expectantly.

"Kate's not here," he said.

The little girl took a look at the book and then back up at him, her eyes huge and filling with tears.

Shit. "She'll be back later," he said quickly, desperately, just about as undone by a three-year-old's tears as he'd been by Kate's.

The little girl opened the book for him, her pigtails bouncing.

Oh no. No, no, no. "I'm not Kate," he said.

She stared up at him, her eyes swimming. "Read," she said soggily.

"You'll stop crying?"

She nodded.

"I mean it," he said, and pointed at her. "One more tear, and it's over."

She flashed a fast smile, the tears instantly gone. "'Kay."

Suspecting he'd been had, Grif crouched low and looked her in the eyes. "If you tell anyone I did this, I'll . . ." He broke off, unable to figure out a threat suitable for a three-year-old that wouldn't scare the shit out of her or scar her psychologically for life.

"Brooklyn? Where are you?" A pretty brunette stepped outside the townhouse next door. "Sweetie, it's Sunday. Kate's at the diner with her family for breakfast— Oh." Catching sight of Grif, she stopped short. Her gaze drank in the sight of him, making him realize he stood there in only his tux pants, which he'd thankfully buttoned.

"Hi," the brunette said awkwardly.

"Hey," he said, doing his best to look like he wasn't some sort of perv.

Little Brooklyn took her book and ran home.

Grif's gaze went to where Kate's car should have been parked. Empty.

Yep, apparently, she'd ditched him for breakfast with her

family. A longer note would have been nice. Like, thank you very much for all the orgasms, Grif . . .

Except she'd say his whole name, Griffin, in that soft voice, and he'd want to give her more . . .

In his experience, women loved to leave long notes. Unless they were upset. He added up the clues and came to the logical conclusion.

She was indeed upset.

He scanned the street out of habit, and zeroed in on the Lexus down the street. That asshole Anders. Stepping off the porch, he strode to the car, rapping once on the window, hard.

Trevan slid the window down two inches and gave him a wary look.

"Why are you still out here?" Grif asked him

"I just came outside."

Grif felt the hood. Indeed, it was cold. Before he could say anything, Dustin ran up to the car, out of breath. "Jeez, dad, why do you always park so far down? It's a long walk."

"It's exercise," Anders said. "You should have run it as a warm-up for practice instead of being lazy."

Dustin rolled his eyes as he got into the car. With a chirp of the tires, they were off. Grif stood there with his hands on his hips, staring after them, spoiling for a fight. He didn't like the feeling much.

Go home, he told himself. *Forget it. Forget her. She wanted you; she begged for you; she promised it was just for the night. Everything is okay.*

But it didn't feel okay.

Kate had to stop for gas and at the store for a birthday card, and then on impulse she ran into the florist to grab her dad flowers. She was quite certain no one had ever given him flowers before, and she wanted to make him happy.

He was getting his life back together, and she was proud

of him. Today was about him and making sure he saw that he had a lot to live for.

She stepped into the diner and eyed her group in the back. Ryan, Ashley, and a black-masked Tommy. Kate waved and headed over to them. "Where's Dad?"

"Restroom," Ryan said as Kate scooted into the round booth and was immediately bombarded by Ashley. "Where were you?" she hissed over Tommy's head. "I had to get the child dressed."

"I'm not a child," Tommy said. "I'm Batman."

"Sorry I'm late," Kate said, and hugged him. "I stopped to get Dad something." She looked at her brother. "Batman again? Did we wash that shirt?"

Tommy looked down at his shirt and did a palm's up. He didn't care one way or the other.

Ryan was giving her a long, steady look. "Sleep well?"

She felt her cheeks bloom. "Yes," she said, and her left eye twitched because there'd been very little sleeping involved in the night's activities.

Ryan stared at her some more. He knew her left eye twitched whenever she lied. "You?" she inquired politely, keeping her eyes wide open so there could be no more twitching.

He smirked.

He'd gotten his bridesmaid, then.

Ashley's gaze was still narrowed in on Kate. "Why is your mascara smudged?"

Kate swiped under her eyes. "Uh . . ."

Ashley leaned in and sniffed at her. "And what's that scent?"

Kate nudged her away and turned from Ryan's knowing gaze. "I didn't have time to take a shower, okay?"

"You smell like a guy," Ashley said. "A really great-smelling guy." Her sister sniffed at her again. "Man, that's good—" She broke off and got an aghast look on her face, eyes wide, mouth open. "Ohmigod!"

"What?"

"No shower," Ashley said slowly. "Flushed face. Smudged mascara. Smelling like a guy—"

"Shh!"

"You got laid!" Ashley whispered. "Ohemgee, you really did!"

"Did what?" their dad asked as he came to the table.

Kate jumped up and hugged him. "Happy birthday, Dad."

He looked touched at the flowers. "What are we talking about?"

She began to sweat. "Nothing."

"Slut," Ashley whispered in her ear.

Tommy popped up between them. "What's a slut?"

Ryan choked on his coffee.

Ashley looked quite pleased with herself.

Their dad looked alarmed. "Er, what?"

Kate inhaled a deep breath for calm. "Nothing," she said, and gave Ashley a say-it-again-and-die look" before rumpling Tommy's hair. "How about eggs?"

"Yes, and bacon," Tommy said, suitably distracted. "A mountain of bacon."

"Sounds good." Kate waved desperately for their server just as the door to the café opened. Kate's heart stopped, just completely stopped as Griffin Reid walked in.

Unlike her, he'd taken the time to shower. And he'd gone home, too, because rather than his tux he was wearing a pair of perfectly battered Levi's and a white button-down. He looked good enough to bring a hot flash. She slid down in her seat a little, waving her menu in front of her face to try to cool herself down. Don't look. If you don't look at him, you're invisible . . .

Her dad smiled and waved him over.

Crap. "Dad—"

Too late. Griffin was moving toward her in that easy, long-limbed stride, his eyes pinning her in place.

Feeling like a bug on a slide, she froze in her seat.

Ryan snickered like he was twelve.

"Ohmigod," Ashley whispered. "It was him! You slept with him!"

"Shh!"

Tommy's brow furrowed. "Is someone going to tell me what *slut* means?"

"You can look it up when you're thirty-five," Kate said, "or when I'm dead. Whichever comes last——" She broke off because Griffin was right there, at the table, those slate eyes on hers, stoic, solemn. Serious. "Griffin," she said, as if just seeing him. "What are you doing here?"

"Maybe the man came to eat," her dad said, scooting over. "Join us, Griffin. The more the merrier."

Griffin eyed the flowers. "I wouldn't want to intrude."

"You aren't," her dad said. "I'd rather we not celebrate, but Kate insists."

"You're turning fifty-five, Dad," Kate said. "We're celebrating."

"And also your one-year sobriety," Ashley said.

The table went silent except for Tommy slurping his water.

"It's a big deal," Kate said softly to her dad. "It's good to celebrate, all of it."

Her dad nodded. "Sit," he said to Griffin. "You look hungry."

Griffin's gaze slid to Kate, and she felt her face heat again. He'd been plenty hungry last night. They both had. She looked into his eyes and realized that he wasn't completely stoic. There was something in his expression. He looked like a storm blowing in and about as cheerful as an open grave, but there was something else as well.

He was deferring to her.

She was quite certain he didn't defer to anyone easily, but he was letting her make this call.

"Kate," Tommy said, pointing to her throat. "Your skin is bouncing."

Kate put a hand to her throat. "It's not bouncing. It's my pulse."

"Why is it doing that?"

"A woman's heart beats faster than a man's," she said. "That's all."

Ryan snorted.

Ashley rolled her eyes.

Griffin's gaze remained on hers, giving nothing away.

And her dad divided a long, careful look between them. "Okay," he said. "What am I missing?"

"Well," Ashley said. "Kate's given up on the whole on-line dating thing and has moved on to real, live dating."

"Yes," her dad said. "I know that. She's dating Ryan." He looked at Ryan. "Right?"

Ryan looked at Kate. *Fix this.*

Kate resisted thunking her head to the table. "Dad, not now."

Ashley began to whisper. "S . . . L . . ."

Kate picked up her knife, and Ashley fell silent.

Not Tommy. Tommy smiled. "It's S-L-U-T," he told Ashley proudly. "*Slut.*"

Kate did thunk her head to the table then.

"You staying?" Ryan asked Griffin.

Kate looked up to see him hesitate—also unlike him. Then he shocked the hell out of her by sliding into the booth.

Their thighs brushed, his hard and powerful, and flashes of last night flickered in her brain. Griffin in her bed, his hands gripping hers above her head, him buried deep inside her, thrusting even deeper, his eyes dark and intense, his voice a husky promise that had driven her wild.

He'd made good on every single hot promise, which begged the question. They'd given each other everything that needed to be given, so why was he here?

Fifteen

Griffin didn't do regrets as a whole, but he was beginning to regret the shit out of his impulse to stop at the diner.

He'd spent a lot of years out in the middle of nowhere with his only family being his fellow soldiers. Their lives depended on getting along, so for the most part that's exactly what they did.

Before that, there'd been his actual family. For much of his teen years his mom and dad had been separated, his mom in New York and his father here in Idaho. There'd been no real sense of a family unit other than his relationship with Holly. There'd never been this sort of family-by-committee feel that the Evanses had.

It was more than slightly terrifying.

Kate was looking at him, her eyes a little glossy as if she was lost in thought. And given the way her pulse was fluttering and the way she licked her lips when he met her gaze, he had a feeling he knew what she was thinking about.

Last night.

She jumped when Ashley snapped her fingers in her face. "Jeez," the teenager said. "Where the heck were you? Disneyland?"

Ryan snorted into his water.

Tommy looked confused.

Griffin met Kate's gaze. He'd wanted to see her again, and here she was, and he still wasn't satisfied. Not by a long shot. And why hadn't she answered her dad about Ryan? Was there still something there? His gut tightened at the thought. Not wanting to examine that too closely, he picked up a menu.

Tommy grinned. "Yay, you're staying!" he said, straightening his Batman mask. "You can be Robin. Robin's very important. Have you eaten here before? Cuz all the stuff is named after people in town." The kid leaned over Grif's shoulder and pointed. "There's the Tommy Ice Cream Sundae, see? It's for me cuz that's what I like the best here. And there's the Eddie, which is a scrambled egg dish made for my dad. I don't know why he's scrambled, but it's really good."

Grif nodded, waiting until everyone seemed busy talking to turn to Kate. Keeping his voice low, trying to be discreet, he said, "We need to talk."

Of course at that very moment, the chatter lulled and all interest turned their way.

"What do you got to talk about?" Tommy asked.

Luckily, the waitress came by right then. Shelly had gone to school with Grif, and she smiled at him. "Hey, hon. Nice to see you. You all ready?"

"One of everything," Tommy yelled with enthusiasm, getting up on his knees in the chair to do it.

Kate corrected his order. "Make that eggs and toast."

"And bacon!" Tommy added.

"And bacon," Kate said.

Shelly looked at Ashley next. The teen tossed her menu down with dramatic flair and sighed. "A grapefruit, I guess."

Again Kate corrected the order. "More," she told Ashley.

"I'm on a diet."

"Another time." Kate looked at Shelly. "Give her the same as Tommy, with a bowl of fruit."

Ashley grumbled a little bit but looked secretly pleased, not letting out a single argument. No one seemed to argue with Kate's authority, Grif noticed, and she definitely had authority here. She ran her world with a sweet warmth that no one questioned.

The only time he'd seen her out of her element had been with him.

Food for thought.

So was the way Ryan was alternately eyeballing Grif and trying to give Kate some sort of secret message that Grif couldn't quite read. Giving up, he lifted his menu and perused it. Then, making sure his face was covered from everyone else, he turned his head to Kate.

She ignored him.

Shelly was at Kate. "The usual?"

"Uh . . ." Kate glanced at the menu.

Griffin leaned in and pointed to something called the Ryan Omelet. The description said: "Laid-back but interesting, layered, and special, this omelet is guaranteed to make you feel good."

Griffin tapped it. "Maybe the Ryan?" he said meaningfully. "Is that what you're having?"

She looked at him in disbelief. "No. I'm not having the Ryan." Then she also leaned in, as if looking at his menu and hissed in his ear, "And if you'll remember, I had the Griffin just last night, so really I shouldn't be hungry for a damn long time!" She pulled back and looked at Shelly. "I'll take the Dell's Mountain Special."

Shelly smiled. "Three eggs, three sausages, three bacon strips, three pancakes, toast, and hash browns. Anything else?"

"Maybe the kitchen sink?" Ryan asked beneath his breath, then jumped as if maybe he'd been kicked under the table.

"Yes," Kate said, and pushed back her chair. "All that

and the kitchen sink, too. Excuse me, I need a minute." And she headed to the bathroom.

"She likes to give herself time-outs," Tommy said into the awkward silence. "Says it keeps her outta jail."

"She should be more worried about the loony bin," Ryan muttered.

Ashley laughed and fist bumped Ryan.

"How about you, handsome?" Shelly asked Grif.

"Just a coffee, thanks," he said, and rose.

He needed a time-out, too.

He waited in the hallway between the two restrooms and across from the kitchen entrance.

"What are you doing?" Kate asked when she came out.

"I told you, we need to talk."

She stared at him as if he were crazy. "Why?"

"Why?" He stared back, a little stymied at this. Wasn't it obvious?

Kate sighed. "Tell me this. Would you want to talk with any other woman you'd gone home with last night?"

This made him blink, and she laughed with little mirth in the sound. "Go home, Griffin."

"I didn't go home with you last night to sleep with you," he said. "I drove you home to make sure you got there safely." And shit, that didn't come out right. He shoved his fingers through his hair. "Things got out of hand."

"Yes," she agreed. "In the best possible way."

"Then why did you sneak out of your own bed this morning like you were taking the walk of shame?"

She stared at him and then laughed again, this time for real. She laughed so hard she had to bend over and put her hands on her knees. Twice she started to straighten up but ended up laughing some more.

"Look," he said, starting to get pissed off. "I was worried that you were upset or something. You'd left your own place and vanished."

She made an obvious effort to get herself under control while he waited with hands on hips. "I'm trying to apologize here," he said, thoroughly irritated.

That got her. She did straighten then, her smile gone. "Don't you dare apologize for the best sex of my life."

He opened his mouth, but she pointed at him. "I mean it," she said.

"Best of your life?" he repeated, losing a good portion of his mad because damn. Hard to be mad after that compliment.

"Yes," she said. "The best of my life." Her mouth twitched. "I'm actually thinking of having it carved on my tombstone."

He rubbed his jaw and eyeballed her. "So while I was stressing over possibly having shocked you into next week, you're . . . okay?"

"So okay." At that, she patted his chest in a dismissive gesture. "And thank you." She started to walk away, but he caught her.

"Wait." He was having a hard time wrapping his mind around this. "So you're just going to sleep with me and be done with it?"

Now it was her turn to blink in surprise. "Uh . . . yes?"

Huh. This had always been his MO, so why this bothered him, he had no clue. None. Zero. Zip . . .

"What's the matter?" she asked.

"Nothing," he said. "Nothing at all." Christ, he was such a liar. A totally fucked-up, turned-upside-down, confused-as-hell liar. Letting go of her, he turned to leave, thinking he was the biggest idiot on earth, wasting all morning worrying. Kate might be sweet and warm and unassuming, but she was sure as hell no pushover. In fact, she'd just completely schooled him.

"I'm not still sleeping with Ryan," she said to his back.

He turned around and met her gaze.

"I mean, we talk about doing it sometimes," she said, and shrugged. "But we haven't. Not in a long time."

"But you . . . talk about it."

"More like joke about it," she said. "But it's been a long time since we actually have. A really long time. Don't forget that part." She grimaced. "Listen, this is new for me. I mean, if you want to chitchat about science, I'm your girl. Or how to get crayon out of your clothes. Or how to corral twenty wild and rambunctious little kids. But talking about this sort of stuff, relationship stuff . . ." She shook her head. "I have to admit, it's out of my league. Way out."

Grif was starting to get an odd feeling. "When you said there'd been two men before me . . ."

"Yeah." She bit her lip. "I didn't actually say two men . . ."

She had his full attention. "A woman?"

She laughed a little, clearly embarrassed. "No. Not that there's anything wrong with that." She squirmed a bit, and utterly fascinated, Grif could only wait her out.

"Okay," she finally said. "The truth is, it was one guy and . . ."

"And?"

"And . . . I sort of counted my vibrator." She closed her eyes, her cheeks bright red. "It's called Magic Mike. That's what the box said."

It wasn't often Griffin found himself speechless, but he was there right now. Also, he was smiling for the first time all morning. "You named your dildo."

"No," she said. "Dildo is a town in Newfoundland, Canada. I have a . . ." She lowered her voice. "Vibrator."

"And you named it," he said with vast amusement.

"The name was on the box! And don't you laugh at me. This is all your fault. You make me so nervous!"

"You weren't nervous last night," he said, still smiling. "You were . . ." Perfect. "Hot as hell."

She took this in for a moment and then let out a small smile. "Really?"

"Really." He tilted her face to his. "Does Ryan know about last night? Do I need to sleep with one eye open?"

"No," Ryan said from behind them. "You can sleep worry free." He paused. "Unless you hurt her." And then he vanished into the men's restroom.

Grif looked at Kate, and she smiled again. "See?" she said. "All is well. So . . . nice seeing you, but I've really got to get back out there."

He caught her wrist and reeled her back in. "How long, Kate?"

"Well, actually, I imagine the food's coming any second, so—"

"No, I meant how long had it been for you before last night?" He was thinking of how quickly he'd gotten inside her, how hard and fast he'd taken her. And then round two.

And round three.

Had he hurt her?

Kate blew out a breath and studied the wallpaper peeling off the wall.

"A few months?" he asked.

"Did you know that over half of all singles in America haven't had a date in a year?" she asked.

Shit. "A year?"

"Yes," she said. "That." Hesitated. "Times two."

Oh Christ. He rolled his neck but couldn't release the kink. He dropped his head to his chest then looked at her. "Did I hurt you?"

"No. No," she repeated softly, and lifted a hand to his face, letting her thumb rasp over his stubble. "You didn't hurt me. You . . . revived me."

Ryan came out of the bathroom and gave Kate a long look. "Eleven days," he said cryptically, and then headed back to the table.

Grif had no idea what that meant, but it put a pensive look on Kate's face. When she caught him eyeing her, she cleared her expression. "So . . . here we are, two people who just happened to sleep together. Nothing more, nothing less."

And that was that. She'd wanted her one-night stand, with him of all people, and she'd gotten it. Exactly what she'd wanted.

As for what he wanted, that was pretty damn complicated.

Or maybe it wasn't.

He'd been here in Sunshine for a few days, and he wasn't itching to race off. He'd settled in and . . . and hell. The truth was he could see himself further settling. Maybe he and his dad would never win a father-son relationship of the year award. Hell, maybe they'd never even learn to have a conversation without growling at each other. But it was still home. His home. Where he belonged.

Which had nothing to do with Kate.

Or did it? He didn't know, and one epiphany a day was his max, so he went to move past her.

Their arms brushed, and she made a sound.

He stopped short, his own heart doing some odd and heavy pounding in his chest. "What was that?"

"What was what?" she asked.

"You . . . moaned."

She let out a forced laugh. "Don't be ridiculous, I didn't—"

He brushed against her again, purposely this time, and she made the sound again before going still, biting her lip. "That," he said, pointing at her. "There."

She closed her eyes. "You know what it is."

Yeah, he knew. He leaned into her. "Say it."

"Chemistry," she whispered, and blushed. "I happen to be a bit of an expert on the subject."

Christ, she made him smile. She made him a lot of things, too many things, and suddenly, he couldn't walk away. "So, as an expert," he said, "what do you suggest we do?"

Kate's heart was pounding, and she had to lick her suddenly dry lips. Anything she might have suggested certainly couldn't be discussed in a family restaurant.

But she could think it. In fact she would be thinking about it, and what they'd done last night, for a long time to come. "I'm not sure what we can do." She held her breath and met his gaze. "You can't exactly fight the laws of science."

His eyes heated and focused right on hers. "No, you can't," he said, low and slightly rough.

She closed her eyes. He'd spoken in that voice last night,

right in her ear, and remembering gave her a shiver. The really good kind of shiver, and she stepped closer.

His big, capable hands immediately went to her hips, his long fingers making themselves at home on her body like it was his. Like she was his.

She shivered again, and their gazes met just as she slid her arms around his neck and pulled his head down.

He was already bending to meet her halfway.

Incredibly aware of the chaos around them and how anyone could come upon them, she let her eyes drift closed. Just a taste, just one more taste, she thought as his mouth touched hers.

Threading his hand through her hair, he tilted her head farther back until apparently he had her right where he wanted her. Then he parted her lips and slowly and completely ravished her. The man could kiss, he was the kisser of all kissers, and the longer it went on the more insistent it became. She melted into him, completely, until at a sound behind them, she broke away with unsure steps, her breathing anywhere but under control.

"Excuse me," a waitress said, skirting around them with a knowing smile.

Holy.

Smokes.

Kate stared up at the man still sharing air with her. He was a sight standing tall in front of her with his usual cool calm gone, replaced by something dangerous, alluring, and hotter than sin.

"That's some science problem," he said. "I don't think we've solved it yet."

She put a hand on her chest to keep her heart from leaping out. "I concur. So . . . what do we do?"

"Solve it," he said firmly.

She paused. "How?"

He gave a slow shake of his head. "You're the expert."

"It's possible the attraction will just wane and die a natural death," she said.

His gaze was on her mouth. "Doubt it."

So did she. "Did you know that most people make a decision regarding whether they are attracted to a person within three seconds of meeting?"

"How many seconds within meeting me did you decide?" he asked.

"Maybe I still haven't decided."

He laughed softly. "You've decided."

Dammit, she really hated that he could read her so effectively. "Well, it took you longer than three seconds," she pointed out. "I had to throw myself at you to get your attention."

His smile faded. "Don't mistake restraint for disinterest, Kate."

Her breath caught on that, and she didn't know how to respond. Hell, she didn't know what to think. What was he saying exactly?

Tracing a finger along her temple, he tucked a strand of hair behind her ear. "We going to solve our problem?" he asked softly.

There was no air in her lungs. None. "I thought this was a one-night thing," she said. "Just a fun adventure."

His lips curved. "A naked adventure."

"Yeah." She couldn't ask for more. She couldn't because she wasn't sure that she'd be able to have another night and not fall for him harder than she already had.

Sixteen

The next day Kate got up at the crack of dawn against the wishes of every single bone in her body. She wanted to lie in bed for another half an hour but that wasn't going to burn calories.

She could think of a way to burn at least 112 calories, but Griffin wasn't in her bed. Which was her own doing.

We going to solve our problem?

He'd asked her that in the diner, and she'd resisted getting serious about the question. In hindsight, she had no idea how. Maybe because of the envelope still keeping her company everywhere she went. This was her year, everything within her told her it was. She wanted to go to San Diego, needed to go, and yet . . . she was afraid. There. The pathetic truth. She was afraid. If she went, would her family be okay without her?

And then there was the real fear. If they were okay without her . . . did that mean no one needed her?

Tired of herself, she got up and ran.

Since she was still a little spooked from the last time and not quite up for the woods, she altered her route, taking the streets to the park instead. The fog hadn't lifted yet, and she slowed to a halt in the middle of the park, realizing that taking the streets hadn't helped all that much.

She still felt like a sitting duck.

With every horror film she'd ever seen running through her mind, she slipped her hand in her pocket and came up with the Mace.

Some men brought flowers.

Griffin had brought her Mace.

She loved that about him.

Larry was asleep on his bench, and she tiptoed past him. The concession stand was closed, of course. Which kind of sucked since popcorn for breakfast sounded pretty good about now.

Turning to go back, she nearly plowed into . . . Larry.

He was large and built like a bull in a china shop. A gentle giant. His long black and silver hair was thick and wild, his eyes sleepy. "You woke me," he said.

She glanced at the bench and saw his bags of stuff scattered around. "I'm sorry."

"You buy me popcorn?"

"They're not open yet."

Larry sighed. He might look like a retired linebacker, but his eyes were sweet, and he hunched a little bit, like he was trying to be more her size than his. She couldn't imagine he'd been the one to chase her last time. For one thing, he moved like a tortoise. And for another, he wore only socks on his feet, as usual. People brought him hand-me-down shoes all the time; he just didn't like them.

"Are you hungry?" she asked. "The diner's offered to feed you breakfast, remember? You just have to show up."

"The diner," he repeated, his brow wrinkling.

"Yes," she said. "Downtown. They'll feed you if you're hungry."

He smiled sleepily at her, reaching out with his big, beefy hand to pat her on the top of her head. And then he turned and gathered all his stuff and walked slowly off, limping slightly in his sock-covered feet.

Watching him go, Kate relaxed her grip on the Mace in her pocket.

Grif found his dad in the barn saddling up his horse.

Donald watched him approach, no expression on his face. "Still here, huh?"

Grif shrugged and crouched down to greet an enthusiastic Thing One and Thing Two when they bounded over. "Seems like." He gave each dog a full belly rub, which had them writhing in ecstasy. "Going out?" he asked his dad.

"I run a ranching empire. What else would I be doing?"

Grif bit back his defensive retort. "Want some company?"

Donald gave him a once-over. "You remember how to ride?"

Grif knew a challenge when he heard one. He saddled up, the motions as familiar as when riding had been a routine part of his life.

They rode in silence. Well, Grif and his dad were silent. Thing One and Thing Two, not so much. Donald had a Chuckit, a plastic stick that allowed him to scoop a tennis ball and throw it for the dogs from horseback.

He made his first toss for Thing One, and the dog leaped into the air, catching the ball with beauty and grace. Thing Two didn't have the same grace or anything close to it. She couldn't jump as high either. So she caught the ball—square in the center of her forehead.

This dimmed her enthusiasm not one little bit, even when it happened for the third time in a row, and Grif couldn't help but laugh.

"Every single time," his dad said, and shook his head, though a small smile cracked his usually grim mouth as well.

Though there was still snow on the upper-elevation peaks, the valley floor was working on a spring bloom. A rainbow of flowers rocked in the wind alongside thigh-high wild grass. An hour later they stopped at the far northern pasture. Griffin took in the quiet beauty and wondered how in the hell he'd ever come to resent it so much in his youth.

"Your ass sore yet?" his dad asked. "I don't imagine you did a lot of riding over there."

"Over there" being anywhere off the continental US, which of course was another planet as far as his father was concerned. "Not on a horse," he said, resisting the urge to shift his weight in the saddle, because the truth was, he was getting sore—a fact he was never going to admit. "I'm fine. What're your plans for this place?"

His father craned his neck and stared at him.

Yeah. Grif had no idea where that sentence had come from either. Except . . . he did. Holly's wedding had made him realize how precious home was, and even though things still weren't great with his dad, Idaho was home. It was where he belonged.

"What are my plans for the ranch," his dad repeated slowly. "Why?"

Grif shrugged.

His dad stared at him some more. "Thought you had job options."

Grif shrugged again. "It's just a question."

"You're thinking of staying here in Idaho?"

"No. I don't know," Grif said. "I'm just thinking out loud." But yeah, he was thinking of staying.

Wanting to stay . . .

And if that wasn't the most asinine thing he'd ever thought, he didn't know what was. He and his dad would kill each other in less than a day.

"You think we could work together," his dad said. And then let out a loud guffaw that pissed Grif off.

"It was just a thought," he said, hating feeling like a stupid, defensive teenager all over again.

Donald Reid took off his cowboy hat and ran his fingers through his still thick but entirely gray hair. "You can't just become a damn rancher. It takes years and a heart for it." He slid Grif a look. "A heart that you've never shown here, not once."

Grif bit back the urge to argue in his own defense, to say, what about all the times he'd taken care of Holly when she'd gotten herself into trouble or how many hours he'd put into this ranch as a kid and teenager, sweat and blood and agony, hours that apparently had gotten erased somehow in the past decade of service to his country. "I'm not saying I want to step in and run this place, Dad." Jesus. "I'm just asking what your plans are."

"And how you might fit into them."

"You just won't let us get along, will you?" Grif let out his own mirthless laugh. "You know, this whole time I thought it was me. For years, I've thought that. But in fourteen years of military service, I managed to get along just fine with everyone, which told me that you're the only person who has a problem with me."

"I don't have a problem with you. I have a problem with your attitude."

"You don't know my attitude now," Grif responded. "You're going off my teenage attitude."

"Which sucked."

"Yeah. And I can't change that. Or apologize for it."

"Why not?"

Grif stared at his dad. "You want me to apologize for being a stupid punk-ass kid?"

"Maybe."

Grif shook his head. "Fine. I'm sorry I was such a pain in your ass. But every kid is a pain in the ass. Parents are supposed to get over it."

Donald Reid was silent at that. He was silent through riding fences and checking on cattle.

And then, two hours later, out of the blue, he spoke. "Wouldn't hurt to put you to work, see how you do."

Not exactly blowing Grif's hair back with praise, but it was all he was going to get. And it was good enough. He wasn't seeking the old man's approval, though it would have been nice. He was seeking . . . his place, he supposed. He still wasn't sure he'd found it, but he'd taken a step anyway.

* * *

At the end of the day, Grif was heading back to the house when a figure at the creek caught his attention.

Kate.

"I'm just checking on the seedlings," she said when he changed course and walked over to her. She gave him a long once over. "Headache?"

He rubbed his temple. "A little." He'd not yet even noticed.

"I keep meaning to ask you," she said. "Are you in physical therapy?"

"Was. Until I got here."

"What were you doing in PT?" she asked.

"A little of everything."

She stood and brushed her hands off on her jeans. "How about yoga?"

"Yoga?"

"Yes," she said. "It's been proven to be very effective against migraines. Have you ever tried it?"

"Hell no."

She smiled. "You're chicken."

His gaze slid to hers, and she laughed. "You are," she said, smiling wide. "You're afraid of the word *yoga*."

"No. I'm afraid of yoga clothes."

"Do you have basketball shorts?"

"Yeah. Why?" he asked warily.

"Put them on, and I'll show you a few yoga moves to ease a migraine. No leggings required," she promised.

"I don't think so."

"Please?" she asked. "Just consider it."

He studied her a moment, ostensibly to do his considering. Instead he was considering how much fun it might be to watch her do yoga. "There should be naked yoga," he said. "If there was naked yoga, I'd be all over it."

She laughed. "Let's start with basketball-shorts yoga."

He had zero interest in yoga, but hell, if she wanted to maneuver him around on a little pad with her hands all over him, who was he to hold back? "If I agree, I'll need something from you in return."

She nibbled on her lower lip as her gaze slid to his mouth.

Yeah, babe. That. Later. "You have to let me show you how to protect yourself," he said.

"So you want to swap tutorials?" she asked.

No, actually, he wanted to swap other things. Like touches and kisses and bodily fluids. "Yeah," he said. "I want to swap tutorials."

Again her gaze dropped to his mouth.

"Chicken?" he taunted softly.

She looked at her watch. "I have thirty minutes. You're first. You can do me tomorrow."

"Gladly," he said, and enjoyed her blush.

Five minutes later he was flat on his back on the deck of the ranch house.

"Such a gorgeous view," Kate said, looking out at the valley below, bordered by the rugged peaks.

His view was far better. She was kneeling at his side, her hand on his abs. From his vantage point he had a fantastic view of her full breasts, and if he wasn't mistaken, she was just a little bit chilly.

"Close your eyes," she said, and leaning over him, began to massage his shoulders. "Just breathe."

He closed his eyes and breathed. And then yawned. "Sorry," he said. "Tired."

"Yawning doesn't necessarily mean you're tired," she said. "It means your body needs more oxygen. Think of your happy place."

Eyes still closed, he slid his hand up the back of her thigh and cupped her ass.

"Griffin!"

"That's my happy place."

"My butt is your happy place?"

"Mmm-hmm," he said with a groan of pleasure at the way she dug her fingers into his biceps.

"Muscle tension is often the root cause of a bad headache," she said.

"Or an IED at ground zero."

She was quiet a minute. "Or that," she said, her voice not as steady as before. "Yoga can alleviate both the cause and the symptom of physiological stressors."

Not wanting to talk about physiological stressors, he opened his eyes and tried to look down her top. "This really would be a lot more fun naked."

Ignoring that, she maneuvered him into several poses, one of which was called cat's pose, where she made him get on his hands and knees and stick his ass in the air and breathe like a woman in labor. He pretended not to get it, making her show him slowly and in great detail what she wanted, and watching her on her hands and knees breathing like that got him hard as a rock.

Totally worth it.

Twenty minutes later she let him collapse to the mat. She leaned over him to knead his shoulders again, digging right into the aching muscles. "Still holding some tension," she said.

Yes, except the source of his biggest tension was considerably south of his shoulders.

"You're lucky to have grown up out here," she said, eyeing the view. "With the horses and miles and miles of land." She inhaled deeply. "Smell it. It's so fresh."

He took a deep breath and smelled horses and dirt. And her, some complicated mix of shampoo and lotion and essence of Kate.

"It's just beautiful," she said softly.

He took another breath and had to admit, it was true. He had never appreciated it when he was younger. He'd been far too busy being pissed off at the world. And at his father for always being on his ass about something. And at his mom for dying. And at school for being torture. Everything.

But now, with the maturity the past decade had given him, he realized he'd missed it and was truly enjoying being back.

"Feel better?" she asked, letting her hands slide off his shoulders.

No. But she still looked hot on her knees. Really hot.

"Griffin?" She cocked her head. "Are you even listening to me?"

"My brain stopped working the second you got on your knees like that."

She snorted, and he sat up and pulled her onto his lap, nuzzling at the sweet spot right beneath her ear.

She melted into him and made his damn day. "I have to go," she whispered, even as she wrapped her arms around his neck, seducing him with nothing more than a smile. Which meant that the joke was on him, because all along he'd honestly believed that everything that was happening— or not happening—between them was his own doing.

But even he had to call bullshit on the notion.

He'd been a hell of a soldier. He knew how to keep his guard up and watch his own six. And yet with little to no effort Kate had taken him down, methodically, thoughtfully, purposely.

Taken down by a second-grade elementary school teacher slash science nerd who had no idea how powerful she was.

She wriggled free. "Sorry," she said. "But I've got to help Ashley with her math, and then it's Bingo Night. We're raising money for the school library." She leaned in and then surprised him by nipping his lower lip, wrenching a groan from him.

"Good?" she whispered.

"So good it should be illegal."

"*Cosmo* said it was a trick to hold a guy's interest."

She had his interest all right. And, he was afraid, his heart as well.

He was still sitting there alone a few minutes later when his dad opened the sliding door and stared at him. "Yoga?" he asked.

"It's a tension reliever."

Donald gave a bark of laughter. "Whipped," he said, and while Grif sat there stunned that he'd made his dad laugh— sure, it was totally at him and not with him, but it was something—Donald vanished back inside.

That night Griffin didn't get a headache, and he slept like a log. He had no idea if it had been the riding, the yoga, or all the fresh air, but he suspected that the culprit was none of the above.

That the honor belonged to Kate herself.

The next day Kate woke at the crack of dawn. At first she thought maybe it was the pressure of the pretty embossed scholarship envelope sitting bedside, the one silently saying, *Psst, only nine more days to grab your lifelong dream . . .*

But then she heard the knock at her door. Staggering down the hall, she peeked out. Grif.

He handed her a to-go mug of coffee. "You've got five minutes."

"Huh?"

"Drink first," he said, and then pushed his way inside. He leaned against the wall, arms crossed, watching her obey his order.

When she had a few sips down and the caffeine had begun to clear her head, she asked, "Five minutes for what?"

He just looked at her, all big, bad, and silent.

Five minutes . . .

Her body tingled. Normally her egg timer was set to about twenty, but she knew firsthand that Grif could get her to the finish line in half that time.

"Time to get dressed," he said. "It's my turn to have my way with you."

"Then why am I getting dressed?"

The corners of his mouth twitched. An almost smile. But whatever had him up and ready this early wasn't all that amusing. Serious Grif was in the house.

And then she remembered. "You're going to teach me how to defend myself."

"Yes."

"I'm not really all that fond of violence."

"You don't have to be." He turned her away from him

and in the direction of her bedroom. When she didn't immediately start moving, he gave her a swat on the butt. "Hustle."

What did it say about her that his comment made her want to hustle to strip rather than the reverse?

He took her to the gym in town and proceeded to give her boxing lessons. Thirty minutes later she was drenched in sweat, and every single muscle trembled.

"How do you feel?" he asked when he'd brought her back home and walked her inside.

"Like a puddle of goo." She blew a strand of hair from her face. "And maybe like I could kick some ass."

He flashed a heart-stopping smile, hooked an arm around her neck, and drew her in close, pressing his mouth to her temple. "That's my girl."

She slid her hands up his chest. "Griffin?"

His voice was morning gruff and caused shivers down her spine. "Yeah?"

"We still have a chemistry problem."

"No shit." His hands went to her hips and squeezed as he glanced at her foyer table. "Kate, would you say that table is . . . sturdy?"

She dropped her head to his chest and half moaned, half laughed. "Don't tempt me."

She felt him smile at her temple. "You want me bad," he said.

"I told you. You can't fight chemistry."

A laugh huffed from him. "So it's not your fault? Is that what you're saying?"

"That's right," she said. "It's your fault."

He only smiled, shook his head, and then quickly left, as if maybe he didn't trust himself with her.

The feeling was mutual.

The next day at dawn, Grif was woken by his phone chirping.

"You have five minutes," Kate said. "I'm on your deck with yoga mats."

He scrubbed a hand over his face. "Are you naked?"

"No!"

He sighed and rolled out of bed, peeking out his window to indeed see her car out front. "This is not how I dreamed of you waking me up, Kate," he said into the phone.

Her breath caught audibly, which only made him harder—a combination of morning wood and Kate's voice.

"Are you coming?" she asked softly.

He groaned. "I will if you will."

"Oh my God. I didn't mean—" She broke off at his low laugh.

"Love it when you talk dirty," he said.

"Just get your ass out here, Griffin Reid. Now."

"And I especially love it when you go all domineering like that."

She hung up on him. Grif grinned and then stood there and recited the alphabet backward until he could pull on a pair of basketball shorts without tenting the front of them.

Holly and Adam came home from their honeymoon the next day, both looking quite relaxed and mellow. Holly hugged Grif tight in greeting then stepped back, grinning up at his face.

"What?" he asked.

"Oh, sorry, am I still doing it?" she asked. "Am I still smiling?"

"From ear to ear," Grif said.

"I know! I can't seem to stop."

Adam laughed at her, and she smacked her new husband in the chest. "Stop it. It's all your fault anyway."

Pulling her into him, Adam nuzzled her ear before nipping it. "I know," he said, sounding quite full of himself.

Grif blew out a sigh. "Didn't you get that out of your system over the past few days?"

"Nope." Adam took a good look at Grif and then his brows went up. "How are you doing?"

"Good," Grif said.

"Really." This wasn't a question, and it sounded rather heavy on the irony. "And why are you good?"

"Why am I good?" Grif asked. "What kind of question is that?"

"I'm sensing a tremor in the force," Adam said.

"What the hell?" Grif looked at Holly. "What did you do to him?"

"Well, I pretty much screwed him deaf and blind, and then—"

"Christ!" Grif covered his ear. "Don't tell me!"

Holly laughed, but Adam was still giving Grif a once-over.

Adam was a little spooky sometimes, knowing things he shouldn't. Grif held his gaze, thinking he couldn't possibly know.

But Adam just stared back. He knew.

"What's going on?" Holly asked.

"Ask him," Adam said.

"All right." She shoved her new husband aside and looked up at her brother. "What the hell is my husband talking about?"

"Nothing."

Holly turned to Adam, who gave her a raised brow. Holly gasped and whirled back on Grif. "You didn't!"

"Going to have to narrow that down, Hol."

She went toe-to-toe with him. "You didn't sleep with her. Tell me you didn't sleep with her."

Well, there hadn't been all that much sleeping involved, but Grif knew his sister had one hell of a right hook, and he already had a building headache, so he kept that detail to himself.

As well as the fact that Kate had given him a third yoga tutorial that morning during which she'd put him through his paces. He'd then returned the favor, teaching her some more self-defense moves. It had been a hot and sweaty forty-five minutes that he knew damn well had left her hot and bothered, and him the same.

And then she'd gone to work, and he'd gone to the shower for a self-serve.

"Dammit, Grif!" Holly said. "I told you she's vulnerable!"

"She's a grown woman," Grif said. "Capable of making her own decisions."

"You were at a wedding, for God's sake. A really, really, really great wedding."

"So?"

Holly stared at him like he was the biggest moron on earth. "So weddings make people even more vulnerable. Oh my God, I can't believe you did this to her."

Okay, this was starting to piss him off. "Jesus, I didn't force her!"

"Of course you didn't! You didn't have to. She has a huge crush on you, and you know that! All you had to do was give her that look."

"What look?"

"You know what look! The look you give women, the one that makes them fall at your feet. She probably leaped right into your arms."

Grif opened his mouth and then shut it.

Adam laughed then sucked it up at a dark look from Grif.

"Women don't fall at my feet," Grif said.

"Suzie Mayers, Tessa Winworth, Sugar Madison, Morgan Yzardo," Holly said, ticking the names off on her fingers. "Tracy Bassinger, Carina Martinez—"

"That was high school!"

Holly let her hands fall to her side, but the temper was still firing in her eyes. "They used to crawl into your window at night."

At the very pleasant memory, Grif smiled, and Holly hit him again. "Ow!" he said. "Watch it. I'm hurt, you know."

"Oh, really? Are you fragile, you big, annoying oaf? Are you taking care of everyone else in your world except yourself, leaving you no time for a real life? Are you feeling lonely and overwhelmed and just a little bit afraid that this is all life is going to offer? Are you living in a small town where your only viable options are your own ex-boyfriend or dating some asshole from Boise you met online?"

Grif went still, his amusement with his sister fading. "Kate's dating some asshole from Boise?"

"Is that all you heard?"

No. He'd heard it all, every word. And an unaccustomed emotion was sitting on his chest now.

Guilt.

Because the truth was, Kate had been vulnerable that night, and he'd known it. She'd also been a little bit toasted. And looking for oblivion. He'd given her everything she'd wanted; he knew that. She'd thoroughly enjoyed herself. Her breathy little pants of "Oh yes, Griffin, oh my God, yes" were still headlining his fantasies at night.

But had he taken advantage of her? He didn't like the thought that maybe he had. He didn't like that at all.

But he also didn't like the thought of her dating some dickwad she'd met online.

"Grif," Holly said far more gently at his silence. "She's not your type."

"And you know my type?"

"Yes. Slutty." She arched a brow, waiting for him to deny it.

"People change," he said.

"Fine," she allowed. "I'll grant you that. Let me come at this another way. I know what's not your type. Sweet, hard-working, dedicated, loyal second-grade teachers from Sunshine."

A direct hit.

Seventeen

K ate was standing in front of her class trying to express the importance of being able to spell the states in the continental US when someone peeked into her room.

Holly.

She was wearing a vistor's pass, which was no doubt thanks to Ryan. Holly and Adam had only taken a few days off. Brady, Adam's helicopter pilot brother, had flown them to Coeur d'Alene for a lux stay at a resort hotel, but it was high season at Belle Haven and even though they'd hired on new vet Dr. Wyatt to help, business was booming, leaving a real honeymoon slated for early fall.

Holly had enjoyed her little trip if her glowing complexion was any indicator. She gave a finger wave to the class, who knew her from visits to the animal center.

Kate moved toward her. "Everyone say hi to Ms. Reid— Actually, she's Mrs. Connelly now."

"Hi, Mrs. Connelly," the kids said in varying degrees of unison.

Holly beamed. "Hi, everyone. I just need to borrow Ms. Evans for a minute."

Every seven- and eight-year-old in the class had lost their train of thought at the sight of her, hoping she had an animal with her. Which she didn't. Unfortunately, Kate really needed to keep them on task because they were running behind today. She took the time to lean into Holly for a quick hug and baby rub on her still flat belly. "I'm so happy to see you," she said, "but we're on a super-tight schedule today."

"Okay, but this is . . ." Holly lowered her voice. *"Muy importante."*

"That means very important," Tommy said out loud, translating for everyone.

"How do you even know that, freak?" Dustin asked.

Tommy shrugged and went back to his coloring.

"Dustin," Kate said, making sure her temper didn't show. "What happens when we call someone a name?"

He put down his crayon, stood up, and walked to the back of the room to the chair facing the wall. He plopped on it and sprawled out like he didn't care that he'd been singled out.

Which Kate knew to be true.

What she didn't know was why. Dustin knew the rules, knew the consequences. And they both knew something else, that if he didn't pass today's spelling test, he wouldn't be allowed to play in his travel team's tournament this weekend.

Why didn't he care?

The answer to that wasn't at all reassuring. She glanced at Tommy, who was ignoring the entire situation, and then shook her head at Holly.

She really didn't have time for this now.

"It'll only take a second," Holly promised.

Kate sighed. There was no deterring Holly when she sank her teeth into something, though Kate couldn't imagine what she was all worked up about. She'd just spent several days alone with Adam, one of the sexiest men on the entire planet. "Can this wait until recess?"

"No, I have to get to work." Holly helped run her father's ranching empire with the precision of a drill sergeant and the care of a den mother. She was good at her job, and doing it in a man's world had made her tough. Few crossed Holly.

Kate loved her like a sister, but even she didn't cross Holly. So she glanced back at the class. "Keep practicing," she told them. "Don't leave your seats." She met Holly's gaze. "So what's up?"

"I was thinking you might tell me."

Kate knew that tone, and she went still. She had no idea how, but Holly knew something had happened between her and Griffin. Luckily, she had no way of knowing what exactly—

"Rumor has it," Holly said, "that you slept with my brother."

Okay, scratch that. Holly knew everything. Kate took another glance over her shoulder at the kids. Of course not a single one of them was paying her the slightest bit of attention. Dammit. Where was a crisis when she needed one? Mikey had been pulling Nina's hair all damn day, but was he doing it now? No, he was sitting in his seat like a perfect little angel, tongue between his teeth, brow furrowed in concentration, actually doing as she'd asked, practicing his spelling.

Even Dustin had settled down and was taking his timeout with surprising grace.

"How did this happen?" Holly asked.

Kate could give her the whole chemistry lesson or tell her the simple truth—it should have been just a harmless kiss, but as it turned out, there was no such thing as harmless as it pertained to Griffin. But she doubted his sister wanted to know that.

"Ms. Evans?" Scott called from the front row. "Can I give Bunny some more water? He looks thirsty."

"I'm sorry," Kate whispered to Holly. "I didn't do it to hurt you."

"Honey, this isn't about me. It's about you, and I'm worried. Grif's only here for the week, or however long the fancy strikes him. You know that, right? Tell me you know that."

"I know that."

"He's not your picket-fence guy."

"I know that, too," Kate said, even though the words sent a little stab of pain into her chest.

"And it's not like I'm not happy you're getting laid . . ."

"Ohmigod," Kate said, feeling her face flush. "I can't believe this is '*muy importante*.'"

"I had to make sure you were okay."

Holly could have no idea how much that meant to Kate, but the fact was that Kate had never been better. She glanced down at the tug on her sweater. Scott. "Yes, you can give Bunny some water."

The boy beamed and ran to the bunny cage on the counter that ran along the classroom windows.

Kate let out a breath and met Holly's gaze. "So how did you find out?"

"Adam took one look at Grif and could tell he'd gotten lucky," Holly said.

"He could've been with anyone," Kate said. "How did you know it was me?"

Holly gave her a get-real look. "You're the only one he's bothered with since he got here."

This gave Kate a little frisson of pleasure.

"And you need to look in the mirror once in a while," Holly said. "A guy would be crazy not to want you." She paused. "But also, I know because I talked to him."

Kate's heart stopped as she imagined how that conversation must have gone, what with Holly's interfering ways and Griffin's ability to be silent until the end of time. "You did?"

"Actually, I hit him."

"You what?"

"Hey, it was my sisterly duty," Holly said. "Don't worry, I didn't hurt him too badly."

"You talked to Griffin," Kate repeated, mortified.

"Well, as much as you can actually talk to Grif. He's not exactly a conversationalist."

Kate closed her eyes. This was true. Griffin wasn't a big

talker. But there were other ways to communicate, and he had those ways down.

"Ms. Evans?" Scott was back at her side. "Bunny's got a problem."

"What is it?"

"You know how he was a little fat? Well, he's not so fat now. I think he's hungry. Can I feed him?"

"Yes, but don't touch him until I get there, okay?"

"'Kay."

"And don't lick!"

"'Kay."

Holly looked shocked. "Lick?" she whispered.

"Long story," Kate said. "Don't ask."

Holly shook her head. "Thank God I'm not a teacher." She took Kate's hand. "I love you," she said. "You know that. And I want you to be happy. But I don't want you to get hurt."

"I'm not. I won't."

"Kate—"

"I seduced him, Hol." Kate closed her eyes and then opened them. "It was all me. I knew what I was doing. I just wanted the one night, that was it. It's done. And we're good."

"It's . . . done?"

"Yep." Done. Well, except for that chemistry problem.

"And you're okay?" Holly asked softly. "Really?"

"Really." Except . . . she didn't have any idea how to get over the memory of being with him. She hadn't had any idea at all that their night would literally move heaven and earth for her, that her soul would be woken up, that her body could hum like that. She hadn't known any of it, but even if she had, she'd still have done it.

Holly sighed and hugged her hard.

"I'm so happy you're back," Kate said.

"Even though I yelled at you in a whisper?"

"Even though."

Holly squeezed her hand. "You know, if you'd asked me, he's not who I'd have picked for you."

Kate nodded. "I know."

Holly stared at her for a long moment. "But I'd have been wrong. He thinks he's an island. He's certainly always been a rock. For me. My mom. Everyone."

Kate nodded. She knew this, too. She'd seen this.

"But he's never had anyone be his rock." She smiled. "Be his rock, Kate."

"Ms. Evans!"

Scott again. He was back at her side, cradling a lump of something in the front of his sweatshirt. "Scott, I told you not to touch."

"Not touching. Carrying." He revealed his precious cargo.

Three bunny babies.

"Bunny multiplied!" he said joyously.

Kate met Holly's amused glance. "Really have to go now."

By the end of the day, Dell had come by to check on the bunnies, and Kate had arranged homes for them when they were old enough to be separated from Bunny.

And she'd nearly recovered from the fact that people knew she'd slept with Griffin.

Nearly, but not quite

All she had left now were parent conferences. There had been four of them each day after school all week long. Today the first one was with Dustin's parents.

Emily Anders was divorced from Trevan so the meeting was tense from the start. They sat at the art table. Trevan's arms were crossed over his chest, his jaw tight, everything about him and his expensive suit saying, *Pissed-off male*.

Kate did her best to put them at ease. "Dustin's doing extremely well in math and science." She handed them Dustin's progress report.

Trevan's jaw bunched as he looked it over. "You're aware that in order to play in his travel league, Dustin needs to maintain a certain grade level."

"Yes."

"So why did you give him a D in spelling?"

"That's what he earned."

Trevan gave her an intimidating stare that Kate refused to let get to her.

"This will take him out of tournament play until the next grading period," he said.

"His homework and test scores are below grade average," Kate said. "I've been offering to help after school, but you've turned that help down."

Emily turned to her ex. "Is that true?"

Trevan ignored her and stared at Kate. "You know he has daily baseball practice for his travel league. It's extensive and time-consuming."

"Oh my God," Emily said. "Are you kidding me? He's eight. I've told you a million times, you're putting too much pressure on him."

Kate agreed. "School is important, too, Mr. Anders."

"So is this," he said, voice low, vibrating with temper now. "He has to do better."

"Yes, he does," Kate said. "Or he's going to miss our next few field trips, one of which is tomorrow. He's going home with some extra credit tonight. You could help—"

"Or you could help by taking some of this ridiculous pressure off," Trevan said. "It's second grade for crissake."

"Second grade is important," Kate said. "But my offer of tutoring is still open."

"My tax dollars pay you to teach him in the amount of time you have," Trevan said.

"You often taken him out early," Kate reminded him. "And he misses valuable class time."

Emily gasped. "Trevan, we agreed that you would no longer do that!"

Trevan's face remained cool and blank, but pure temper sparked in his eyes. He'd slipped up, and he clearly blamed Kate for making that public.

Emily drew a deep breath, and ignoring her ex now, she

spoke directly to Kate. "You've been very generous with your time. We're grateful." She rose and gave Trevan an expectant look.

Grim-faced, he rose, too. "Teaching is your job, Ms. Evans. Not the school play or Bingo Night or running through the park feeding all the bums. My job is parenting. You do your job and I'll do mine." And then he left the classroom without another word.

Kate let out a breath.

"I'd apologize for him," Emily said into the silence, "but I no longer have to do that."

Kate smiled and did her best to shrug it off. "I know it's not easy to hear your child needs extra help."

"No. But you're a lot kinder than I could ever be," Emily said, and left.

Kate didn't feel kind. She felt a little shaken, a feeling that didn't improve when she called for the next parents to come into her classroom for their conference and saw that among the others waiting for her was Griffin, wearing a guest tag in what she recognized as Ryan's handwriting, complete with a smiley face alongside his name.

Eighteen

Grif questioned his sanity while waiting in the hallway of the elementary school for Kate. He'd had breakfast with Adam and Dell then spent the day working on the ranch with his dad.

It had been a good day. A damn good day. And he had no idea the last time he could have said that about a day with his dad.

He had things he could be doing and absolutely no business waiting here for a woman who'd already gotten what she wanted from him.

But there was something niggling at him. His sister had gotten into his head. She'd accused him of taking advantage of Kate, and now he kept thinking about that.

Kate had promised she was fine, had even joked about their chemistry still being a problem, but was she really okay? She wasn't a one-night sort of woman, and now he was wondering if maybe she was just pretending all was good just to assuage his guilt. Maybe . . . maybe she was secretly pining away for him.

He watched yet another parent come out of her classroom. It had been some sort of parent-kid afternoon, and he'd seen the way Kate handled herself and others.

Effortlessly.

Every single kid got a kind word. Every parent the same. Never a lack of patience or an awkward moment.

Nope, she only exhibited those particular personality traits with him.

Which for some reason made him like her even more. He looked at his watch. She'd been on her feet all day. That had to be exhausting. And doing it while dealing with kids . . . well, that was Grif's very own definition of hell.

But she didn't look strained. She looked . . . sexy and adorable in yet another colorful cargo skirt, cardigan sweater, and leggings. Her hair was up, prim and proper today, and she was apologizing to one of the parents for having to wait to speak to her.

Grif watched as the parents filed out with smiles on their faces, each thinking that their kid was the shit. It couldn't possibly be true, but Kate made them believe it.

"You didn't like school much, did you?"

Grif looked down at Tommy. The kid was wearing jeans that were slightly too big on his scrawny frame so that when he walked, he had to hitch them up or lose them. One of his battered sneakers was untied. And in complete opposition to the bedraggled, vulnerable appearance he gave off, his hoodie featured the Incredible Hulk in all his green fierceness.

"I like school," Tommy said.

This surprised Grif, given that Tommy never seemed to actually be interacting with anyone other than himself. "You do?"

"Yeah. The library's full of books, and you can pick whatever you want. And there's Internet on the computers in there so I can play games. Words with Friends is my favorite. I'd rather play on a cell phone, but my dad says I can't have a cell phone yet, so I play it on my iPod Touch when I'm at home." He shrugged. "And I like the brownies.

And Mrs. Hinkle. She's the cafeteria lady. She doesn't make me eat my veggies if I don't wanna."

Grif nodded. "That's a most excellent cafeteria lady."

"You don't like veggies either?" the kid asked, tilting his head up. As he did, his hood fell back.

There was a bruise under his left eye, and it looked new. "When I was your age," Grif said, "I used to sneak my veggies to the dog beneath the table until I got caught."

"You get in trouble?"

"Always." It was the truth. Holly could have murdered someone and gotten away with it, but Grif had lived on his father's shit list. It was just a matter of how far up or down on the list he was at any given point. "How about you?" he asked. "You get in trouble?" He paused. "Maybe today?"

Tommy went still then pulled his hood back up over his head. "No. I don't really get into trouble very much."

"Maybe someone caused you some trouble, then."

Tommy didn't answer that one. Instead he walked down the hallway and out to the playground.

Grif went with him and then crouched down to look into Tommy's face. "He bothering you?"

"No."

"Tommy."

Tommy looked away. "I hit him first," he whispered.

This shocked Grif into a short laugh. "Yeah?"

"He was picking on Gwendolyn. She's in my class. He told her that her dad works for his dad and is a complete loser and that so was she. I looked for an adult like we're supposed to, but there was no one."

"And?"

"And Dustin was still too close to her, so . . . I pushed him, and then his elbow hit me in the eye when he went down."

"That was nice of you to stick up for your friend."

"No man left behind," Tommy recited. "Even if it's a girl, right?"

"Right," Grif said.

Tommy nodded, then nibbled on his lower lip, pride gone, replaced by unhappiness. "He cried," he whispered. "He tried to hide it, but I saw."

Grif let out a long breath. "You have your iPod Touch with you?"

Tommy pulled it out and Grif took it. "I'm loading the Find My Friends app and putting myself on it. Next time you look around for an adult and can't find one, you'll be able to find me. You text me, and I'll come. No matter what. Okay?"

Tommy looked awed. "'Kay. Will I be able to see how far I am from you? Like exactly?"

The kid was so much like Kate, with his need for the little details, Griffin's heart clenched a little. "Yes, exactly. And let's do this, too . . ." Grif loaded a good map app as well. "Now you can see mileage from one place to another, any place."

"Cool!"

Just then Ashley zipped into the parking lot and honked for Tommy.

Tommy waved at her. "Gotta go," he said to Grif. And with the resilience only a second grader could exhibit, he ran off.

Grif watched Ashley wait until Tommy had his seat belt on before ripping out of the lot, and that's when he caught sight of the Lexus changing spots from the far north part of the lot to directly behind Kate's car.

Someone else waiting on Kate, he thought, and then she was walking out to her car. When she caught sight of Anders, she stood at her car door while the guy approached.

Grif didn't know what the guy was saying to her so he moved closer and was glad for it when he saw Kate stiffen. The dickwad was in her face, yelling at her about his son's grades and some missed tournament. It wouldn't have been surprising for her to be shaken at the confrontation.

But that's not what happened. Nope, the curvy little dynamo's eyes were calm but flashing a steely determination, her shoulders squared.

She wasn't shaken or afraid. She was annoyed as hell, and it made Grif grin.

He loved her 'tude. The only thing that could improve this scenario would be for her to use one of her new self-defense moves he'd taught her to flatten the guy. Yeah, Grif would really enjoy that.

Kate glanced at Grif as he moved in close to her side, giving him a narrow-eyed look that said, *Don't you dare interfere.*

Yeah, she was made of damn sturdy stuff, and she knew how to handle herself. She'd been born handling problems, and this was just that. Just one more problem in a long line of problems.

But that didn't stop Grif from staying right at her back. He was close enough to catch the scent of her—a sexy-smelling shampoo, some sort of lemon disinfectant, and, if he wasn't mistaken, crayons.

Trevan gave him a fuck-off-and-die look. "This is a private conversation," he said.

"Then take it down a notch," Grif suggested.

"Don't tell me what to do."

"Okay," Kate said quickly, turning to Grif and putting her hands on his chest. "I need a moment."

Grif shrugged, easy. "Take as many moments as you need."

"Alone," she said.

"No."

Kate inhaled deep. "Griffin, there's confidentiality involved here. Give me a minute. Please?"

He stared down into her eyes, saw her courage and tenacity, and couldn't say he was surprised. She was incredibly strong, much stronger than he'd given her credit for. Nodding, he stepped back. Not far, and not out of intimidation or hearing range, but enough that Kate gave him a nod of thanks.

Then she turned back to Asshole Dad of the Year. "I thought I was perfectly clear the other afternoon about what

Dustin needed to do in order to get a passing grade," she said. "It wasn't a difficult task."

"What are you saying?"

"I'm saying that maybe Dustin doesn't want to be a baseball star. Maybe he did this on purpose so that he wouldn't have to play this weekend."

Anders frowned. "You don't know what you're talking about."

"Your son is smart," Kate said. "Very smart. So you tell me—why isn't he passing?"

"Exactly. What kind of a teacher are you?"

"A good one," she said, not taking the bait. "You should talk to him. And I hope you do it gently and with genuine compassion, because he needs that. And he needs that from you."

Griffin stood rooted to the spot, struck by how fierce she looked standing there defending one of her kids. And not even a particularly good kid. In fact, Grif had a feeling that that was exactly why she was being so adamant.

Griffin had been that kid. But he'd never had a teacher go to bat for him the way Kate was for Dustin.

"Dustin's going to be big in baseball," Trevan said. "I played baseball for Arizona State; it's in his genes. I'd have gone pro if my knee hadn't blown out, but Dustin's going to take it all the way. He wouldn't screw that up on purpose."

Yes, he would, Grif thought. If pushed too hard, the kid would do exactly that. Just like Grif had when he'd been pushed by his father. He'd ended up turning his back on both the ranch and Sunshine.

"There are things just as important as baseball," Kate said with surprising gentleness. "Dustin's really great with the animals. He's especially into the S&R dog demonstrations we've been having with Adam Connelly at Belle Haven."

"I don't give a rat's ass how good he is with animals. Fix this, Ms. Evans. Or else."

Kate said nothing, and Grif had to admire her restraint.

He didn't have any such restraint. So when Trevan headed to his car, Grif stepped into his path.

"Grif," Kate said warningly.

He gave her a look and held up a finger. He only needed a second. Putting a "friendly" hand on Trevan's shoulder, he leaned in like they were best buddies. "If I see you watching her," he said, "or parking in front of her town-house or hassling her in any way again, you'd best make sure you life insurance is paid up."

"You threatening me?"

Grif glanced over Trevan's head and found Kate's eyes narrowed on his. He smiled at her.

She didn't return it.

"Yeah," Grif said to Anders. "I'm threatening you. Now smile at the pretty lady, get in your car, and drive away."

Trevan did, leaving a good part of his tires smoking on the asphalt while he was at it.

"What was that?" Kate asked.

"What was what?"

"That ridiculous my-dick-is-bigger-than-your-dick pre-sentation."

He choked out a laugh. "Did you just say *dick*?"

"Would you rather I have said *penis*?"

"Actually," he said. "I prefer *cock*."

"Fine. What was that ridiculous my-cock-is-bigger-than-your-cock presentation?"

"Why Ms. Evans," he said, grinning wide. "I do believe you have a potty mouth. I like it."

Not amused, she crossed her arms over her chest. "An-swer my question, please."

Please. God, she was such a polite tyrant. "You re-ally think that was some sort of macho display for your benefit?"

"Either that or you were peeing on me to mark your ter-ritory."

Not exactly pining away for him, he realized, and he began to wonder if he'd been entirely off base with his worries. "I just came by to see if you were doing okay, and I saw him tangling with you."

"I can handle myself."

"I can see that." And he could. It was attractive as hell.

"And why wouldn't I be okay?" she asked.

Yeah, genius. Why wouldn't she be okay?

She arched a brow and crossed her arms over her chest. "It can't be because a grumpy dad yelled at me," she said, "since you had no way of knowing that was going to happen here today. So what is it? Why wouldn't I be okay?"

He was quickly his losing footing in this conversation. How did that always happen with her?

"Please tell me it's not because we slept together. That you're not thinking I might not be okay because of that."

"Uh—"

"Because I already told you that it was one of the best nights of my life," she said slowly, and then she went still. "Oh, I see," she said. "I think I get it."

Good. He was grateful she got it, because he didn't.

"You still think I can't handle that. The one-night thing. Is that it, Griffin?"

Yeah, he'd stepped into it, right up to his big, fat mouth. "Kate—"

"Oh no," she said. "Don't you *Kate* me." She hitched her bag farther up on her shoulder and turned to her car.

Walk away, Soldier. Take your losses. Instead, he asked the question now haunting him. "How did you know?"

"How did I know what?"

"That Dustin doesn't want to play baseball. How did you see that?"

She turned back, some of her temper appearing to fade as she searched his gaze.

"He's a little punk," he went on, needing an explanation. "It'd have been so easy for you to dismiss him, not really deal with him, just give him his detention or whatever and put him out of your mind to concentrate on the better-behaved kids, the ones who want to be here."

Her eyes held his. "I don't usually take the easy way out, Griffin."

No. No, she didn't.

"And anyway, when you've been a teacher for any amount of time," she went on, "you learn to read kids. Or anyone, really. So it was no great mystery. A kid that age isn't all that complicated. There isn't a big, long list of things that could be making him act out like that."

"But you put baseball at the top of the list."

"It was a guess," she admitted.

"A good one," he said. "A smart one. No one else would have seen that."

She shrugged then studied him. "This hits home for you." She let out a sigh, unlocked her car, and tossed her purse in. "I don't leave any kids behind, Griffin. I'm sorry that it happened to you. It shouldn't have."

He wasn't easy to read, he'd made sure of it, and yet she read him like a book.

"Have you ever tried talking to your dad about it?" she asked.

"You mean the brick wall?" He blew out a breath and shook his head. "This isn't why I came here."

"Fine. Then let's talk about why you did come. To make sure I wasn't secretly devastated about our one night, right? To make sure you haven't ruined me for all men?"

He grimaced and shoved his hands through his hair. "Okay, how about we leave it at the fact that I'm a complete idiot and move on."

Finally, he'd reached her. Her mouth curved, albeit slightly, but he'd take it. "I'm willing if you're willing," she said.

He nodded and turned to go, but he couldn't stop himself from stepping in it one last time. "Oh, and online dating is dangerous."

"More dangerous than dating, say . . . you?"

Touché. "We haven't dated," he said.

"True."

"We should change that."

She actually paused, and he went for it. "Have dinner with me, Kate."

"I've got a lot to go over in regards to my upcoming parent-teacher conferences . . ."

He knew a blow-off when he heard one. He'd certainly given enough of them in his life. Studying her for a moment, he said, "You change your mind about me?"

"No. No," she said again more firmly. "I really do just have a lot of work."

"I could help," he said in that voice that had gotten him what he wanted more than once. "I'm an excellent . . . debriefer."

She gave him a considering look, and as he'd intended, a sense of playfulness came into her gaze. "What would this debriefing involve?" She wanted to know.

He stepped closer and was gratified to hear her breath catch. "Personal, hands-on techniques come to mind," he said.

"Oh," she breathed, sounding a little short of air and also intrigued.

He smiled. "We'll discuss at dinner."

"Now?" she asked.

"Now."

Halfway out of town, Kate's cell phone rang. It was Holly. "Hey," Kate said, going for casual. "What's up, everything okay?"

"Depends," Holly said.

"On?"

"You. Are you okay?"

Kate looked over at Grif, who was driving. "I'm okay." And excited. And terrified. "Why?"

"Are we still best friends?" Holly asked.

"Well, of course!"

"Then when were you going to tell me you're on a date?"

"I just texted you five minutes ago that I'd be out tonight."

"With my brother?"

Kate twisted and looked behind them. "Are you following us?"

Griffin, much more used to Holly's tricks, didn't even glance in the rearview mirror.

"I'm not following you," Holly said.

"Let me guess," Kate said dryly. "There's another rumor?"

"Adam asked Grif to go on a quad ride with him tonight, but Grif said he was busy. Grif's never too busy for a quad ride. I took a wild guess."

She glanced at Griffin. He was driving in his usual Zen-calm zone. Kate didn't have a Zen-calm zone. "Was I this annoying when you were dating Adam?" she asked Holly.

"More," Holly said on a laugh. "Listen, I just want to say that I love you. And take things slow, okay?"

"I will." Kate looked at Griffin again. "I'll take very good care of your brother, but he's a big boy now, Hol."

Holly laughed.

Griffin slid Kate a long, slow, thoughtful gaze that gave her a hot flash. She hung up with Holly and pocketed her phone.

"I'm a big boy?"

Kate thought about just how big and shifted in her seat, earning her another one of those looks, this one accompanied by a low, sexy laugh.

He drove her into Boise, where they went to a tiny little blues club she'd never been to before. They enjoyed great food, great music, and fantastic wine, and when she curled up with him on a comfy love seat to watch the musicians, kicking off the heels that were killing her feet, Grif pulled her feet onto his lap.

"What are you doing?" she asked, shocked. Panicked. Her feet were . . . well, not pretty. She'd spent years standing on them all day in classrooms. Not even Ryan would have touched her callused stumps.

But Griffin wrapped her foot in his big, warm hands and dug his thumbs into her arch.

She moaned so loud that he grinned and leaned over her to kiss her, probably to shut her up.

Later he drove her back to her car. When they reached the school, he woke her up, and she was mortified that she fell asleep on him. He unlocked her car for her and nudged her inside.

"Be careful," he said, and hooked her seat belt.

To her surprise, he followed her home. "Is this where we get to the hands-on debriefing?" she teased as he walked her inside.

He smiled. "You're too tired for what I have in mind."

She was getting less tired by the second. "What exactly do you have in mind?"

"A proper debriefing is . . . intense," he said. "You need to be on top of your game for that."

Her good parts quivered, and she pressed him against the door. "You think I'm off my game?"

He stroked a hand down her back and palmed her butt in a possessive nature that was shockingly thrilling. "I think you're exhausted," he said. "Understandably so." He patted her butt then and tugged off her sweater. He hung it up on its hook, his thoughtfulness warming her and making her suddenly not so tired. Because for the first time in recent memory, someone was taking care of her. She felt safe. Cared for. Cherished.

And this was a problem. A big one, given the man making her feel these things. The man she'd originally pulled into her orbit for nothing more than a tryst.

After all, he was leaving.

She was leaving.

And she was in over her head . . .

As if he sensed her sudden melancholy, he paused. "You okay?"

She managed a laugh. "I thought guys only asked that question in romance novels."

He looked at her for a long moment. "We'll do just about anything to get what we want, Kate. You should remember that."

She sucked in a breath. "What if what you want is the same thing I want?"

This earned her another steadying gaze. "I don't think that can be true," he said.

"Is that why you haven't tried to get back in my bed? Because you think I don't want what you want?"

"I didn't want to push you," he said.

"I'm not easily pushed." She put her hand on his chest. "So I'm going to ask again, what if we want the same thing?"

He stared down at her for what had to be an eternity, during which she let her hand shift a little, gliding from pec to pec.

"You're going to get your way on this, aren't you?" he murmured, voice low and a little husky.

"I usually do." She kicked off her shoes. "Don't try to fight it, Griffin. I'll be gentle."

He moved so that his forehead rested against hers as he slid his hands into her hair, his fingertips against her scalp. "You're daring me."

"Yes," she said, not opening her eyes, enjoying the bliss caused by his touch. Even without looking, she felt him smile. After a moment he tugged lightly on her hair until she met his gaze.

"I stayed away to give you time to think," he said.

"Thinking's overrated."

This startled a laugh out of him, and she soaked up the sight of his genuine amusement. He was just too damn sexy for his own good, certainly too sexy for her own good. When he let her inside his personal space like this, when he so rarely let anyone in, letting her see the private side of him, every last defense around her heart melted away.

Just melted away . . .

"Griffin?" she whispered, suddenly serious.

His smile faded. "Yeah?"

She backed him to the foyer table. "Remember when you asked me if this table was sturdy?" She patted her hands on it. "It feels sturdy.

His eyes were serious now, very serious, with only the slightest quirk of his lips as he stepped into her and kissed her hard. "You're going to be the death of me," he whispered against her mouth.

"I know," she said, sliding her hands up around his neck. "But it's a good way to go, right?"

Apparently he was too busy divesting her of her clothes to answer. He started with her blouse. He smiled at her pretty pink bra and then took that off, too, tossing it over his shoulder. "Do your panties match?" he asked.

"There are some things a man should find out for himself," she said demurely.

His hands slid beneath her skirt and pulled her leggings down and off. He shoved up her skirt and eyed the matching scrap of pink. "Nice. Lose 'em." Then, before she could, he tugged the silk down her legs. And then her skirt as well. Which left her bare-assed on the wood. Putting a big hand on each of her thighs, he spread her legs and then stepped between them, his jeans rubbing up against her heated flesh.

Heaven . . . "Griffin?"

"Yeah?" He trailed hot kisses up her cheek to her ear, melting her bones.

"You want me bad," she said, rocking against him, pulling his head down to hers, pressing a kiss to first one corner of his mouth and then the other.

He closed his eyes, tilted his head back, and swallowed hard as if unused to such a tender touch, which of course only made her want to be all the more tender.

"I do want you bad," he whispered as she planted tiny kisses along his jaw and down his throat. "Very bad."

"Good." She pushed up his shirt, reveling in his rock-hard abs and leanly muscled chest, leaning in to take a nibble right above his collarbone, and when he sucked in a breath, she soothed the ache with her tongue.

Her efforts tugged a deep groan from Griffin. He tore off his shirt and shoved his hand into his front pocket, coming up with a condom.

"You think of everything," she said.

"Yes, would you like to know what I'm thinking now?"

She had a pretty good idea. "If I didn't know the truth," she said. "I'd swear you were once a Boy Scout."

He dropped his forehead to her shoulder and huffed out a laugh, his chest rising and falling as he fought for control. "Don't play with me right now," he warned. His taut body wasn't up for teasing.

Neither was hers. She popped open his jeans and reached inside. "I don't play." She stroked him, and he swore roughly. Picking her up, he turned and pinned her against the wall. Her fingers tangled in his hair as he lowered his mouth to hers, kissing her into submission.

"Bed," he growled against her lips, and carried her to her room. He dropped her onto the mattress and then crawled up her body, kissing every inch of skin he passed, stopping at every spot where she gasped or squirmed, starting over when he felt like it, until she was writhing and panting beneath him. The feel of his hard body pressing into hers, combined with the way he devoured her, sent jolts of pleasure through her, coiling low in her belly.

"The condom," she finally gasped.

He was one step ahead of her, and then his weight settled on her. Opening her thighs for him, she urged him closer. "Hurry."

"Hell no." Cupping her face in his big hands, he moved as calmly and deliberately as he pleased. "We have time." And then he held her gaze as he, just as slowly and steadily as he did everything, slid into her.

He stilled then, a look of impossible control crossing his face. But if he was learning her body, she was doing the same with his. She knew how to wrestle his hard-earned control away, and she gradually arched her hips, taking even more of him deep inside her.

Eyes hot, he bent over her, and then it wasn't just his control snapping but hers, too, as they both fought for release. When it came, it was with shocking force, knocking them both into oblivion.

Much later she felt him lean over her to kiss her good-bye, a deliciously hot kiss that left her stirred up all over again. "Uh-oh," she whispered.

"What?"

"It's still here. Our chemistry problem."

He smiled a little tightly in silent agreement, and then he was gone.

Nineteen

K ate woke up deliciously sated and with a smile on her face. Sex absolutely did a body good. Normally, she might have spent a few moments wondering what last night had actually meant—or not meant—but she decided if she didn't think about it too deeply, she could take it in the spirit she'd originally intended.

Naked fun, and not as the possible beginning to something between them, because that would end in disappointment.

Not that any of that mattered at the moment, because she was running late. She made the usual run to her dad's, where she speed-read Ashley's practice SAT essays, fed everyone, grabbed Tommy—Captain America today—and ran out to Ryan's car.

Thirty minutes later, Kate's class was humming with the wild energy of twenty second graders getting ready to go on a field trip to Belle Haven.

Their new vet, Dr. Wyatt, usually came to her class for monthly visits, but at least twice a year Kate brought the kids to the animal center. They got a lot from watching responsible adults handle all the animals, and Kate got a lot out of letting the kids run themselves ragged on the large acreage.

With budget cuts, Kate had to rely on parents to drive the class, and as a result, she was humming with her own wild energy—worry. One of the parents who'd signed up to drive hadn't yet shown up.

Trevan Anders.

She got him on his cell phone five minutes before their scheduled departure time, and he said he was unable to get away from work. He expressed polite regret and offered to make it up to her over dinner, where he hoped to also apologize for his behavior the day before in the parking lot of the school.

The man was as hot and cold as a sink valve, and he gave her a headache. She'd meet him for dinner approximately never.

"Do we have to cancel?" Tommy asked solemnly at her side, having apparently sneaked up on her.

She looked down into his green eyes. The Captain America sweatshirt was a direct contrast to the seriousness of his gaze. "We are not canceling," she said. "Even if we have to walk there."

"It's seven point five miles."

That got a smile out of her. She wasn't the only one in the family who knew all sorts of random facts. "How did you know that?"

He pulled out the iPod Touch he'd gotten for his birthday. "Grif loaded a Find My Friends app and a map, too, and I marked out all my favorite places."

Her heart clenched. God, she loved this kid. "We're not walking," she promised, and called Ryan's cell phone.

"Five days," he said.

Like she didn't know she had five days left to accept her full-ride scholarship to UCSD. "Not why I'm calling," she said.

Luckily, he agreed to step up to the plate, leaving his district meeting early to meet Kate and her class in the school parking lot. The other parent drivers were loading up their cars when he arrived. He ended up with five kids in his truck—including Dustin, who immediately began playing with all the rear control panel buttons of his new car.

"Stop that," Ryan told him, and shut the back passenger door. Standing by his driver's door, he eyed Kate. "You owe me," he said.

"What do I owe you?"

The kids were inside his car with the windows up, but ever vigilant, Ryan pulled out his phone and sent her a text.

"Seriously?" she asked, lifting her head and meeting his gaze after reading the obscene suggestion. "Is that all men think about?"

"Yes. And food."

"Good. Because that's what you're getting. Food."

Ryan sighed. "Fine. Pizza. Loaded. And beer."

"Done."

"That was too easy," Ryan said. "I should have demanded both."

Clearly things hadn't worked out with the bridesmaid from Holly's wedding. Probably it was his charm. The drive to the animal center was uneventful. The center was large, and right out front were Brady and Dell, working with a couple of horses in the pens.

As Kate ushered her class past them and inside, Jade stood up from the front desk and waved. She ran the ship here at Belle View with the same drill sergeant ability with which Holly ran her dad's ranch. Each kid was given a lanyard with a nametag to wear around his or her neck. Jade walked them through an examination room and taught them about some of the equipment.

Then they went out back. In the big barn, they got to meet a bovine and her new calf, who were at the center for some special care after tangling with a coyote. And then Lulu the sheep, who'd just given birth to two lambs out of season.

Back outside, they found Adam in the huge open yard teaching a survival class with Griffin. They'd rigged some sort of climbing wall and were working the ropes. Adam stood at the bottom, belaying Griffin, who was thirty feet above them in the air, clinging to the inverted wall by nothing but his fingertips.

"Wow," her class breathed in unison.

Yeah. Wow . . . Kate watched him swing and then reach for the next tiny little handhold, holding her breath until he pulled himself up with ease. She wondered if he knew she was there, and then he met her gaze, his own sparking a fire inside her.

Yeah. He knew she was there.

"I could do that," Ryan said in her ear.

Kate turned and met his gaze. "Yeah?"

"Totally."

"Except for your fear of heights," Kate said.

"Yeah. Except for that."

Dr. Wyatt brought out a big crate of kittens, eight weeks old and ready for adoption. The kids sat around the box and took turns petting and holding them. Dr. Wyatt told them that they could have first dibs, if any of their parents were in agreement.

Dustin had pushed his way to the front and was cuddling one, a black little girl with bright blue eyes who looked up at him like he was her mama. "I want this one," he said.

"Let your parents know," Dr. Wyatt said. "If they approve, she's yours."

Dustin ducked his face down, but not before Kate saw his expression. He knew his dad would never approve a kitten.

Tommy looked at Dustin for a long moment and then at Kate. "Dad would let me get one, right?"

"Shut up, Captain America," Dustin said, and swiped his arm across his eyes.

Tommy reached out and stroked the black kitten. "If I adopted her, you could come see her every day. If you wanted."

Kate's heart swelled in her chest, both with love and pride. Dustin buried his face in the kitten's fur and didn't say anything for a long moment before giving a barely there nod.

Kate let out her breath and swallowed the lump in her throat. She thought of her dad and hoped like hell he could handle one more living creature in his house . . .

After that, Brady's wife, Lilah, took the kids across the way to Sunshine Kennels to visit the animals there. Kate and the other parent drivers ended up in the employee kitchen with some of the staff. Dell came in and pinned Jade to the fridge for a kiss.

"Hey," Adam said. "I'm the newlywed."

Dell pulled back from a now dazed-looking Jade and grinned down into her face. "Just saying hi."

Jade rolled her eyes, but still gave him a dopey smile.

Everyone but Ryan and Kate drifted out of the kitchen. Ryan handed her a bottle of water. "Figured you were thirsty. What with all that panting you're doing over Reid."

She snatched the bottle. "I'm not panting."

"Drooling, then."

She ignored this. Because okay, she might have drooled a little bit over Griffin on the ropes. She was definitely lusting. Every time she thought about Griffin and what he'd done to her last night—what he always did to her—her legs got all watery and she went damp in areas she had no business going damp in during daylight hours. "It's not a thing." She lifted a shoulder. "Or it's not a real thing."

Ryan looked at her for a long moment. There was a lot in his gaze. Affection. A touching amount of concern. And then, wariness just as Kate felt a change in her force field.

She didn't have to turn around to know who'd come up behind her and now stood at her back. It was utterly unnecessary because her happy nipples told her exactly who it was.

"Griffin," Ryan said.

"Ryan," Griffin said.

Kate sipped her water like her life depended on it.

"Kate," Griffin finally said.

Slurp . . . She couldn't speak, not when she'd just realized that she was standing between the only two men she'd
ever slept with. Ryan had been a good lover, fun and easy
to be with.

But Griffin . . . Griffin was magic.

And she was sandwiched between them. A virtual hot
guy sandwich. Her hands trembled a little bit, but before
she could put down her bottle of water, it was taken out of
her fingers by a big, callused hand and set on the counter
for her.

She met Griffin's gaze and straightened, lust immediately taking a backseat to concern.

He had a headache.

She saw it in the tight lines of his mouth, in the shadows
of his eyes, and in every movement that he didn't make.

"Well," Ryan said. "This is a whole heck of a lot of fun,
standing here awkwardly staring at each other and all, but I
really should . . . something." And then he left.

"You have another migraine," Kate said, pushing Grif to
a chair.

"Little bit."

She moved to the freezer and found a bag of peas. She
dimmed the lights. Griffin had sprawled himself out in the
chair, long legs in front of him, head back, eyes closed.
Stepping between his legs, she gently pressed the cold bag
to his temple.

His hands went to her hips, and he leaned forward and
pressed his face to her stomach.

She closed her eyes and ran her hands over his shoulders. She heard the smile in his voice when he said, "Your
tummy's rumbling."

"It's working at producing a new layer of mucus," she
said. "It has to do that every two weeks to avoid digesting
itself." She paused. "Everyone's stomach has to. Not just
mine." Shut up, Kate . . .

He laughed softly as his hands slid beneath her sweater
now. His rough palms brought goose bumps to her body as
he headed north, stopping just short of her breasts.

"Really?" she asked, her calm voice belying her suddenly racing heart. "You can think about sex right now?"

A low laugh gusted out of him, his breath warming her skin through her sweater as his thumbs brushed over the heavy undersides of her breasts through her bra. "I can always think about sex."

"That's . . . inconvenient," she managed. It certainly was for her.

He let out another low laugh. "You mean because I'm torn between throwing up and taking you right here?"

He was talking the big talk, but there was no way he was up to anything but a very long nap. "Do you have meds?" she asked.

"Not with me. The headaches are fading. Mostly."

His thumbs were rubbing back and forth over her upper ribs, not quite touching her breasts. Her nipples were reacting like they were going to get luckier than was possible standing here in the animal center. "What's your pain level from one to ten?"

"Eleven," he said calmly. "But that's only because there's a hot poker behind my eyeball and I can't see out of it."

She wanted to get him back to the ranch, but she was afraid that he wouldn't get any TLC there from his father. She would have liked to take him home, because she happened to have plenty of TLC for him, but she also had twenty kids to think about. "You need to lie down."

"Yeah. And you probably need to get back to the kids."

She hesitated, and he met her gaze. "I'll be fine." But he didn't remove his hands.

"Griffin—"

"You always say my full name," he said softly, pressing his face between her breasts just as he shifted his hand northward and let his thumbs scrape over her aching nipples. "Like you're going to put me in the corner."

She had to lock her knees. It took her two tries to speak. "That's not where I'm thinking of putting you right now."

He smiled, but it faded fast. So did the color from his face.

"Oh, Griffin," she whispered.

"You're the only one who ever calls me that. The only one . . ." Turning his head, he kissed her breast, and then the nipple poking at the material of her sweater. When he nipped it lightly with his teeth, she gasped. He kissed it again, and then with a sigh he removed his hands from under her clothes and gave her a little push. "Go. I'll be fine. I'll be so fine, I'm coming over tonight to show you how fine."

"Another date?"

His pain-filled gaze met hers. "Yeah. Another date."

She didn't answer. Didn't know if she could. Or should. Another date . . . It was either going to kill her or . . .

She decided she didn't need to worry about the or. He was sick with a migraine. He could be a big talker all he wanted, but he wasn't immortal.

When she got outside, Ryan and Jade had the kids in the yard. Kate went straight to Adam. "Griffin's—"

"Sick. I know." His dark eyes met hers. "I've got him, Kate."

Good. That was good. Because now she could walk away. Walking away from Griffin Reid was the smart thing to do.

And Kate always did the smart thing.

Griffin woke up at midnight in his own bed. This time there was no musical laughter from outside his window. It was pitch-black out there, and the only sound was an incredibly obnoxious chorus of crickets and a lone wolf howling his frustration at the moon.

Grif rolled over to go back to sleep and caught sight of a covered plate on his nightstand with a note attached to it. And Adam in a chair by his bed, feet up on the mattress, head back, fast asleep.

Though Grif didn't move, Adam woke suddenly and fully from one breath to the other, calmly opening his eyes and landing them right on Grif. "You back?" he asked.

"Yeah." His headache was gone. This one had been less

intense and hadn't lasted as long as usual. Grateful for small favors, he sat up. "How did you get stuck with baby-sitting duty again?"

"Maybe I just like to watch you sleep." Adam pointed to the covered plate. "Your other guardian angel left that for you. The pretty one."

"Kate?"

"You have a third guardian angel? No!" He sighed when Grif didn't smile. "Yeah, Kate. She stayed until she fell out of the chair when she dozed off and I made her go home."

Grif peeked under the foil. A homemade turkey club sandwich.

Adam clapped him on the shoulder and headed to the door. "Glad the headaches are getting better. Cuz you're really putting a crimp in my sex life."

Since Adam's sex life was with Grif's sister, this made him wince. He inhaled the sandwich, then rolled out of bed and strode to the window.

He'd slept a solid ten hours.

Also better than usual . . . He figured that could be attributed to just about anything; the passing of time, being here in Sunshine without the stress of daily military life, having friends and family, and . . . and hell, maybe it was also the yoga. In spite of himself, he smiled. It wasn't yoga.

But he was pretty sure it was Kate.

Twenty

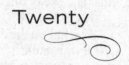

Kate was lying in her bed when she heard it. Something small hitting her window with a little ping.

And then again.

Sliding out of bed, she ducked low and grabbed her handy-dandy baseball bat from beneath her bed. The last time something had woken her up in the middle of the night, it had turned out to be a black bear digging through the trash Dumpster at the end of the row of townhouses.

He'd been deceptively cute and incredibly messy, spreading out the trash across the four small front yards of their building and leaving a bunch of piles of steamy bear poo while he was at it.

The bat had been useless against the bear, and she wasn't sure what use it would be now either, other than to boost her courage.

She peeked out the window. Not a bear, but something just as dangerous.

Griffin.

He stood in the small yard, hands on hips, staring up at

her. Shocked, she shoved up her window. "What are you doing?"

"Chemistry problems."

She stared at him, straightening up in worry. "Are you sleepwalking? Did you take pain meds? Are you hallucinating? Ohmigod, did you drive yourself here in your condition?"

He flashed a smile that stopped her heart. It was rare to see him smile like that, which was probably a good thing since she could feel her brain cells sizzling and popping one by one at the sight, and she wasn't sure how many she had to spare.

"I like your pj's," he said, and she looked down at the little cami and boxer shorts she wore. Not much coverage, but then again, he'd seen it all before. In fact, he'd kissed it, nibbled and licked it, teased it . . . every single inch.

"You going to come down?" he asked, the small smile still playing over his lips, though his eyes were serious, so very serious. He'd asked calmly, even easily, as if he was asking if the sky was midnight black or if it was a Tuesday.

But there was nothing calm inside of her. The man stirred her up, turned her upside down, and in general wreaked havoc on all her senses.

And he knew it.

Just as she knew that if she took this leap, there was no more telling herself this was just fun or chemistry. If she did this, the game changed.

Grif watched Kate war with herself. As far as he was concerned, she could take her sweet-ass time about it since he happened to be enjoying her snug white camisole with the tiny delicate straps very much. The material was a little thin and she was a lot cold.

"It's midnight," she said.

"Yes. You turning into a pumpkin?"

"Griffin," she said on a laugh. "What's this about?"

"Told you. Chemistry."

"I'm not dressed."

"I know," he said. "That's my favorite part."

She shut the window and vanished from sight. There was a pause, and he knew it could go either way for him. But then he heard her flying down the interior stairs.

Her front door opened.

She'd pulled on jeans and a sweater, which wasn't a surprise. It was a little much to have hoped she'd come out in her sexy pj's.

She walked straight to him, close enough to share air, and stared up into his eyes.

There was something about how she did this, how she looked at him as if he was important, as if he meant something to her. Not because he'd been a soldier or because he'd done anything for her. It was simply that she liked him. Him. Which reached inside and squeezed something deep.

Until recently, his world had been made up of people who reported to him or he reported to. Either way, few ever dared to go toe-to-toe with him.

And yet Kate did. She wasn't intimidated or afraid. She was cautious—she was smart to be—but it didn't hold her back.

Nothing did.

She had this sweet, warm, open personality that drew people in like bees to honey, but there was more to her than that. So much more. She might be quiet and sometimes reserved, but she wasn't shy. And she wasn't vulnerable or weak either.

In fact, it was possible that she was the strongest person he'd ever met.

"Hi," she whispered.

"Hi," he whispered back.

Smiling, she reached up to brush the scar over his temple. "Better," she said with relief. "You're really okay."

He was better, yes. As for being okay, that remained to be seen. Because typically, when he was with her, he never felt okay. When he was with her, he was on a roller coaster, an out-of-control roller coaster, and while he loved a good thrill, sometimes she terrified the shit out of him.

Like now. Standing there, all soft and warm from her bed, a little mussed and a whole lot sweet with the TLC she was doling out. He felt like he needed to get control of this ride and quick. She gave to everyone around her but never did anything for herself. Tonight was for her. Catching her hand in his, he slid his thumb over the pulse at the base of her wrist. "Ready?" he asked.

"For what?"

He smiled and watched her gaze drop to his mouth.

"Oh boy," she whispered.

He stroked a finger along her jaw. "Still with me, Kate?"

"You say my name a lot," she said.

"I like your name."

"Studies show that saying a person's name creates an instant link between you," she said.

He smiled. "I'm making you nervous."

"Yes."

"I like you a little nervous. Kate."

She let out a low laugh and turned to take him inside, but he stopped her.

"No?" she asked.

Hell, yes. But no. This time was for her. "Dinner," he said.

"It's late. I can cook."

Oh yes, she could. She was cooking his brain pretty good just standing there. "I don't want you to have to do anything," he said.

She gave him a melting smile, and he decided she was giving him too much credit. "Kate, if we go inside, you'll be dinner."

"Oh," she breathed softly, and stared at his mouth. "Well, if you're hungry . . ."

With a laughing groan, he opened the truck door and all but shoved her in. He drove them through town and up into the hills, turning off the paved road onto a dirt one. They headed up and then up some more, the truck rocking from side to side, making Kate grab the oh-holy-shit bar on the door, but when he glanced at her, she was grinning from ear to ear.

"Faster," she said.

With a laugh he did as the lady directed.

When Kate was as good and lost as she'd ever been, Grif put the truck in park and turned off the engine.

The night was dark. She couldn't see, but she could hear the tall trees swaying lightly in the wind. The only other sound was her accelerated breathing.

Griffin reached out, and her body quivered in anticipation, but he stretched for something behind her.

A condom?

God, she hoped so.

But he came up with a . . . down jacket.

"Here," he said, and handed it to her, followed by a hat, scarf, and gloves.

All about six sizes too big. "What are we doing?" she asked, disappointed to be putting clothes on instead of taking them off.

He laughed softly, assuring her that he'd read her mind. Then he slung the scarf around her neck and leaned in close to zip the jacket up to her chin. "Gloves," he ordered.

She slipped into the gloves while he waited. "What about you?" she asked.

"I'm warm-blooded."

No kidding.

He pulled her out of the car. "It's like forty degrees," she said.

"Thirty-five," he said, lifting his hand like a wolf sniffing the air. "Maybe thirty-six." He brought her to the back of the truck, opened the tailgate, and then lifted her up to sit. Then he hopped up beside her with ease. He spread out a blanket behind them.

"Okay," she said on a laugh. "If you think I'm baring any of my very special places out here, you are sorely mistaken."

He flashed her that devastatingly sexy grin of his. "Special places?" Still grinning, he kissed her. "No," he murmured against her lips. "No baring of your special places. Close your eyes, Kate. Trust me," he said when she hesitated.

She closed her eyes.

His hands went to her shoulders, pressing, urging her to lie back. She felt him hover over her for a moment, and her mouth tingled for the touch of his.

Every part of her tingled for his touch.

She could feel the warmth of his breath. The heat of his body. There in the dark they shared air for a few beats, her mouth parting in anticipation, but then he flopped over onto his back at her side and her eyes flew open. She gaped at him, heart racing, body aching. "What was that?"

"A tease."

"Why?" she demanded.

He laughed low in his throat, sounding very male. "I'm ramping up the anticipation."

If he ramped it up any more, she wouldn't need him; she'd simply spontaneously self-combust. "So we're not going to . . ."

"No."

He said this so firmly it took her a moment for the word to sink in. "But . . ."

He sat up and opened a backpack she hadn't even noticed he had. "Hungry?" he asked.

"Yes, but not for food."

At her grumpy tone, he laughed again. "Be good."

"I'm not feeling good," she grumbled. "In fact, I'm feeling decidedly bad."

"I love it when you're bad, Kate," he said. "Love it to the bone, but this isn't about sex."

"You've got me in the bed of your truck out in the middle of nowhere under the stars," she pointed out. "What is it about then?"

He didn't answer at first, just handed her a foil-wrapped something that turned out to be a chicken and cheese burrito from the town diner—her favorite. It was still warm, as was the to-go mug of hot chocolate he handed her next. She took a sip and stared at him. "You added cinnamon."

"Adam said you like that."

"You asked Adam what I like?"

Looking a little uncomfortable, he lifted a shoulder, and for some reason that relaxed her a little bit. She wasn't the only one out of her element here. Something to think about. Later. For now she was going to enjoy this unexpected gift of a fun evening. She took a big bite of her burrito and watched the sky. "You could have skipped all the trouble, you know. I was a sure thing."

He looked at her for a moment, and then he took a bite of his food. He chewed and swallowed before speaking. "You work your ass off at school, at your dad's . . . hell, you work your ass off at everything you do so that everyone has what they need—all the time."

She made a dismissive gesture. It was her life.

"I just wanted you to have a night," he said. "No responsibilities, nothing on the agenda. Just an easy, no-strings-attached, fun time."

She stared at him, touched. "Thank you," she said, voice husky with the emotion clogging her throat.

He lifted a shoulder, clearly not wanting to discuss it. She took another bite of her burrito. It was heavenly. So was the company.

"So," he said, waiting until her mouth was full. "A sure thing, huh?"

She choked, and he laughed.

"Maybe that was too broad a statement," she said, swiping her mouth.

"Oh no, you can't take it back now, Ms. Evans." His eyes were dark and full of wicked trouble.

"Fine," she admitted. "I was hoping for . . ." She lowered her voice. "Another round."

"Of what?"

She blushed and he looked vastly amused. "Kate, I've had my mouth on every inch of your body. You've had your mouth on my—"

She covered his mouth with her hand, and he laughed, pulling free. "You should be able to say what you want me to do to you."

"It's the teacher in me," she said. "I get used to second-grade speak, which does not involve a lot of sexy talk. I have to be really careful." She slid him a look. "Which must be a world away from your world."

"I don't know," he said. "Sometimes my world involves a whole lot of being careful, too."

She looked at his scar and lost a bit of her appetite. Yeah, he had experience with needing to be careful. "Except in your world, there's a lot higher stakes than teaching a kid a bad word."

He shrugged at the truth of that.

"You ever think about what happened?" she asked quietly.

"You mean about what almost happened?" He shook his head. "Other than being grateful that I'm still breathing, no. I try not to."

She'd finished eating, so he took the foil from her hands and tossed it into the backpack. Then he quite possibly cemented a place in her heart when he pulled out a bag of cookies. They were heaven, and she didn't realize she was hogging them until he said, "If I reach for one, am I putting my fingers at risk?"

"No." She laughed. "I can share." She handed him a single cookie, making him laugh.

"I like food," she said unapologetically. "Even though the sheer quantity of what I consumed is going to make my stomach rumble."

"Because it's regenerating its lining," he said, still grinning. "Like it does every two weeks."

"Are you mocking me?"

"No. I like your science facts, Ms. Evans. I like them very much."

"Come on," she said doubtfully.

"I really do. Got any facts about cookies?"

"Yes, actually," she said smugly. "The average person eats about thirty-five thousand of them in their lifetime."

He looked impressed. "No shit?"

"Well," she said. "That's average, you understand. I single-handedly decimate the equation."

He laughed again, and she smiled at him. "I love the sound of your laugh," she said. "And I loved tonight. Thanks for doing this, Griffin, for giving me a late-night picnic in the mountains. It's been so nice."

"Nice?"

"Well, yes." She took in his grimace. "What's wrong with nice?"

"I was hoping for a better adjective."

"Fun. Exciting," she said. "New."

He met her gaze. "No one's ever taken you on a late-night picnic before?"

"No."

"Never?"

"Never."

He took her drink out of her hands. "Close your eyes like before."

"Why?"

He just waited, and she sighed and closed her eyes. Then once again he laid her back.

"What are we doing?" she asked, feeling him lie down beside her.

"You can open your eyes now."

She blinked and stared up at the most magnificent, amazing night sky she'd ever seen. Black velvet scattered with millions, trillions, of diamonds. "Wow," she whispered.

"Yeah," Grif said, coming up on an elbow to soak up the sight of Kate, face tilted up to the sky, expression rapt and full of wonder. "Wow."

She nudged him with her shoulder. "Stop. I'm not really a wow kind of woman."

"Yes you are," he said, leaning over her.

She sucked in a breath with that beautiful mouth, her lips parting in anticipation.

Just a taste, he told himself. *That's all. You're keeping this fun. Light. Easy.*

Nothing more.

Even knowing he was full of shit and asking for trouble, he held her gaze with his own as he lowered his mouth to hers.

It was far too easy.

God so easy.

Because this was Kate, sweet, soft, trusting Kate, whose hands were clutching his biceps, her breath halted in her chest.

She was so sweet he ached. "Kate," he whispered, then he touched his lips to hers again, forcing himself to take his time, to savor every single heartbeat, because this was it, this was all he was going to take from her.

But then a quiet moan escaped her and her hands tightened on him.

She wanted more, too.

She was dangerous. More dangerous than anything he'd ever faced. The feel of her curvy body beneath him, the scent of her skin . . . He'd kissed lots of women, but over time they'd all ran together in his head.

Not Kate Evans.

With Kate he remembered each and every look, each and every touch. Each and every kiss. And this one, here with her under a million stars was a world-class kiss. He was already hard. Hell, he'd been hard since he set her on the tailgate—but he wasn't going to get any relief tonight. This was just about her tonight.

Not him.

Still, he groaned when she pressed herself up into him, with a soft sound from deep in her throat that shot need straight through him. Trying to get even closer, she tightened her grip, like she wanted to crawl inside him. Knowing he had to stop this now before he took it too far killed him. "Kate."

In answer, she nipped at his bottom lip and then sucked it into her mouth.

Damn, she was no help at all. She had her tongue down his throat, her knee sliding up the length of his thigh so that she was open to him, her hands beneath his shirt, and oh Jesus, they were heading south, her fingers running along the button fly of his jeans. He thrust helplessly into her palm before he ruthlessly clamped down on the hunger roaring through him, desperately trying to access his common sense.

She popped open the top button and was going for the next before he managed to catch her hand. "No," he said, his voice low and raspy.

She blew a strand of hair from her face. "No?"

"This is about you, about showing you a good time."

"Yes," she said. "And I was just getting to the good-time part."

He laughed and dropped his head to her shoulder. "This is about you, Kate," he repeated.

She stared up at him, her eyes twin pools of mystery. "So you're only going to . . . give?"

"Yes."

"And I'm supposed to just take it?"

"Yes."

His voice was a little rough, but he couldn't help it. She stared at his mouth as if she liked the sound of him like that, a little out of control. And then she lay back, legs and arms spread, looking like some sort of jean-clad goddess beneath the starlight. "Well then, get to it," she said.

Oh Jesus. Yeah. It was official. She was going to be the death of him.

When he didn't touch her, she opened one eye and looked at him, and then she narrowed her eyes as she got it. "Are you kidding me? Why did you get me all worked up then?"

He considered her lush, gorgeous, prone body. "You're worked up?"

"Very!"

"You should tell me about it. Slowly and in great detail."

She stared up at him and then closed her eyes again,

lying back all trusting. "You know so much, figure it out for yourself."

He was smiling when he kissed her this time. Smiling. He couldn't remember smiling while kissing a woman before. But then again, everything with Kate was either a surprise or new. He was the most jaded, cynical bastard he knew.

Except with her.

Twenty-one

Kate smiled when she felt Griffin's mouth cover hers, but the smile was short-lived because he kissed her with devastating care and seriousness, and oh Lord, the man could kiss. He had her panting in seconds. Rocking up, she tried to wrap her arms around him, but he took her wrists and held them over her head, pinning her body with his.

"Don't move," he said.

His commanding tone caused a very secret little thrill. "I'm not very good at following orders," she whispered.

"Move, and I stop getting you worked up."

His stern expression started a slow burn deep in her belly. "Well, hurry up and get back to it, then," she said.

"Still trust me?" he asked again.

"Yes."

He held her gaze for a long beat and then bent to her. Still holding her wrists pinned over her head, his warm breath tickled her ear as his teeth nipped her earlobe. Then his lips slid down her throat as he peeled open the jacket and slid a hand beneath her sweater.

The slow burn in her belly spread both north and south

with shocking speed. Did she trust him? With her life? Yes. With her body? Yes.

With her heart? She'd have to be a fool— "Oh," she breathed, startled when his clever fingers peeled her bra down and teased her nipples. And then again when he unbuttoned her jeans and slid down her zipper. She should have been cold, but instead she was on fire, from the inside out. "Hey, you wouldn't let me—" Her words ended on a breathy moan because he stroked a long finger over her.

"You're wet," he said, a naughty accusation. "I bet it was the cookies."

She choked out a half laugh, half moan. "You said we weren't going to—"

"I said I wasn't going to," he corrected, placing soft, wet, devastatingly hot kisses along her neck, dipping his tongue into the hollow at the base of her throat. "But you are, Kate. You're going to a lot."

"Ohmigod," she managed, already shockingly close to orgasm. Her hands still pinned, she arched into his other hand, the one currently the center of her entire universe. His warm breath on her throat raised goose bumps along her skin. The hand he had in her pants moved possessively, hungrily, stroking her with knowing precision. She shuddered and spread her legs a little wider. Then, afraid that he'd stop, she closed them tightly, holding his hand to her.

"I'm not going anywhere," he promised, and then he kissed her long and wet and deep, his fingers having no problem within their confined space, setting a rhythm that had every coherent thought vacating her brain. It also had her entire body trembling on the very edge, and she cried out, rocking into him, helplessly anchored by his body. "Griffin—"

He didn't answer. Instead he guided her movements, taking total control until she was gasping for air in jerky little puffs that dissipated in the chilly sky. She felt her muscles tighten, her toes curl, and she wrenched her mouth from his. "I'm going to—"

"Good. Come."

She was already shuddering as he ground against her, his tongue in her mouth moving with her hips as she did just what he'd demanded and came for him. Hard.

She had no idea how much time went by before she relaxed her body and blinked open her eyes.

He nuzzled her neck. "Still with me?"

"I haven't the foggiest," she said, surprised to find her voice hoarse. That's when she realized, she'd been making all sorts of ruckus. Embarrassed, she tried to turn away, but he tightened his grip, smiling against her.

"Stop it," she said, shoving at him. "It's all your fault. I'm not usually so noisy."

"It worked to our advantage. You kept the bears scared off."

With a horrified gasp she tried to sit up.

He held her still, grin flashing, the bastard. "Just relax a minute." He zipped the jacket back up to her chin but not before pressing his face to her throat and inhaling deeply. "God, I love the scent of you."

"A male emperor moth can smell his female emperor moth seven miles away," she said inanely, her hands coming up to hold his head to her.

"Lucky male emperor moth." He gave her one smacking kiss and grinned.

She studied his face. "You're feeling pretty damn sure of yourself."

"Making a woman scream his name does that to a guy."

"I did not scream your name," she said.

"Do you see any bears?"

She smacked his chest, and then she fisted her hands in his shirt, trying to tug him over her. "Tell me you have a condom."

"I have a condom."

"I love that about you," she said fervently.

"We're not using it."

She went still then pushed him away. "Okay, I don't love that. Why aren't we using it?"

"Already told you." He hopped out of the truck bed and reached a hand back to help her. "Tonight's about you." He opened the door for her and then walked around and slid behind the wheel.

Tonight's about you . . . She stared at him as it sunk in that he was completely serious. Not sure if she was touched or frustrated, she frowned. "So you brought me up here to what, make out with me and give me mine but not get yours?" She gestured vaguely to his lap, where he was still noticeably hard.

"Yeah." He slid her an amused look. "Haven't gone home in this condition after a date since I was a teenager," he admitted.

Touched, she decided with a laugh. She was definitely touched.

And still very aroused.

Which was why, half an hour later, when he walked her to her door, she grabbed him by the front of his shirt and tugged him inside, and then kicked her door shut and pressed him to it.

He arched a brow.

"Whatever I want," she reminded him.

He could have easily moved away, but he didn't. "What do you want?" he asked, voice low.

"You," she said.

"Are you going to be rough?"

"Yes," she said.

"Excellent." He ran his hands down her back to her butt and lifted her so that she could wrap her legs around him. "Where to?"

Because she was in charge. Nearly vibrating with the power, she pointed to her bedroom.

Griffin carried her to the bed and let her slide slowly down. At the full body contact, he groaned and pulled her in closer, kissing her deeply and so hotly that heat and desire once again flamed through her body. "Strip," she said, enjoying her power.

"Yes, ma'am." Pulling his sweatshirt and T-shirt over his head in one economical movement, he tossed the balled-up shirts behind him.

She slid out of the jacket he'd put on her and let it hit the floor.

He kicked off his shoes and socks.

She pulled off her sweater.

He unbuttoned and unzipped his Levi's, and she went still in the act of tugging off her camisole. Lord, he was smoking hot in those battered jeans and nothing else.

"Don't stop," he said.

She had no idea when she'd relinquished the reins to him, but as usual, he'd taken control like he meant business. She lost the camisole and shimmied out of her jeans. This left her in a pale blue bra and matching panties, which caught his attention so thoroughly that he nearly fell over trying to lose his jeans and forest green knit boxers at the same time, but there he was gloriously naked.

"You win," she said.

"Yes." He pointed to the bed. "There," he said. "You'll be my prize."

"You said I could have whatever I wanted."

"Yeah," he said softly, wrestling her to the bed when she didn't move fast enough. "Whatever you want. Just name it." He stroked the hair from her face. "Tell me, Kate."

His voice was rough. Strained. She already knew that he liked to talk during sex, and he especially liked her to talk. But she thought actions were better than words, and she rolled him so that she was on top. Because what she wanted was to ride him like a bronco. "Is this okay?" she whispered.

His hands slid up her ribs, unhooked her bra in a blink of an eye, and sent it sailing across the room. He tugged her down and kissed her, hard.

Apparently it was okay.

"I love this," he said, stroking a finger over the pale blue cloth barely covering her mound. Then he ripped it off her and hooked his hands around her thighs.

She startled. "What are you—"

"Up," he commanded, and scooted her higher on his chest, then higher still, maneuvering her to his shoulders, which apparently wasn't enough because he kept pulling until she would have fallen right onto his face if she hadn't grabbed the headboard and dug her knees into the bed to stop her upward progress. "Griffin—"

"Further. I want my mouth on you." And with one last tug, he had her right where he wanted her—with her knees hugging his ears.

With a gasp, she tried to back up, but he had a big, callused hand on each butt cheek and held her still. She looked down at him to give him a stern look, but instead she was absolutely taken apart by the rapturous look on his face as he kissed her.

There.

And then licked.

And then sucked.

He watched her as he worked her. Watched and groaned, God, he was good at this. So damn good. Incoherent, she let her head fall back, and she gripped the headboard for all she was worth as he took her right outside of herself. She was still panting and shuddering when with a flick of his wrist, he showed her the condom he held between his two fingers.

He really was magic.

She slid down his body to straddle his hips. He rocked into her, and she looked down at his most impressive erection nestling between her spread thighs. "Must have," she said, and opened the condom. When she fumbled with it, he helped her stroke it down his length, the both of them breathless by the time they finished.

Then he lifted her up and impaled her on him.

Her moan mingled with his, but she gripped his biceps. "Easy," she gasped out. "I don't want your headache to come back."

His answer was to thrust into her, hard, and her eyes rolled back in her head. With a low, laughing groan, he tugged her down to him, his hand in her hair, holding her head still as his mouth took hers. The deliberate sucking on her tongue matched his body's movements, the delicious glide in and out, and took her to a whole new level of need. The feel of him, the taste of him, was intoxicating, driving every inch of her out of her mind. Completely. She'd never felt so utterly . . . taken. It was hot and so intensely erotic she wasn't sure she would survive. Everything combined into a sexual pull; the silkiness of his hair sliding through her fingers, the rough scrape of his stubbled jaw, the hard strength of the arms that surrounded her. "Griffin."

"Tell me."

"I— You—" She closed her eyes. "I want you so much." So much it scared her.

"Show me," he said. "Love me."

I do, she nearly said.

But that wasn't what he meant. He meant with her body, of course. She knew it. She also knew he was a force to be reckoned with. The pure physical energy of him when he was fully dressed and upright nearly overwhelmed her. But like this, naked and sprawled out beneath her for her plea-sure, he was unbelievably, dangerously seductive. Love him?

Done.

He was spreading wet, hot kisses alongside her throat. God, she loved when he did that, and her eyes drifted shut as he skimmed warm, strong hands from her stomach to her shoulders and then entangled his fingers in hers. He gave one tug and she fell forward onto him.

Opening her eyes, she found his face only inches from hers. Deep gray orbs stared back at her as he shifted, bring-ing their locked hands between them. Using his for lever-age, she pushed herself upright and inhaled sharply as the movement buried him even deeper inside her. He let her set the pace, watching her intensely as the tension inside her built until she came and took him right along with her.

Twenty-two

When Grif got up for water and came back to the bed, Kate was exactly as he'd left her—sprawled out on her belly, face smashed into the pillow, dead to the world.

Bare-ass naked.

Several things warred for space in his head. Male pride over putting her into a sexual coma and the very caveman-like urge to climb back on the bed, yank her up to her hands and knees, and take her again, from behind this time.

And then there was the most confusing of all. The desire to simply pull her in close and never let her go. He settled for covering her with a blanket so she didn't get cold before pulling on his clothes. He went to turn off the lamp by her bed but was sidetracked by the letter lying there.

It had been folded and unfolded so many times that it was tearing along the two creases. As he reached for the lamp switch, the words *Scholarship* and *Teacher of the Year* caught his attention.

She'd been accepted into what looked like a prestigious science program out of the University of California at San Diego. There were notes in the margins on housing info, class schedules, etc. And someone had drawn an umbrella on the beach.

"Hey," Kate said sleepily. Sitting up, she brought the sheet with her, tucking it beneath her armpits.

He smiled at the modesty. "Seriously?"

She blushed. "Maybe I'm not always comfortable being naked." Then she held out her hand for the letter.

He didn't hand it over. "You should be comfortable naked; you're amazing."

She bit her lower lip and blushed some more. Then she took the letter from him and carefully folded it up, slipping it under her pillow.

His brows went up.

She hugged herself.

Using her own tactic against her, he waited her out, and finally she blew out a breath. "It's a master's program."

"It's more than that," he said. "It's a full-ride scholarship to a special master's program combining science and education."

"Yeah." She stroked the top of her pillow, and his heart did that squeeze thing that tended to happen around her. "It's like a dream summer camp," she said. "But it's for a year, studying under scientists I've admired for a long time. I'd get to do things like watch frogs having sex and study the mating habits of fruit flies."

He stared at her. "And that interests you."

She laughed, that sweet, soft, musical laugh that always touched him, even when it was at his expense. "Very much."

"So why aren't you going?" he asked.

"Who said I wasn't?"

He pointed to her pillow. "Because you're hiding it like it's a top-secret mission."

Again she stroked her pillow, but this time she said nothing.

"What's with the umbrella on the beach?" he tried.

More nothing.

"Maybe you think you're not good enough," he said.

Her eyes flashed at that. Good. She knew she was good enough.

"I really think this might be my year," she said.

"Your year? How may years have there been?"

"It's the third year," she admitted.

"You've put this honor off for three years?"

She lifted a shoulder, looking as defensive as any of her second graders.

"And the umbrella?" he pressed again.

"That was my dad. He's been leaving me little hints, like the umbrella. He says I've wasted enough of my life raising him, that it's my turn to fly."

Grif agreed wholeheartedly, but as someone who'd been told what to do for far too much of his life, he knew when not to do the same. "So what's the real reason you haven't gone? Don't you want to?"

"I do," she breathed, her entire heart in her eyes. "More than anything. But . . . Ashley's going through a phase, and she's sort of falling apart—"

"Falling apart is the very definition of being a teenage girl." He knew this firsthand as he'd been there for most of Holly's formidable—and terrifying—teenage years. "And she's your dad's problem. You're her sister not her mother."

"And Tommy—"

"Is a great kid," he finished. "He's just different. But he doesn't give a shit about that, so you shouldn't either."

"I don't."

"Then what?" he pushed.

"Well, it's a lot for my dad—"

"Bullshit," he said. "Again, you're Tommy's sister, and you're not your dad's wife. And you said yourself he wants you to go. Kate, you've taken care of them a long time, and you've done a great job. But from what I can see, they're getting on just fine."

"Because I make sure of it."

"So trust yourself; you've set them up to be just fine in your absence."

She stared up at him, eyes unfathomable. "You really think I should go."

"Hell yeah. Do you like San Diego?"

"Love it," she said, then gave him an embarrassed laugh. "In pictures anyway. The truth is that I've never been. It's a dream of mine though, to be on the beach. I want to see the sun set on the water."

He smiled. "You want some more fun."

She smiled back and sat up, hugging her knees to her chest. "Not that this, tonight, wasn't a whole bunch of fun. But . . ."

"It doesn't compare to a Pacific coast sunset."

"Actually," she murmured. "It was pretty darn close."

"Pretty darn close?" He'd just put on his clothes, but he made a show of kicking off his shoes, which made her laugh.

"That wasn't a challenge or anything," she said, but her breath caught when he put a knee on the bed.

"Pretty darn close?" he repeated softly.

"Well . . ." She lifted one creamy shoulder and let the sheet slip a little bit. "Maybe I'm not remembering clearly."

"Let me help you remember." He fisted the sheet and pulled, wrenching a laugh-filled gasp from her. Then he wrapped his fingers around her ankles.

And tugged.

She gasped again as he came down over the top of her, pinning her to the bed beneath him as his hands slid up her body to cup her face. "You'll remember this time," he said.

And then he set out to prove it.

Grif left Kate's bed before dawn. It took a shocking amount of discipline, but staying wrapped up in Kate's soft, warm body seemed more dangerous to his well-being than heading back to the ranch and working his ass off.

Which he'd been doing every day. He'd found that though Reid Ranching ran smoothly in general, there was a definite disconnect between Holly in the office and his father's crews in the fields. This was mostly because their ranch manager had left a month ago to move to Colorado and they hadn't replaced him, instead various ranch hands had stepped up.

But Donald Reid wasn't the most patient of men, and he was preoccupied with his hobbies, his girlfriend, and enjoying himself.

So Griffin had inadvertently stepped into the role. Over the past two days he'd been spending a lot of time going through barn inventory for Holly, who'd been freaking out about quarterly paperwork and taxes.

By seven thirty he was in her office with the spreadsheets she'd been hounding him for.

She snatched at the iPad like it was the last donut in an assorted box. Unfortunately, the real box of donuts on her desk was empty except for a few crumbs.

"You're a lifesaver," she said, and shocked him by rounding her desk and giving him a big hug.

"Does that mean you'll stop yelling at me via text all day long?"

She stepped back. "I don't yell. I direct."

"You're bossy as shit," he said, and opened her pencil drawer, stealing the candy bar she always had hidden there.

"Hey! That's my emergency chocolate!"

He bit into it. "Should have saved me a donut. Besides, it's not good for the baby."

Ignoring his comment, she clicked and read through the iPad inventory files. "Griffin—"

"If you're going to tell me I did it wrong, get some other sucker to do your bidding."

"No." She lifted her head, her eyes shining with emotion.

"Uh-oh," he said. "What are you doing?"

"Nothing." She reached for the box of tissues on the desk.

"Shit," he said. "What is it? Baby hormones? Do I need to kick Adam's ass? Dad's? What?"

"No!" she said on a watery laugh, and blew her nose. "Nothing like that." She hugged him again.

"Okay, now I'm really freaked out," he said, freeing himself. "Two hugs in the same day and not a single smack."

She smacked him. "I'm just happy to have you here, you stupid jerk. Helping. Being a part of the family. It feels good." She searched his gaze. "Doesn't it?"

He blew out a breath. He knew where this was going. "Holly—"

"He put you on the payroll, you know."

"What?"

"Yeah," she said, and turned her computer to face him, showing him the payroll files. "You'll be getting your first check this week, along with the rest of us."

He stared at his name on the report, under which the title read *Ranch Manager*. "He didn't even ask me."

"He won't." This time she patted his chest gently. "He wants you to stay. I want you to stay." She put his hand on her belly. "The baby wants you to stay."

"The baby is a bean."

She laughed. "Fine. But everyone else wants you to stay."

He blew out a breath. "I don't know what to say."

"Say you'll think about it."

He was surprised that he felt utterly calm at the very thought. "I'll think about it."

She beamed at him. "Good." She smacked him again. "Now go buy me another candy bar."

Kate got up, showered, and made her usual stop at her dad's. She was shocked to find him in the kitchen stirring oatmeal on the stove. Ashley was pouting at the table, but she was at the table.

"He said I had to eat it," she grumbled. "And FYI, oatmeal's disgusting."

Kate hugged her dad and looked in the pot. It did look disgusting, but she said, "Yum."

Her dad slid her an amused look and scooped her a bowl, too.

It was overdone, but Kate choked down every bite.

Five minutes later, she and Tommy slid into Ryan's car. She was sipping a coffee, desperately trying to get rid of the oatmeal sticking to her gut like lead. Plus, it was career day at school, always a circus, and she needed the kick of caffeine because she'd spent most of the night being ruined for all other men by Griffin.

Ryan glanced at her over the top of his sunglasses.

"Don't say it," she warned.

"I don't have to. The smile says it all."

Kate grimaced. "I know." She'd seen the smile in the mirror when she'd been dressing. She hadn't been able to get it to go away.

Ryan let out a huff of annoyance. "It's like you're just showing off now."

Kate sipped some more coffee.

"Where's mine?" Ryan asked. "Coffee might help ease my pain."

"You're not in pain. And you told me to stop babying you."

He stared at her.

"Well didn't you?"

"Yeah." He put the car in gear and pulled out, looking a little broody. "I just didn't think you'd really do it."

"Shouldn't say stuff you don't mean," Tommy piped up from the backseat.

Ryan glanced at him in the rearview mirror. "Now you listen?"

Tommy grinned.

Ryan sighed. "I bet you'd throw me to the wolves in a heartbeat."

Tommy adamantly shook his head. "Nope. No man left behind," he said. "That's the man rule."

"Excuse me?" Kate asked. "Man rule?"

"Grif said," Tommy said. "Never leave a man behind."

Except he was leaving her behind. Any day now. Which was okay, she reminded herself. They'd had their night. Hell, she'd even had a second and third night . . . "Or a woman," Kate said. "Never leave a woman behind either. Or a child."

"Well, duh," Tommy said.

Ryan made a play for Kate's coffee, but she merely held it out of his reach and then went back to drinking it.

"Mean," Ryan said.

"I'm your friend, not your mother."

"Huh?"

"Nothing," Kate said, feeling both amusement and a pang of yearning.

They pulled into the school. Ryan put the car in park and held Kate's wrist when she would have gotten out with Tommy.

"What?" she asked.

"Four more days."

"I know."

He met her gaze, his own void of its usual sarcasm. "Do you?"

"Yes," she said.

"Then turn in your acceptance!"

She nodded. Seeing her dad trying went a long way toward easing her mind. "I will."

Ryan blew out a sigh and thunked his head against the headrest a few times.

"You're going to shake something loose," she said, and handed him her coffee.

"Bless you," he said fervently. "Sometimes I don't know what I'd do without you."

She met his gaze and saw the exact moment it hit him.

"I didn't meant it like that," he said quickly. "I want you to go. For you." He squeezed her hand. "We'll deal, Kate. We'll all deal. We'll be fine."

Yes. But would she?

A few minutes later Kate was chitchatting with her career day parents when her gaze collided with Griffin's. Her greedy nipples tingled. "Hey," she said in surprise.

"What are you—" She broke off when someone tugged at her sweater.

Tommy.

He smiled up at her. "You know how you always tell me I can be anything I want when I get all growed up?"

"When you grow up, and yes."

"I want to be a soldier and save people, just like Grif."

Ah. It was starting to make sense now. "Tommy, did you invite Griffin here today as your career guide?"

Tommy beamed at her. "Yep."

Yep. She straightened and met Griffin's gaze. He looked at her right back, giving nothing away.

She, on the other hand, was pretty sure she was giving everything away. How could she not? The last time she'd seen him she'd been bouncing on him like he was a wild bronco ride at the fair.

She tried to ignore this as the first parent walked to the front of the class and talked about being a doctor. He'd brought a poster chart of hereditary features and was showing the kids how they got their eye color, blood type, and other traits. Unfortunately, he was also nervous, spoke in a monotone, and kept dropping the poster.

The kids were shifting around and whispering. Kate shushed a few of them and gave Griffin a quick glance. She couldn't imagine how different this situation was from his usual world.

He was facing the front, listening politely to the doctor, but then, as if he felt her looking at him, his gaze slid to her.

Had she thought he kept everything hidden? Because everything he felt was right there, and it stole her breath.

The doctor finished, and the next parent moved to the front of the class. A banker. Kate bit back her sigh as the kids got even more restless.

And then it was Griffin's turn. Unlike the others who'd stood at the dry erase board and given dry, boring speeches, he went to the reading corner and sat in a circle with the kids huddled close.

There he taught them how to build a camp with makeshift items he found in the classroom, such as jackets and coats and umbrellas.

"Where're our guns?" Dustin wanted to know. "We need guns."

"No guns," Grif said.

"Why? Soldiers use guns."

"They also use their brains."

Profound silence met this. Then, from Mikey, "Well, that's no fun."

"Guns are no fun, kid," Grif said. "Trust me."

"You been shot at? Blown up?"

"Both," Grif said.

"Wow," the kids all said in unison.

"Cool."

"Awesome."

Grif shook his head. "Not cool. Not awesome." He pulled off his baseball cap and shoved his hair from his forehead, showing them the long, jagged scar. "Another half an inch to the left and I'd have lost an eye," he said matter-of-factly. "Half an inch to the right and I've had lost my head. Can't live without a head."

The kids were mesmerized.

Griffin then proceeded to get the students to help him create a maze with the desks, after which he had them all tie their shoelaces together so they were hooked in one long line. "Now you learn how to get through the maze together," he said.

"Why together?" Dustin asked. "That's stupid."

"You're on a baseball team," Griffin said. "You should know the benefit of being able to work as a team. What would you do if you got lost?"

"Send the best guy ahead," Dustin said.

Griffin shook his head. "The best guy protects the unit. You need to be able to count on each another." His gaze met Kate's across the room.

She knew he was thinking of when he'd been hurt, down with a migraine, and she'd taken him home, stayed with him.

She'd known what he gave her. He made her feel smart, sexy, worthy. But she hadn't known what she gave him. Who would have thought she gave him anything? But she'd had his back, and at the thought she felt such a surge of pride that she beamed at him.

He didn't quite return the smile, but the very corners of his mouth quirked.

He was actually getting into this a little, she thought, maybe even enjoying himself.

"What if you don't like the person you're tied to?" Nina asked, looking at Dustin at her side with distaste.

"You don't have to like him," Griffin said. "You do have to trust him."

Nina gave Dustin a long look of extreme doubt.

"You don't have to be best friends or even alike," Griffin said, and paused to let that sink in. "In fact it's better if your unit is made up of very different people. That way everyone brings a skill set to the table. Now get ready, we're timing this." He pulled out his phone and brought up a stopwatch. "Go," he said.

Pandemonium.

He whistled, and when he had all of their attention again, he shook his head. "Epic fail. You can't just run around like crazy ants; you have to work together. Try again." He reset his watch, counted down, and said, "Go!"

He let them go wild for a minute longer than he had the first time before stopping them again. "Better," he said. "Now pretend someone's injured." He pointed to one of the kids, Jessica, who was just about as fierce as they came.

She immediately pouted. "I don't want to be injured. I want to be on the rescue unit."

Griffin looked around him for another victim. The first person he laid eyes on was Meggie. Also fierce.

"Why does it have to be a girl?" she demanded, hands on hips. "And anyway, my mom says girls are better than boys at everything."

"Well, you've got me there," Grif murmured, and he pointed to the first boy.

Tommy.

Tommy grinned, and Kate's heart squeezed as Grif put a protective hand on the boy's shoulder. "Tommy has a broken ankle, and you can't just shove him along with you," he said.

"If the best guy went ahead," Dustin said. "He could get help."

Progress, Kate thought. He was actually starting to think of others.

"No man left behind," Grif reminded him. "Ever." He set his timer again. "Go."

The recess bell rang, and the kids whooped and filed out of the classroom. Tommy stopped to give Grif a fist bump and a gap-toothed grin.

Grif hadn't been sure he'd have a damn thing to offer when Tommy had first asked him to do this. But he couldn't turn the kid down. So he'd made sure that Tommy had done well at the drills, and he had. The kid might be different but he was good different.

Grif hadn't been at all like Tommy when he'd been young. Grif had always been at the top of the food chain, but something about Kate's brother had grabbed at him from the first. Maybe because deep down he felt a little like Tommy now, trying to fit into an alien world.

Grif held back as the last of the parents left. He thought the morning had gone well, but what did he know? When he'd been a student here, a good day at school meant he had not been sent to the principal's office.

Kate went to the back closet for her coat. "I'm not on recess duty today, but I like to be out there with the kids—"

He nudged her into the closet and out of view of anyone who happened to be walking by the classroom.

"What are you doing?" she gasped.

Pressing her against the coats, he looked down into her face. "You gave me a look earlier."

"What look?"

"You know what look," he said. "The one that said you wanted to eat me for lunch."

"Oh, you mean this one?" And then she gave him a repeat of the look.

Pushing her farther into the closet, he shut the door behind him.

"Oh no," she said on a laugh. "Don't give me dirty thoughts right now. We can't—"

He kissed her. God, he loved kissing her. And doing it in the dark on the fly was even better.

"Going to miss this," she whispered, pressing close.

Still cupping her face, he pulled back slightly, but he couldn't see her face now.

"When you leave," she clarified.

He traced a thumb over her jawline. "I don't think I'm the one going."

He felt her go still. "What?"

"I'm getting comfortable here," he said much more casually than he felt. He lifted a shoulder, happy now for the dark, not willing to show her, much less admit, how much her thoughts on this mattered to him. "I might stick around."

"Wow," she breathed. "I did not see that coming."

This threw him because it was a nonreaction. He'd expected something else. Something more. "And . . . ?"

"And now I'm really having dirty thoughts," she whispered, her voice holding an emotion that he couldn't decipher without a translator. But some words didn't need translating.

"I love your dirty thoughts," he said, understanding she wasn't ready to discuss his possibly staying in Sunshine. That was okay, neither was he. "Tell me."

"It's nothing we can discuss in school," she said primly, even as she pressed her body close.

Okay, now they were talking.

"It involves some dirty words."

"Ah, now you're just teasing me," he said, and bent to her. "Tell me one."

"No."

"Come on. Just one."

"All right." Going up on tiptoe, she pressed her body to his from chest to thigh and everything glorious in between, and put her mouth to his ear and whispered one word softly.

His favorite word of all. He tightened his grip on her. "Ms. Evans, I believe we need to discuss this in more detail."

"We do," she agreed.

"Tonight."

Kate's heart had skipped a beat. Hell, it had skipped a whole bunch of beats. He was thinking of staying? He was asking her out again? She was dizzy with it all. "Can't," she said. "It's Friday."

"What, no being down and dirty on Fridays?" he teased. "It's what Fridays were meant for."

"It's the night I cook for my dad. I make up a bunch of casseroles for him to use during the week."

"I'll buy him cooking lessons," Grif said without missing a beat, and slid his hands up her blouse.

He was thinking of staying . . . "He's a terrible cook," she murmured, locking her knees when the pads of his fingers slid over her nipples.

"Hence the lessons," he said in his sex voice, making her go all trembly.

"I also have to help Ashley with college stuff," she said. "We're planning a road trip to tour some colleges in the fall."

"You'll be dissecting calves and frogs in the fall," he reminded her. "You should make it a summer tour instead."

For some reason, the thought brought panic, and she pulled back. "It's not that simple."

He went still for a beat and then backed from her. "Nope," he agreed. "You just have to want it bad enough."

"Want what?"

He opened the closet door and met her gaze. "You're afraid to go."

"What? That's ridiculous." She laughed, but it sounded hollow and fake even to her own ears. "I'm not afraid. I can't just leave, Griffin, not without making sure everything's going to be okay."

"You're afraid," he repeated.

Yes. Okay, yes, she was afraid. Hell, she was terrified. She'd never even been out of Idaho for God's sake, and here she was planning to go to California on her own for a year. But instead of admitting that, she crossed her arms and got defensive. "Says the guy who doesn't even know me."

He merely arched a brow. "Is that how you want to play this, Kate? That we're still just a chemistry problem, nothing more?"

"We are just a chemistry problem."

He shoved his fingers through his hair and then met her gaze. "You put on a good show, Kate, of making it about everyone else. Your family, your work . . . chemistry. But it is a show. Behind the curtains, it's all you and your fears."

"Don't be ridiculous."

But he was gone.

Twenty-three

Still shaken, Kate shuffled into her dad's house, arms full. She had casseroles for the next week, a big, fat book of the best colleges in the country, and the Flash costume Tommy had ordered from her Amazon account.

Channing Tatum immediately wound himself around her ankles, and she stepped on his paw, nearly killing them both.

"You stole my damn chips again," her dad said from where he was sitting on the couch with his laptop.

She'd found them in his mailbox. The postal carrier had a huge crush on him and was an enabler. "Sorry," she said, not sorry at all.

He sighed. "Heard you had quite the lineup at career day."

"Yes, we had a doctor and a banker."

"And a real life warrior," her dad said, getting up to help her. "Tommy stole Ashley's makeup when he got home and used it for camouflage."

"Not makeup, dad," came Tommy's muffled voice. "War paint."

Kate turned around. What appeared to be every sheet

and towel from the house had been used to make an impressive fort behind the couch.

"He's working on setting up an army base," her dad said.

"Outpost," Tommy corrected, again muffled.

That's when Kate realized she smelled something burning.

"You're just in time," her dad said. "I've got something in the oven."

He looked pretty darn proud of himself, and Kate bit back her sigh. "Is it the something that's burning?"

"What?" Her dad sniffed the air. "Shit."

"Shit," Tommy repeated from the depths of his fort.

"No swearing!" Kate said.

"Dad!" came Ashley's shriek from upstairs. "You're burning something! Again!"

Eddie and Kate were already rushing into the kitchen. Smoke was billowing out of the oven. Her dad ripped open the oven door and reached in.

"Dad! Oven mitts!" Kate yelled, then nudged him out of the way, grabbed the mitts, and pulled out . . . a ruined lasagna.

Her dad looked down at the charred mess and scratched the top of his head. "Huh. I have no idea why that keeps happening."

"It's called a timer," Kate said, and set the dish on the stovetop, next to the pot with the morning's oatmeal still stuck in the bottom like cement.

He shook his head. "Guess it's takeout tonight. I'm getting good at that." He flashed her a small smile and opened the junk drawer, stuffed to the gills with so much crap it took him a moment to get it open. Then he began to fish through the mess for the take-out menus. "I was watching a special on the travel channel," he said. "Did you know San Diego is the eighth-largest city in the states? It's the country's premiere beach destination." He glanced at her. "You send in your acceptance yet?"

He knew she hadn't. "No."

"How many days left?"

"Four."

Her dad tossed a Chinese, an Italian, and a Mexican menu onto the counter. "Don't you think you've wasted enough of your life raising me? Come on, Kate, it's your turn to fly."

"Dad, we both know I can't go anywhere. Not until you can be the parent again."

He turned off the oven and waved the oven mitts around to dissipate the smoke. "I am being the parent, Kate."

"You just about set the house on fire. Again."

"Don't be silly," he said. "The fire alarm didn't even go off."

That's when the fire alarm went off.

This was followed by a solid twenty minutes of insanity. First Tommy came racing into the kitchen and straight out the back door, where he grabbed the garden hose, cranked it on, and then tried to reenter the kitchen to be the hero.

Then Ashley made a dramatic entry, coughing and waving a hand in front of her face. "I just washed my hair! Do you know how bad smoke sticks to freshly washed hair?" she shrieked over the fire alarm.

Kate climbed up onto the cabinets and waved a magazine at the fire alarm until it stopped.

Her father called the fire department to ward off the emergency run.

Much later, after they'd ordered Chinese, cleaned up the kitchen, gone through some of Ashley's homework, and dealt with an algebra crisis, Kate sat next to her father on the couch.

He stroked a hand over her hair in silent apology for the night. With a sigh she set her head on his shoulder.

"I want you to go to UCSD," he said quietly.

She was still reeling from her last conversation with Griffin. He'd accused her of being afraid to go for the master's program.

And then there'd been his other bomb. The not leaving bomb . . .

But did that change anything? Her heart said oh hell yes. Her brain said absolutely not. His staying couldn't, shouldn't, change a thing. She'd gotten what she'd wanted from him. A good time. A great time. The end. Right? "I want me to go, too," she told her dad. "But—"

"No buts," he said. "I know you're afraid we'll fall apart, and who can blame you? But we're going to be okay, Kate. You've spoiled us long enough."

"What does that mean?"

He sighed. "You've been a steady rock for the family when I couldn't be, always showing how important and valuable each of us is. But it's okay to move on with your life. We're ready to try things on our own for a bit."

"But Ashley's college and Tommy—"

"Honey, taking care of people isn't doing everything for them. That's enabling. We'll manage. We'll miss you," he said, his voice a little thick now. "So much. But you have to go. For all of us."

She swallowed hard. "You're sure."

"No." He gave a low laugh. "You know we'll call you too much. We'll drive you crazy from afar. But you need to go." He hugged her. "I'm proud of you. And I love you, Kate. So much."

"Love you, too, Dad."

Tommy came into the room as Superman complete with red cape and turned on the TV. Then Ashley stuck her head in the room. "Kate, where's my cheerleading uniform?"

"Again?" Kate asked. "You lost it again?"

Her dad put his hand on Kate's knee. "I've got this," he said. "I did laundry this morning. It's been washed and is all ready for practice tomorrow."

"Impressive," Kate murmured.

He smiled and pointed to his phone. "I downloaded a homemaker app. It gives me daily lists."

Ashley rolled her eyes and vanished.

"In five seconds she'll be yelling thank you," her dad said. "Five, four, three, two—"

"Noooo!" came a bloodcurdling scream from the direction of the laundry room.

Tommy turned up the TV.

Ashley reappeared in the doorway with her cheerleading uniform—which had been shrunk to the size of a small child.

"Shit," her dad said.

"Shit," Tommy said.

Later that night, Kate stood at her kitchen counter eating ice cream, having a stare down contest with the scholarship letter lying on the tile.

Was she afraid? Hell yes. But anyone would be, she told herself.

Four more days . . .

The question was: Could she do it in spite of her fears? Could she really walk away? For a year?

Not walk away, she corrected. She'd still be a part of her family's life, a part of Sunshine. She'd always have that.

Wouldn't she?

The late-night knock surprised her. Moving through her townhouse, she pulled the front door open a crack and squeaked in surprise when Griffin pushed his way in.

"You didn't look to see who it was," he said, not sounding at all happy about that.

She shut the door behind him. "Well, hello to you, too."

He turned to face her, hands on hips, brow arched, and she sighed. "Okay, so I assumed it'd be Ashley with another homework emergency," she admitted. "Or my dad demanding to know where I'd hid his stash. Or—"

"Stash?" Grif's frown deepened. "I thought he's sober."

"He is. I meant his potato chips." She shook her head. "And not that I'm not happy to see you, but what brings you here?"

His gaze caught on the scholarship letter on the counter and nudged it. "You accept yet?"

She went back to her ice cream. "You're starting to sound like my dad and Ryan."

"You should do it, Kate."

Yes, but I don't know if I can walk away from you for a

year. "I don't want to talk about it." She licked her spoon clean and then felt Griffin come close, so that their toes touched. Well, her toes, his work boots. Tipping her head up, she met his gaze.

"You should do it," he said again, softly.

She took him in, from his hair—way longer than a military cut now—to the healing scar, to his firm-but-oh-so-giving mouth. Her heart sped up a little as she let her biggest fear escape. "I'll be gone a year."

"So what?"

She sucked in a breath at that. "So what?" she repeated. Ouch . . .

His hands gripped her arms. "I'm saying I don't care how long it takes, Kate. I'm saying so what. It's something you want, and I'm one hundred percent in favor of you doing anything you want."

"But . . ." She held his gaze. "This. Are you saying you don't want . . . this?"

"No. I'm saying this isn't going to hold you back."

"It's a year, Griffin."

He put his hands on her hips and lifted her to the counter, then stepped between her legs and cupped her face. "All my life," he said, "people have been waiting on me. My sister. My dad. Any woman in my life." He paused and let that sink in. "I think I can do the waiting for a change."

She stared at him, her hands slack as he took the ice cream from them. "You okay?" he murmured.

"I don't know." She shook her head. "I really didn't see you coming."

"Back at you." He slid one hand up her back and into her hair, the other arm wrapping low on her hips so that he could lift her up.

She wrapped her legs around him and cupped his face as he carried her into the bedroom. "You're good for me," she said. "I hope you know that."

Closing his eyes, he pressed his forehead to hers. She clutched at him. "So good," she whispered. And she spent the dark hours of the night showing him so, over and over . . .

* * *

The next day Griffin sat in the ranch office staring at the computer screen until the numbers blurred. Holly and Adam were spending the day looking at houses, and Grif was supposedly holding down the fort.

His mind wasn't on the task. Instead it was on a certain strawberry blond second-grade teacher who'd blown his mind—and other parts—all night long. He'd extracted a promise from her at dawn as he'd left her boneless and sated in her bed—dinner tonight.

Another date.

It was crazy. And necessary. As necessary as air.

He accessed the payroll accounts to get that running—a pain in his ass—and was immediately stymied by the lack of a password. He searched and found a sticky note from Holly that his dad had the password in his desk.

Simple enough. He looked down. Thing One was sleeping on his left foot. Thing Two was on his right. They didn't have a foot fetish; they had a Grif fetish. "We're on the move guys."

Neither dog so much as blinked.

Pushing away from Holly's desk, Grif pulled his feet free and stood up. Both dogs leaped to their feet like they'd been shot, and scrambled to follow Grif to his dad's office.

Empty.

Grif walked over to the pristine desk and pulled open the top drawer. No sticky note with a password, just a manila file labeled: Medical Shit.

The two words, reeking of cynicism and annoyance, had him opening the file because it would be just like the senior Reid to have had another heart attack and not told a damn soul including his own kids.

There was a stack of EOBs—explanation of benefits— at least an inch thick. Grif scanned the dates and relaxed marginally.

All from Donald's last heart attack. Nothing new.

Grif set those aside and skimmed the rest, and then

his gaze caught on what should have been an innocuous detail—his dad's blood type. Grif's mom was an O. The paper in front of him stated that Donald was an O as well, which was surprising because that meant their children would also be O.

But Grif was not. He was blood type A.

And as he knew from the doctor's lecture at career day, when two people with blood type O mate, the result was always blood type O offspring.

Always.

Thing One nudged at him, adding a little let's-go-out-and-play whine. Thing Two joined in.

But Grif just stared at the file.

He wasn't Donald Reid's biological child.

Twenty-four

G rif didn't know how long he sat there at his dad's desk, memories barraging him. Being five years old and standing in front of this very desk, a muddy frog dripping from each hand as his father yelled at him for his "un-Reid-like behavior."

Or at age twelve being caught joyriding in his dad's quad without permission in the middle of the night by a deputy sheriff. Donald Reid's idea of punishment for that had been to leave Grif in police custody until the next day, in a cell with some serious delinquents five years his senior who'd enjoyed tormenting him during those long hours before dawn.

At seventeen he'd been pulled over on prom night with a bag of weed in his truck—and the mayor's daughter. Donald had let the law fully prosecute Grif that time, and six months later when he'd turned eighteen, he'd left Sunshine, still thoroughly pissed off.

He wasn't exactly sure what he was now, but pissed off didn't begin to describe it.

"What the hell are you doing in here? This is my office."

Grif looked up as Donald strode into the room looking pretty pissed off himself.

Perfect, they were going to start off hot. Worked for Grif, who stood, medical file in hand.

"Hey," Donald said. "That's mine."

"Yeah, it is."

Donald's face went red, the precursor to a full-blown temper. "Get the hell out."

"Oh, I intend to. But this first." Grif tossed the open file on the desk.

Donald stood on the other side of the desk, hands on hips. "Why are you searching through my things?"

"I wasn't searching through your things. I was trying to do payroll, and Holly told me you had the password."

"So you just helped yourself to my desk to find it?"

"You weren't here and it had to be done. Dad."

Donald finally clued in to the fact that he wasn't the only one running a little temper. "What the hell is your problem?"

"You," Grif said.

Donald narrowed his eyes. "You want to be very careful how you speak to me, boy. I can still take you."

Boy. It was always "boy" or "kid," or on occasion "little asshole punk." There'd been other nicknames over the years, none flattering. Not that he'd deserved one, Grif could admit.

But apparently, he'd never deserved "son" either. "You're careful not to call me son."

Donald shook his head. "What the hell are you mumbling about?"

Grif pointed to the blood work in Donald's medical file. Tapped the blood type. "This."

Donald stared down at the file. "I already told you why I didn't tell you about my little heart thing."

"It was a heart attack, not a little heart thing, and I'm not talking about that." Grif shoved his fingers through his hair and pushed away from the desk. He went to the window and stared out at the land that he'd actually started to believe could really be his home.

An illusion. This place wasn't his, and he sure as hell didn't belong here.

"The password's in the other drawer," Donald said.

"Forget the password. Jesus." Grif turned to face the man who for better or worse had been the only father he'd ever known. "I'm talking about the fact that you're not my biological father."

The high color in Donald's cheeks drained, and he put a hand out to grip the desk.

Grif searched for some sympathy for the man but found none. "So you knew."

"Yes."

Yes. Just like that. Grif was having a hard time breathing. "I had a right to know, too."

"It wasn't my secret to tell."

The silence shimmered between them for a moment and, if anything, made Griffin all the more furious. "Bullshit," he said. "Mom's gone. Why keep it a secret?"

Donald said nothing, and Grif could actually feel his blood pressure change. "What the hell, Dad—" He broke off. "Or should I say Donald?"

The man had the good grace to wince. "I'm still your dad," he said. "There's no need for all this melodrama."

"Melodrama?" Grif's head began to drum in tune to his pulse. "I want to know who my real father is."

"Was."

"He's dead, then?"

Donald crossed his arms, his expression going bulldog stubborn. Grif recognized the look from years of butting heads with that expression.

"It doesn't matter," Donald said. "None of it matters. I came into the picture before you were born, and I'm on your birth certificate. That's all your mom wanted you to know."

A variety of scenarios crossed Grif's mind, not a single one of them good. "Did he get her pregnant and then desert her? Was she . . . raped?"

Donald turned away. "No."

"No? That's all, just no?"

Donald sucked in a deep breath and appeared to stare out at nothing for a long moment. "She was just pregnant when I met her. She said she was a package deal or nothing at all. I took the package deal. The end."

Grif stared at his stiff spine. "But once I came, you felt differently. You were pissed off that you were stuck with me. You didn't want to be responsible for me."

"Don't you put words into my mouth."

"Then give me your words."

Donald didn't give him any words. He didn't move a muscle.

Grif shoved his fingers through his hair in agitation at the exact same moment Donald made the same move. Grif dropped his hand. Apparently, some things didn't require blood. "We've been at each other for as long as I can remember," he said quickly. "At least now I know why." He paused. "You don't know who he was."

"No. She never told me."

"And you don't know what happened to him?"

"I said so, didn't I?"

Like banging his head against a brick wall. Grif sank back into the chair. "You have to give me something," he said hoarsely.

Donald said nothing.

"I need to know," Grif said. "I deserve to know."

Donald turned back, eyes shuddered, face hard. "What you deserve to know is that I loved your mom. I'd have done anything for her, would have turned myself inside out for her, but she loved . . . him. Whoever he was. I never got that piece of her, so yeah, maybe when I looked at you, I saw him. Maybe I was hard on you because of it, and maybe I was not the perfect father. But what's done is done."

Donald Reid was as old school as they came, stoic and gruff. The admission came out short and abrupt, like it had cost him.

Grif didn't care. He gave the medical file a shove. It slid across the smooth surface and hit the floor, scattering. And then he walked out, slamming the door behind him.

Holly stood in the hallway staring at him, eyes wide and filled with tears. "Grif—"

He'd have stormed right by her except she didn't deserve that from him. He sighed. "You heard."

"You were both shouting." She reached for him. "My God, Grif— Are you okay?"

"Yeah," he said. And then gave a short shake of his head. "No."

From inside the office came the sound of glass shattering, as if maybe something had just been flung across the room and hit a wall.

Holly gasped.

Grif just walked away.

Kate looked at her watch for the fifth time in as many minutes. It wasn't like her to watch the time, but nor was it like Grif to be late.

Another ten minutes ticked by and she looked at her watch again, just as her phone vibrated with a text from her date.

Can't make it.

She stared at the abrupt words. She was still staring at it when her phone rang.

"Is Grif there?" Holly asked, sounding off.

"Hol," Kate said, straightening. "Honey, what's the matter?"

"I need to talk to him, and I thought you guys had a date."

"We did," Kate said. "He didn't show."

A weighted silence.

"Holly," Kate said softly, a very bad feeling sinking in her gut. "What it is? What's wrong?"

Another heavy silence, filled only with a muffled sob.

"Okay, now you're scaring me," Kate said. "Tell me what's going on."

"I can't," Holly said. "This . . . it has to come from him. Kate . . . ?"

"Anything," Kate said, and meant it.

"My dad and Adam are out looking for him, and there's no better trackers . . . except Grif himself. Which actually means—"

"That he's not going to be found until he wants to be," Kate said quietly.

"Exactly. Do you have any ideas?"

"I'll get back to you." Kate hung up, and with her heart thumping with anxiety and worry in her chest, she drove to her dad's. He was in his usual place on the couch with his laptop.

"I'll have you know," he said without looking up, "I've got dinner cooking and the timer's on, thank you very much. Also, I did laundry, and no one's whites turned pink. And," he went on when Kate started to speak, "I mastered Ashley's chemistry. She even said, and I quote, 'Wow, Dad, you're nicer than Kate,' end quote." He beamed.

"That's all great, dad. Where's Tommy?"

"No, I don't think you're listening. You can call UCSD. You're still within the deadline, right? How many days left?"

"Three," she said. "Dad, I need to see Tommy."

Her dad looked up, finally clued in by her shaky voice. "He's cleaning his room. You okay?"

"Yes." She stared toward the hall and then stopped. "He's cleaning his room? How'd you get him to do that?"

Her dad smiled, but he was already back to typing on his keyboard. "Told him he couldn't wear any superhero clothes until it was clean. Superheroes do not live in filth."

Impressed, Kate knocked on Tommy's door, and at the annoyed "I'm working in here!" she let herself in.

Tommy was wearing his new Flash costume, and his room was indeed clean. "Hey," Kate said. "You remember that app that allows Griffin to find you?"

"No man left behind," Tommy said. "It's genius."

"Does it work in reverse?"

Tommy cocked his head and studied her. "Huh?"

"Can we find Griffin?"

"Sure," Tommy said.

Sure. Relief filled her as together they leaned over Tommy's iPod Touch. He brought up the app, waited for it to load, and then tilted the screen her way. "He's at your place."

"No he's not. I was just there."

"Not your house. Your place."

Kate stared at the blinking dot on the map. He was at the dam.

Tommy grinned. "Are you two playing hide-and-go-seek?"

"Something like that." She kissed the top of Tommy's head and ran out, wondering what Griffin was doing and what had happened.

And hating the knot in her gut that told her it was bad.

Twenty-five

Griffin had driven off-road for a while before going it on foot. He was ignoring his phone and the flurry of texts coming from Holly, each more demanding than the last.

Call me.

Dammit, Grif . . . I want to talk to you.

You're still my brother, you stubborn ass, CALL ME.

He lost track of time. He'd have preferred to lose track of where he was, but he never got lost. At least not physically.

Mentally was another thing altogether. He was definitely lost. Only yesterday he'd believed he could belong here.

But he'd never belonged here.

Only yesterday he'd known exactly who he was and what he wanted. He'd even thought maybe he was falling in love.

He hadn't known shit.

Now he was someone else entirely, with no real idea of who that person even was. So how could he be home? How could he be in love?

And yet here he was, sitting on a dead tree that wasn't even his place. It was Kate's. But Kate was his comfort right now, and this was as close to her as he could get.

He had no idea how long he sat there before he heard running footsteps.

Kate came up the path at a dead run, skidding to a stop at the sight of him.

"Hey," she said, breathless, clapping a hand to her heart. "It's true, you're here."

He knew on some level he'd wanted her to find him, or he'd have simply climbed the condemned tree house behind him. She was afraid of heights; she'd never have even looked up there.

When he didn't speak, she sank down next to him. "Holly called," she said. "Looking for you. Everyone's looking for you. Adam, your dad—"

Grif made an involuntary sound, which pissed him off. He was good at being stoic, good at holding his shit in.

Except with her.

When the fuck had that happened?

She'd gone quiet at the sound he made, and when she spoke again, it was softly and with great care. "I got worried," she said. "And went to see Tommy. We used that app you loaded for him."

"Smart," he said, impressed in spite of himself. "But Holly shouldn't have called you."

"We're best friends, Griffin. She was scared. Crying actually."

Guilt hit him. Holly was just as shocked as he'd been and just as confused and hurt—and he'd been deleting her texts.

"Griffin." Kate reached for his hand. "What happened?"

"Holly didn't tell you?"

"No. She said it was your story to tell."

He let out a low breath. "I found a medical file at the ranch office earlier. The blood types of my parents didn't match up to mine." He met her gaze. "They're both blood type O. Their baby would be an O also. But I'm an A."

She absorbed the unexpected shock of that. "But you look just like your mom."

"I'm hers," he said.

She turned her head and met his gaze. "But not Donald's."

He shook his head.

"You two talked?"

"More like yelled." He scraped a hand over his jaw. "He says he doesn't know much, that my mom was pregnant when they got together."

"So he took you on as his."

"No." Griffin shook his head. "He never really did that."

She wrapped her arms around him, but he held himself still. He didn't want to be comforted. He didn't want to be touched.

Kate did both anyway. Crawling into his lap, she straddled him and cupped his face. She met his eyes, and he realized he already was touched, to the bone, by her. And nothing was going to change that.

Leaning in, she kissed him with devastating softness. "I'm so sorry, Griffin," she whispered against his mouth, and kissed him again, just a sweet, warm, loving brush of her lips to his.

"Don't." Her gentleness was going to undo him. He was vibrating with emotions and pumping adrenaline, and when she looked at him like that, the signals in his brain crossed because he wanted to strip her and take her right here, losing himself in her.

Holding his gaze captive, Kate stood up, pulling him with her. She kept tugging until he was wrapped in her arms.

Ah hell. Dropping his head to her shoulder, he pulled her in tight, because this, this was what he'd come for, and for the first time in his recent memory he let himself take comfort from someone.

From her.

She pressed her lips to his jaw and whispered, "Come with me." She led him along the path. Back through the park, past a sleeping Larry. Then through the woods, along the path to her townhouse, never letting go of his hand.

She could take away his pain, if he let her, at least for a little while. But only a real asshole would let her do that.

And yet when she entangled their fingers and pulled him along like one of her errant pupils, he went inside her townhouse.

And then inside her.

He was gone when Kate woke up. She knew it before she even opened her eyes because when he was in bed with her, his energy took up all space and then some.

She loved that, loved being surrounded by him.

But that energy was gone now. She was alone, and there was a terrifying finality to the feeling. Anxious, she showered quickly and then dove for her phone when it rang. "Griffin."

"Nope," Ryan said. "And you sound way too eager. Do we need to have a how-to-play-hard-to-get discussion?"

Kate blew out a sigh and dressed while holding the phone in the crook of her neck. "What's up?"

"Two days left."

"I know that! I know that better than you!"

"Then what's the hold up?" he asked.

"What's with wanting to get rid of me so badly?" she countered.

"Hey, I don't want to get rid of you. The loss of your presence for a year will leave a huge hole in my heart."

"Aw," she murmured. "Really?"

"No. But if you get this degree, I can get a huge grant for a new science program."

Kate shook her head and disconnected. She shoved her feet into her boots and headed out into the morning rain. It took her ten minutes to get to the ranch. She found Griffin in his bedroom at the ranch, packing. "Whatcha doing?" she asked with what she thought was remarkable calm.

"Going to DC," he said, tossing clothes into a duffel bag.

"DC," she repeated. "For . . . ?"

"A job."

She stared at him, but he never even looked at her. "Huh," she said. "Because yesterday I thought we were going to give this a shot. And then you did me, what? Twice last night? And now you're gone? Just like that?"

He stopped and looked at her then. "You have your thing to go do. We aren't going to tie each other down."

She felt her chest go tight. "You said it wouldn't matter if I went."

"Things change."

This stunned her for a beat. Stunned and hurt. But he was the one hurting, she knew, and he was reacting instead of thinking. "I never viewed you as tying me down. Unless . . ." She infused some playfulness in her voice. "You want to . . ."

"Stop, Kate."

Okay, so he wasn't in a playful mood. Neither was she, actually. "Griffin, don't make a hasty decision."

"It's already made."

If she thought she'd been hurt a minute ago, it was nothing compared to this. He'd already left her. She actually couldn't breathe as she turned to the door to get out, to get away before he could see those emotions she couldn't begin to hide.

He inhaled sharply and then reached out and snagged her. "I'm sorry," he said. "I have to go."

"Because I'm not important enough to be the reason for you to stay?"

"You're important," he said tightly, whipping her around to face him. "You're so damn important to me that I'm actually not sure I can take it."

"You were taking it just fine," she managed to point out.

"Because I thought I knew who I was."

"You still know."

He was already shaking his head. "No, I don't. And I'm done here in Sunshine."

"You mean you're done with us."

He stared at her. "Us?"

"Yes. I actually thought you had real feelings for me."

"I do have real feelings for you," he said. "But I have things to take care of. I have a life to lead. And that life isn't here."

"Why, because you're not Donald Reid's blood?" she asked. "What does that matter? This is your home."

"No," he said with terrifying stillness. "It's not. I don't belong here. I never did."

She stared at him, at the absolute, resolute determination on his face, and she knew she was talking to a brick wall. A brick wall that had just broken her heart. "So. DC?"

"Teaching and training," he said curtly.

"Just like that."

"I've been entertaining offers since I got here, you knew that. Just as you knew I was here for two weeks max, that we could never have been more than a two-week thing."

Bullshit. Such bullshit. "So this is it, then?" she asked. "We're . . . done?"

A muscle ticked in his jaw, nothing more.

She stepped close and put a hand on his chest to feel his heart beating steady and sure beneath her palm, which was reassuring, because for a moment she'd thought maybe he'd turned to stone. "I'm in love with you, Griffin."

He closed his eyes.

"What?" she said quietly. "Do you not want to hear me say it, or do you not want me to feel it?"

"I have nothing to offer you," he said just as quietly. "I'm a soldier, or I was. Now I'm . . . hell. I have no idea, but it's nothing much."

"You offer me the same things you've always offered me," she said. "No one but you has ever taken me outside all the daily grind and responsibility. You make me more than a teacher or a sister. You make me feel sexy and fun. Griffin, when I'm with you, the rest of the world just drops away. It has nothing to do with the fact that you could be dropped anywhere in the world and find the explosives or that you can make a shelter out of nothing. You have value outside of being a soldier. So much."

He was already shaking his head. "Kate—"

"No, please. Please, don't," she said. "I don't want excuses about why you can't love me. I've probably heard it all before."

She started to leave, but he caught her at the door, pinning her between the hard wood and his even harder body. He stood with his chest to her back, a hand holding the door closed on either side of her head. "I love you too, Kate."

Her heart stopped.

"I love you so goddamn much it hurts," he said.

This had her heart starting again, at full speed, thundering in her ears. *Don't overreact*, she told herself. His declaration had clearly been made under extreme emotional duress. On a normal day he'd never have admitted it to her, and she knew it. "But?" she managed. "Because I definitely sense a but at the end of that sentence." She paused, but he didn't say a word, and it hit her so hard that she could only spin to stare at him in shock for a long moment. "I just figured it out," she whispered. "The difference between us."

He just looked at her.

"Yeah, you give off this badass, adventurous vibe," she said. "Like you're up for anything. But you're not."

"Kate—"

"No, it's true. You're only adventurous physically. But not with your heart. That's me," she said. "I'm the adventurous one." God, who'd have thought it? "I'm the one," she repeated, rubbing her aching chest. "Because I'll follow my heart anywhere." She sniffed. "I'd follow it to DC if that's what worked. I'd do whatever it took."

There was a beat of stunned silence, and she had no idea who was more shocked, herself or Griffin.

"Kate," he finally said, sounding raw to the bone. "Your life is here. You love it here. You're going to get your master's and then come back and get married and have kids and a great life. Right here in Sunshine."

"First," she said fiercely, finding her mad. "You don't get to tell me what I'm going to have. And second, I don't necessarily dream of children and a white picket fence." She paused, waiting for him to look at her. "But I dream of you, Griffin."

He opened his mouth and then shut it. Apparently, she'd rendered him speechless.

"I don't want you to plan your life around me," he finally said.

She'd argue that he was worth it, but there was no point. She couldn't make him want this. And even more important, she couldn't take this thing with him backward. She couldn't go from what they'd had these past two weeks, with the crazy need, the lazy lovemaking in the middle of the night when he'd spent hours worshipping every inch of her, back to boundaries and bare-minimum contact. She couldn't pretend to be okay when she knew there was more. He'd ruined her for other men, damn him. "Explain one thing to me," she said. "Explain how you not being Donald Reid's blood is chasing you out of here, out of Sunshine, when you'd decided to stay."

"I told you. I don't belong here now."

"That's just dumb. Sunshine's still your hometown. Nothing changes that. Not even blood."

He let out a low laugh, utterly without mirth. "Even the fucking name of the town . . ." he muttered, and scrubbed a hand over his head. "Look, you love it here," he said. "You love to cook and feed your family and teach the kids, and you're . . . hell, Kate. You are Sunshine. But not me. I was wrong before. I can't . . . I don't fit into this cozy little world; it's not me. It's not my perfect little world like it is yours."

She stared at him. "There is something seriously wrong with you if you think my life is perfect."

"You have a family who loves and adores you."

"You think Donald doesn't love you?"

He shrugged. "I thought I could come here and make it right. But I'm not his son. I'll never be his son."

"Griffin . . . look at who you've become. You're brave and strong and giving and heroic . . . You're the best person

I know. So does it really matter who provided the one-in-a-million sperm that hit the egg?"

He stared at her for a long beat during which time she allowed herself a kernel of hope because she could see things in his gaze. Affection. Need. Even love.

But then that all vanished, and his expression went blank. The soldier's expression. "This wasn't my intention," he said. "Falling for you."

"No?" she asked. "What was your intention?"

He didn't answer her directly. "I got carried away in the moment. You were so . . . open and warm and—"

"Oh my God. If you say sweet," she warned.

A very small smile curved his mouth. "Hot. Smart. Irresistible." His smile made its way to his eyes. "A pain in my ass." He held her gaze. "You're dangerous to me, Kate."

He was a demolitions expert, and he thought she was dangerous. It was a bitter pill, even though she knew exactly what he meant.

She was dangerous to his heart.

Well, join the club, she thought.

"I have to do this," he said. "I have a flight out tomorrow."

"So this is good-bye, then," she said with far more calm than she felt. Stupid man . . .

"We'll see each other," he said.

"When? How?"

"You want a plan?" he asked.

"Yes."

"I can't give you one. We'll be on opposite sides of the country. But there's e-mail," he said. "Skype. Texts."

As sure as she knew she loved him, she also knew she'd never be happy like this. She shook her head. Going to him, she cupped his face, kissed him softly, then headed to the door.

"Kate."

She walked out and he didn't stop her. Driving home on autopilot, she let herself in, slid to the floor, and let herself have a good cry. Then, still sniffling and hiccupping, she went to her computer and did it. She hit Send on her acceptance letter.

She stared at the sent e-mail until it blurred, and then she called Ryan. "Did it."

"Did what?" he asked.

"Sent my acceptance letter."

There was a beat of silence. "Are you crying?" he asked warily

"No."

"Good," he said with a huge sigh of relief.

She burst into tears.

"Ah, Christ," he said. "What the hell happened?"

"Griffin said I was a pain in his ass."

"You're a pain in everyone's ass."

"I b—broke up with him," she sobbed.

There was a pained silence. "Is that why you sent your letter?" he asked.

"No." She swiped her nose on her sleeve. "I want to dissect cow brains."

"Good answer. Do you need anything?"

"If I said yes, would you come over with ice cream?"

"No. But I'd send Holly."

She disconnected.

Twenty-six

H olly showed up at Kate's less than an hour later. Her eyes were as red-rimmed as Kate's, and she held a gallon of ice cream.

"He's still my brother," Holly said.

"Of course he is," Kate said.

"And he's still your . . ." She trailed off when Kate's eyes filled and she shook her head.

"Oh, honey," Holly whispered, reaching for her. "He'll come around."

Again Kate shook her head.

They watched *Friends* season ten on DVD, their go-to stress reliever. Later, after Holly was gone, Kate's phone rang. She allowed her heart to leap into her throat, but it wasn't Griffin. And why would it be? She'd walked away, told him to go. He wouldn't want to cause her any further pain. He'd give her what she asked for.

Damn, stupid, shortsighted, stubborn man.

It was her dad, and he sounded a little stressed as he asked her to come over ASAP. Kate rushed over there and then came to a startled stop in the kitchen when her dad,

Tommy, and Ashley popped up with a cake and yelled, "Surprise!"

Well, Ashley and Tommy yelled *surprise*, her dad yelled *congratulations*, and then he sighed. "We forgot to work on that part." He pushed the lit cake toward Kate. "Ryan told us you'd accepted at UCSD. We're celebrating."

"We didn't burn the cake," Tommy said proudly.

"And it only took three tries," Ashley said.

Kate blew out the candles and tried to smile, but she got all choked up and couldn't talk.

"Uh-oh," Tommy said, and well-versed in women, even at the tender age of seven, he hauled out a box of tissues and gingerly pushed it toward her before escaping the room.

Ashley went to the freezer for ice cream, making Kate laugh through her tears. "I'm okay, Ashley."

"Okay," her sister said, obviously relieved that they didn't have to talk about it. "Well . . . I've gotta . . ." She gestured vaguely to the other room and then vanished.

Kate blew her nose and looked at her dad. "You want to run off, too?"

"Nah. Not much scares me." He paused. "You're still worried about going?"

"No."

"You upset with us?"

"No! Never."

He gave her a long look.

"Okay, sometimes," she admitted, "but that's not it."

"Griffin?" he asked.

She went still and then pulled free.

"Bingo," he said quietly. "You broke up?"

"We weren't ever together, not really."

He looked into her eyes for a long moment. "I see."

She didn't know how he could when she didn't.

"I really hope you're going away for you," he said. "Not because you need to run away."

"I don't need to go anywhere. Griffin's going. To DC for a job—" She broke off when her phone rang.

It was Kel, the local sheriff. "Dustin Anders has gone

missing," he said without preamble. "Do you have any information on where he might be?"

The incident command was set up outside of the Anders's home and, by the time Kate drove home, the search had been organized and was under way.

Trevan grabbed Kate by the arm the second she arrived, dragged her off to the side of the controlled chaos. "He's not with you?" he demanded.

"No. Why would he be?" She struggled to free herself, but he held tight.

"He left the house to see you," Trevan said, low and rough in her ear. His face was hard and carved from stone, his expression dialed to pissed off. "So where the hell did he go?"

She felt a presence at her back and knew without looking that it was Griffin.

"Let go of her," he said with dead calm.

Trevan's eyes darkened, but he let go of Kate.

"Why was Dustin coming to see me?" Kate asked Trevan.

"He'd finished his math and wanted to show you. Wanted to make sure you knew he was trying to pass."

Kel appeared and nodded to Trevan. "Need to ask you a few more questions."

Trevan gave Kate one last hard look and went with Kel. When they were gone, she turned to face Grif.

He had his blank face on.

She didn't have a blank face or anything close to it. Tension shimmered between them. Or maybe that was just her need to smack him. "I had that under control," she said stiffly. "In fact I was just about to use one of the moves you taught me to level him flat as a pancake." She was proud of her even voice when she really just wanted to throw herself into his arms and seek comfort. Griffin gave good comfort.

But he wasn't hers.

"I'd have liked to see that," he said. "Sorry I robbed you of the pleasure."

"You're forgiven." She paused. "For all of it."

"All of it?"

"For you being a complete stubborn ass and all."

"Ah," he said, something funny in his voice that she couldn't quite place. Tension, certainly. Regret? Maybe . . . She tried to figure out what he might be thinking, but she'd never had much luck with that. Her stomach jittered. Nerves, unhappiness, emptiness, pick one.

So this is what it felt like to have a hot fling go bad . . .

"Adam's got a crew in the woods and search dogs," he said. "I'm going to join him."

That's when she realized he was dressed in S&R gear. Nodding, she hugged herself as he started to go. Then he paused. "This isn't your fault," he said.

She shook her head. "You don't know that. Maybe he ran away because of his bad grade in spelling."

"Don't do that, Kate. Don't doubt yourself. You know who you are and what a great teacher you are."

She looked to the woods instead of into his eyes because she was afraid she might break. "Just find him."

She'd never asked him for a single thing, and they both knew it. A muscle in his jaw bunched, but he didn't say anything else before he left.

The street filled with people who wanted to help, including her family, Ryan, Holly and Jade, Donald Reid. Hell, half the town, it seemed. With dark coming, people organized into search groups and fanned out in every possible direction.

And then the unbelievable happened.

Tommy came up missing as well.

It was like a nightmare, a bad *Criminal Minds* episode. One minute he was there, and then the next he was gone. Kate turned in a slow circle on her street, the warm, cozy, wonderful street she'd been so happy living on, as a shiver of dread raced up her spine.

This isn't your fault.

Grif had told her that himself, and he never said anything that wasn't one hundred percent true.

But she still felt responsible.

Tommy had gone after Dustin himself. She knew that. No man left behind, but the thought of him out there in the woods terrified her. She called Griffin.

"I already know," he answered. "I'm on it."

"Your app," she said. "You can find him that way, right?"

"Yes. Kate, I want you to trust me on this. It's going to be okay," he promised, sounding so calm and absolutely confident that she found herself nodding as if he could actually see her. She did trust him. Damn him. She disconnected and then nearly jumped out of her skin when someone slid an arm around her waist.

Ashley.

Her sister smiled wanly at her and handed her a steaming cup of hot chocolate. "You holding up okay?" she asked.

"Yes. It's going to be okay," Kate assured her. "I think Griffin and Adam know where they are."

Ashley nodded. "Just in case, I've got Dad researching all the known trails that fan out from these woods." She made Kate take the mug. "Drink it," she said. "You're cold and the sugar will help."

Kate took a sip, looking at her sister over the lid of the cup.

"I know," Ashley said. "I'm good in an emergency, right? Who knew?" She paused. "They're going to find them. Tommy's going to be okay."

Kate's throat went tight. "I know."

"He has to be." Ashley swallowed hard and looked away. "We've already lost mom. We can't lose him, too."

Kate set the mug down and hugged her sister hard. "We won't." Her phone rang from her back pocket.

"The boys are safe, and physically okay," Adam said.

Kate let out a relieved breath and had to lock her knees. "They're together?"

"Yep. Grif's got them. He just called it into me and wanted me to call you right away. Kel's calling Trevan Anders now."

She hung up and realized Adam had said "physically

okay," which relieved a lot of her angst but certainly not all, not by a long shot. She wanted to go to them but, one, she didn't know where they were, and two, she had Ashley standing there looking terrified. She gave her the news and then they told their dad.

Ashley let down her tough-girl guard to shed a few tears. "I do love that little freakazoid." She clung for a moment. "Kate?"

"Yeah?"

"I don't wanna go away to college." She said this in a rush and then sucked up another breath. "That's your dream, not mine."

Kate squeezed her and pulled back just enough to look into Ashley's eyes. "You've been holding on to that."

"Yeah."

Kate smoothed Ashley's hair back from her face. "Are you ever going to tell me what your dream is?"

"WSU Spokane."

Washington State University was only thirty minutes from home. A good, solid school.

"I could commute," Ashley said. "And stay at home. I love it at home. Is that weird? Wanting to stay close to Dad and Tommy? I just feel like it's my place, you know?"

Kate swallowed the lump in her throat and smiled, then pulled Ashley in tight again. "It's wonderful. I—" She broke off, going still. Her place. "Oh my God." She pulled free.

"What?"

"I know where they are." She should have known sooner. Clearly Griffin had caught on immediately. With "physically okay" echoing in her brain, she took off running around the back of her building to the trail she used for her torture slash exercise. Past the park and Larry's bench.

Larry sat up as she passed.

"Hey," he said. "Popcorn?"

"Later, Larry, I promise!" She kept going, up to the dam, and once there, she pulled out her phone, calling Griffin. She heard it ring in her ear and . . . nearby.

From her place, her spot. Her tree.

She disconnected and stared at Griffin, who pointed up to the tree house.

She craned her neck. "Tommy?" she called. "Dustin?"

There was no movement, but she sensed four eyes peering down at her in the dark. "I know you're up there."

Still nothing, and Griffin just raised a brow at her.

"No one's mad," she said to the silence. "Everyone just wants to see you both." She paused. "Please don't make me climb up there. Because I will, and you both know I hate heights. I might cry all over the both of you."

The beat of silence was short this time, and then there was some rustling. Tommy's face appeared, pale and anxious. "Dustin wants you to pinkie swear that he's not in trouble. Not for this and not for before."

"Before?" Kate asked.

"When he almost got caught by you the last time he hid up here."

Kate went still. "The day of the wedding? When someone ran behind me in the woods? That was Dustin?"

Tommy nodded solemnly.

Kate let out a long, shuddering breath. "Dustin?" she called. "You have no idea how happy I am that it was you that day. You're not in trouble for that. And you're not in trouble now. Pinkie promise."

"You have to come up here to do it," Tommy said.

"Tommy," Kate said. "I'm not going up there. Now get down here. I want a hug, and then I want to smack you upside the head. I am not climbing a tree."

"Have to," Tommy said solemnly.

Kate looked at Griffin. "Can't you do your S&R thing?"

"I already did."

She rolled her eyes and turned her attention to the tree. "I'm in a skirt."

"I won't let you fall," Griffin said.

Famous last words. Because it was far too late. She'd fallen for him a long time ago. But then again, he knew that. He knew everything.

The stubborn ass.

Saying not a single word, he crouched down and put his hands together, fingers laced. A foothold.

A stubborn ass who was still there for her when she needed him. "Are you going to pinkie swear not to look up my skirt?" she asked him.

"I don't make promises."

Of course not. She placed her boot in his hands and her hands on his very capable shoulders. He hoisted her with ease, holding her perfectly still, perfectly steady as she fumbled to pull herself up, knowing the whole damn while he had a view straight up her skirt. She was wearing a peach lace thong today, which was a little bit like wearing nothing at all. Was he kicking himself for what he'd given up? Wishing he'd thrown himself at her feet and declared his undying love? Planning to fling himself to his death now that he'd let her and her peach thong go?

Hopefully all of the above, she thought, and if he got a case of blue balls from the view, she wouldn't mind that either.

As if maybe he'd read her mind, he gave her a sudden, unexpected—and entirely unnecessary—boost, and she fell into the tree house. She sat up and stared at Tommy and Dustin. Dustin's face was streaked with dried tears.

"He hurt his ankle," Tommy said. "Not bad, but it's a little swollen. His dad's going to kill him cuz he has a game tomorrow."

Dustin nodded jerkily, terrified. "I won't be able to play."

"Your dad's worried sick," she said. "He just wants you back safe and sound. You've been gone awhile." She gave Tommy a long look.

"No man left behind," he said in soft apology. He turned to Griffin, who had pulled himself up as well and was in the doorway. "Right, Grif?"

"Right," Griffin said. "Except next time, you call when you're on a mission, secret or otherwise. That rule is just as important as no man left behind. Do you understand?"

"Yes," Tommy said solemnly. "I understand. Incident Command needs to know."

"Exactly," Griffin said.

Kate executed her afore-promised pinkie swear, which turned out to be a complicated handshake that she was pretty sure she couldn't have replicated to save her life. Then she nodded to Griffin.

Around them, the area had filled with the crowd from the street, led by Kel and Trevan, with Donald Reid and the other volunteer searchers right behind.

Her dad was there, grabbing Tommy and hugging him close.

Trevan didn't grab or hug Dustin. "You sprained your ankle?" he demanded, hands on hips. "How are you going to play?"

"Shut up," Emily told her ex-husband, and hugged Dustin so tight he squeaked. "Honey, why did you run away like that?"

Dustin pulled back and looked at his mom. "I don't want to play on the travel team anymore," he said in a tight whisper.

There was an awkward silence in the crowd as Emily whirled on Trevan. "Tell him. Tell him right now that he doesn't have to play."

"Of course he has to play," Trevan said. "We paid for the entire year." Trevan studied Dustin. "You'll be fine to play."

Dustin looked at his feet and nodded.

Trevan looked at Emily. "See? He'll be fine."

Emily made a disgusted sound. "He wants to be a better student. He wants a kitten."

"A kitten," Trevan said, horrified. "Why?"

"Because he's eight," Emily said. "And if you won't stop this madness, then I will. I'm withdrawing my permission for him to play ball."

Dustin looked up at his mom, his expression both shocked and hopeful. She hugged him again. "It's over," she said. "I promise you."

Trevan swore in disgust, turned on his heel, and strode off.

Kate let out a breath and glanced at her dad, who was still hugging Tommy close. At the sight her throat tightened and her eyes burned with tears. She'd never been so thankful for him, imperfections and all.

With the drama over, people were heading back to their cars. She watched as Griffin turned and looked at his own father. Was he as moved by all that had transpired as she'd been?

Griffin stilled then frowned. "Dad?"

Donald's complexion was seriously off-color, and even as the thought registered in Kate's mind, Donald staggered back, bumping into Adam and Holly.

"Dad," Grif said more loudly, and ran toward him, getting there in time to catch the older Reid as he collapsed.

Twenty-seven

G rif got to the hospital just behind the ambulance and experienced a terrible déjà vu as he strode inside.

Only a few months ago he'd been in a different hospital on the other side of the world. Alone. At the time, he'd told himself it was for the best. He hadn't wanted anyone pacing the ER wondering if he was going to live or die.

Now he was on the other side of the fence, surrounded by the people who'd meant the most to him for much of his life.

Holly and Adam sat a short distance away. Adam had an arm around Holly, his mouth pressed to her temple, whispering something that had her nodding, meeting his eyes with gratitude and love.

There were lots of others nearby as well, including much of the ranch staff. And Deanna. She was a mess, sobbing all over her sister, and on Grif, too, when he tried to console her.

"He's going to be okay," he said.

She clung to him, her head on his shoulder. "I know."

"He's too ornery to die."

Now she both cried and laughed. "I know that, too. Grif . . ." She pulled back, her mascara smeared, her eyes filled with genuine grief. "He loves you. You know that, right?"

"Yeah," he said, knowing that's what she wanted to hear. Because he had no idea what he knew.

Kate was there, too. She'd set aside whatever she thought of him and had insisted on coming with him to the hospital. She brought him a bottle of water and sat next to him quietly, not expecting him to talk.

So he had no idea why he did. "The last things I said to him," he started, remembering their fight in the office. Christ. He was such an asshole. He shook his head, unable to speak past the lump in his throat.

Kate's hand closed over his. "He's got quite a way with words himself," she said quietly but with irony thick in her voice. "I'm sure he gave as good as he got." She squeezed his hand, and he met her gaze.

She didn't smile, offer any empty platitudes, or even try to keep his attention. She simply sat at his side and gave him all the strength she had to share. Grateful, knowing he wasn't worthy of that strength, he closed his eyes and leaned back to wait, incredibly aware of their entwined fingers.

He then spent the longest three hours of his life waiting for a report, and when it came, it wasn't surprising.

His dad had indeed suffered a second heart attack, and though the general consensus was that it was another mild one, it wasn't good news. When he was finally cleared for visitors, they were told only two at a time. Grif let Holly and Adam go first. Now that Grif knew Donald was out of the woods, he wasn't in all that big of a hurry to piss him off and maybe make things worse.

A little while later, Holly and Adam came back out. Holly pulled Grif to his feet, and holding his hands, she looked up at him. Her eyes were red but she smiled. "He's going to be okay."

"Good."

"He's asking for you."

Grif gave a slow shake of his head. "Not a good idea, Hol."

"It's the best idea." Going up on tiptoe, she kissed his cheek. "You're family, Grif," she whispered against his jaw. "You always have been; you always will be. For better or worse." She kissed him again. "He's asking for you," she repeated softly.

Grif was halfway down the hall to ICU before he realized he was still gripping Kate's hand tightly and that she was practically running at his side to keep up with his long-legged stride.

He slowed his steps and tried to let go of her hand.

She held tight.

She gave him a small but genuine smile, and he realized it was him holding on to her.

They entered his father's hospital room. Donald opened his eyes and managed a charming smile for Kate, who bent over him and kissed his cheek. "Gave us a scare," she said lightly.

"Ah, you should know better," Donald murmured, voice raspy. "I'm far too handsome to die."

"You mean ornery, don't you?" she teased.

He winked at her. "You know it." He squeezed her fingers. "Darlin', would you mind giving me and the boy a minute?"

"Not at all." Kate hugged him then hugged Grif as well.

Grif almost didn't let go. When she was gone, he walked to the side of the bed. The last words he and Donald had spoken to each other bounced around in his head uncomfortably. At the time he'd thought if he never had to speak another word to this stubborn old coot again, it would be too soon. Now there was too much to say, and he didn't know where to start.

A nurse popped her head in. "Only a few minutes," she said sternly. "He needs rest."

Grif nodded.

"Keep him calm. No riling him up."

Grif nodded again, but he'd have better luck walking to the moon. If he so much as breathed, he riled the man up. Bracing himself, he sat in the chair by the bed. "You in any pain?"

"Yes. But not in the way you think." Donald shifted around and swore.

Grif stood again, leaning over him to hold him still. "Don't move. You're not supposed to move."

"Dad," Donald snapped. "Would it kill you to still call me dad?"

Grif stilled.

"And sit for crissake. If you're going to hover over me like a grandma, then just get the hell out now."

Grif lowered himself back to the chair. "I see all that go-go juice is making you sweet and affable," he said, nodding to the multiple IVs.

Donald actually smiled at that. "There you are. My cynical, sarcastic son. Was worried you'd already left."

Grif bent forward, planted his elbows on his knees, and rubbed his temples.

"Headache?" Donald asked.

"If I say yes, will you lie back and relax before your nurse guts me?"

"In a minute," Donald said, and his voice changed, going very serious, "Nurse Ratchet's going to come back and drug me again so listen carefully because I'm not going to be able to repeat myself." He drew in a deep breath and paused.

Grif braced himself, having no idea what he expected to hear. Get the hell out of Dodge, maybe?

"When I met your mom," Donald said, "she was just pregnant."

"You told me that already."

"She put my name on your birth certificate."

"Yes, I've seen it."

"Jesus, I said listen, not talk." Donald sighed. "I loved her. I loved her more than anything or anyone since."

"You two fought all the time."

"She hated Idaho," Donald admitted. "She went back to New York, and after that we got along again."

"From two thousand miles away."

"It worked for us," Donald said. "I kept her secret. And I'd do it again in a heartbeat." He paused. "Or for as long as this heart will beat," he added dryly, meeting Grif's gaze. "I did it for her, but that doesn't mean I didn't love you as my own. I did. Even when you were a punk-ass. And I should get extra credit for that, by the way. Because you were a punk-ass. You really were one hard fucker to love."

Grif dropped his head between his shoulder blades and let out a low laugh. It was true. He was a hard fucker to love.

"Anyway," Donald went on. "If all you want to remember is me not telling you a secret I'd promised to hold, then the hell with you. I didn't tell you because it didn't matter; it didn't change anything. We are father and son." His eyes were sharp and penetrating. "You get me?"

Grif nodded. "I get you."

Donald held his gaze for a long beat and then gave one short nod. "There's more."

Grif braced himself.

"Whoever you're biological dad was, he knocked your mom up and left her. That's on him, not you. And you're not just his. You're a product of environment, which means you have the mountains in your blood. The ranch in your blood. And me. Goddammit, you have me."

Grif couldn't have spoken to save his life, he was that shocked. And moved.

And when Donald reached out, Grif grasped his father's hand tightly.

"You were never my dirty secret," Donald said in that same voice that had flayed Grif alive more times than he could count. "And if you felt like you were, well, that's on me. I thought of you as mine. And that's the biggest reason I kept the secret. The angry, pissed-off teenage Grif couldn't have handled the truth. He'd have left and never come back."

Grif absolutely knew that to be true. He squeezed his dad's fingers and then leaned over him again, this time for a hug.

The last week of school flew by so much faster than Kate could have imagined. It was a blur of packing, end-of-year celebrations, and family time.

No Griffin time though.

He hadn't left ASAP as planned, instead staying until his dad was out of the hospital and well on his way to a full recovery. She hadn't actively avoided him, but their paths hadn't crossed. And she couldn't help but notice he hadn't actively sought her out either.

Clearly there was nothing to say.

She'd made the big decision to go to UCSD immediately. She'd gotten an off-campus studio apartment and was going to take a full summer course load to get a jump start on her curriculum. She was starting next week.

Once she'd made the decision to go, she was ready. No looking back. Looking back made her heart hurt. She'd miss her family and friends, but she'd see them. They'd come to visit, and she would do the same. It was going to be good for all of them, and she'd be back. That wasn't what hurt.

No, what hurt was knowing that she'd gambled on Griffin.

And lost.

Grif and Adam sat on their respective ATVs at the top of the ridge, staring down at the valley below. It was just past the ass crack of dawn and steam was rising from the rocky land as the sun slanted over the peaks.

"Going to miss any of it?" Adam asked.

Like a limb. "Maybe."

Adam gave a small smile. "Liar."

Grif shrugged. "It's the way it is."

"It didn't have to go this way."

"Got to have work," Grif said.

"Could have found work less than two thousand miles away."

This wasn't anything Grif hadn't said to himself a million times over the past week. "I'm not going to be all that far."

"Would you be going if Kate wasn't?"

Grif hesitated. "I don't know."

"Yeah, you do," Adam said.

Yeah, he did.

"Look," Adam said. "I'm the guy no one expected to find happiness with a woman. But I did."

"So what are you saying?"

"That if I can, anyone can," Adam said.

Grif slid him a look. "You needed a woman to be happy?"

"Don't piss me off," Adam said mildly. "You know what I'm talking about."

Yeah, he did. From the moment he'd first seen Kate again the weekend of Adam and Holly's wedding, he'd been on a crazy ride. At first he'd actually been cocky enough to think Kate couldn't possibly give him anything other than a good time.

But she'd given him a hell of a lot more than that. For whatever reason, she'd seen something in him that she'd wanted, and she'd gone for it. She'd believed in him. She'd given him so damn much. She'd given him all of herself, every corner of her heart and soul.

He'd taken both, without giving a thing in return. And then, when the going had gotten tough, he'd tossed it all aside. He'd change that if he could, but he had no right to her now. None. "I'm not going to be the guy to hold her back."

"So don't."

Grif thought about that and realized Adam was right. When Grif had come for the wedding, it had been with wariness and no expectations. Things had been black and white. He'd been hurt. He'd just gotten out of the military for the first time in his adult life. Neither of those things had been by choice.

But coming back here had been a choice. His first in a string of good choices, he knew now. His second good choice had been Kate.

Ah, who the hell was he kidding? He hadn't been smart enough to pick her. She'd picked him. He'd gotten lucky is all. She'd picked him, and then she'd added color to the black and white that was his world. She'd added dimension. She'd added . . . life.

And now that life didn't work without her in it.

"I screwed things up," he admitted.

Adam shrugged. "Fix 'em."

"It's not that easy."

Adam slid him a glance. "No shit."

It took him another few days, but Grif figured out what he had to do.

Grovel.

He knocked on Kate's door armed with what he hoped was an irresistible bribe. Ice cream. He'd added a card to the bag and hoped for the best.

Kate opened the door looking a little harried in faded jeans, a long-sleeved T-shirt that he was pretty sure was his, and bare feet. She stared at him.

"Hey," he said, and thrust out the bag.

She looked into it.

"It's double fudge," he said.

She pulled out the card. It had a heart on the front but was blank on the inside because he'd forgotten to sign it. She looked up at him.

He grimaced. "I meant to write on that."

This sparked some interest. "What were you going to write?" she asked.

Good question. He tried to see past her, but she was blocking his way in. "Maybe we can do this inside."

"Do what?"

"Talk."

She gave him a bad moment when she hesitated, but she did eventually step aside and gesture him in. "How's your dad?" she asked.

"Fine." He nodded. Christ, he was an idiot. "He's going to be okay."

"And you and your dad together?"

He blew out a breath. "We're going to be okay, too." He paused, hesitated really, which he rarely did, but he was feeling way out of his league. "I'm sorry for pushing you away, Kate. Everything I said about how I feel about you is true," he said.

She nodded, and then . . . turned and walked off.

After a beat of hesitation, he followed her to her room. She was sitting on her bed looking down at her tightly clasped hands. "Even the pain-in-the-ass part?" she asked.

He let out a small smile. "Maybe especially that part." He crouched in front of her and put his hands on her thighs. "Kate."

She looked at him.

"I love you, Kate."

Her eyes filled, but no tears fell.

"And I didn't just get carried away in the moment," he said. "I was with you because I wanted to be. I was wrong and—" He paused as she pushed him away and continued on with her packing as if he hadn't spoken. Packing everything including her snow boots. Huh. He stared at her suitcase. "Does it snow in San Diego?"

She parlayed this with a question of her own. "You still taking that job in DC?"

"Yes."

She fell quiet. He was so used to her chattering, the silence seemed wrong.

She zipped the huge suitcase and nodded. "You'll be happier there."

"Kate—"

"I don't think there's anything left to say. We were a thing, a hot one, but it burned out."

He actually looked down at himself to see if he was bleeding.

"It's over," she said quietly.

"It'll never be over," he said. "A part of us will always care no matter where we are or what we're doing."

She turned away at that, neither denying nor confirming his words. "Good-bye, Griffin," she said instead, politely moving back to her front door and holding it open for him.

Grif drove home. He wasn't sure how long he sat in his truck like a shell-shocked idiot, thinking so hard his windows fogged.

He knew he'd let Kate down, but damn. It couldn't be too late. He could still become the man she thought him, no matter whose blood flowed through his veins. Pulling out his phone, he punched in a number. When Joe answered, Grif didn't hesitate. "About the job."

One week later, Kate entered her tiny studio flat after her first day of school, dropped her books, kicked off her shoes, and then went perfectly still.

There was a man sitting on the small love seat.

Griffin.

He rose and immediately dwarfed the living room. He pulled her heavy bag from her shoulder and let it fall. Then he tugged off her sunglasses. He didn't smile at her gaping shock. He just looked at her, very serious.

"What are you doing here?" she whispered.

"Looking at you. You're a sight for sore eyes, Kate."

Her heart was pounding so loudly she barely heard herself say, "How long are you going to look at me?"

He smiled then, as if she were being funny. "Long as you'll let me," he said.

"And then?"

"And then I'm hoping you'll let me put my hands on you."

Oh God, it was too much, and she turned from him to

take a badly needed moment. But now she was facing the small mirror over her desk, and she couldn't handle looking at her reflection, seeing Griffin behind her. Gripping the desk for desperately needed balance, she bowed her head.

He came up behind her. Circling an arm around her waist, he kissed her just beneath her ear. The feel of him, the scent of him, everything about his nearness made her weak in the knees. Her eyes drifted shut, and she very nearly tilted her head to give him better access, but she controlled herself. Still, there was no holding in her moan. She'd missed him so much, too much. "Griffin."

"Missed you, Kate," he murmured.

For a moment she closed her eyes, allowing herself to savor the sensation of his embrace, but she couldn't let him do this to her, refused to let him destroy her again. Lifting her head, she met his gaze in the mirror. "Why aren't you in DC?"

"Decided against the bitch of a commute," he said lightly.

She wasn't amused. "I don't understand." And she wanted to understand. She needed to understand.

"I didn't take the job," he said. "I don't care about it. You're the only thing I care about, Kate." He smiled a bit wryly. "I'd move to the moon to be with you. Or, as it turns out, San Diego."

They were surrounded by the complications of her new life, and yet he still managed to make it all sound so simple. She closed her eyes again, but Griffin cupped her face, waiting her out.

"You caught me off guard," he said when she opened them again. "Knocked my sorry ass for a loop the way you reeled me in."

"I reeled you in?"

He laughed. "In the best way. You embraced me, compromised me . . . loved me."

Kate couldn't speak. She could scarcely breathe. "I also seduced you."

"My favorite part," he said. "When I got hurt, I went to Sunshine because it was 'home,' but I was wrong. Home is wherever you are, Kate."

Her heart squeezed tight, so damn tight that she couldn't talk, and Griffin studied her for a long beat. "If you're not ready for this," he said quietly, braced for something. "Just tell me."

Rejection. He was putting on a good show, but he wasn't sure about his reception here in her world. "There's no ranch here to run," she said. "What will you do?"

He shrugged. "I like the beach. Always did think I'd make a great lifeguard."

She stared at him. He remained utterly still for her inspection, his eyes unwavering and intense, and . . . vulnerable.

No, he was nowhere near as laid-back as he wanted her to believe. In fact, she was pretty sure he wasn't breathing, waiting on a response from her. "You'd move here for me," she said cautiously, needing this spelled out.

He gestured to a pack on the floor near the love seat. "Already did."

"Just for me," she murmured, marveling at the truth of it. Turning to face him, she sighed in pleasure as his warm, strong arms closed tightly around her. "For my dream . . . Oh, Griffin."

"Is that 'oh, Griffin, how romantic' or 'oh, Griffin, you're an idiot'?"

"Both, but mostly the first."

He chuckled, the sound raw with relief as he rubbed his jaw against hers. Then he buried his face in her hair, letting out a long, ragged breath that seemed to come from the very bottom of his heart and soul. "About your dream," he said. "I was hoping it might include me."

She slid her fingers into his silky hair and lifted his head so she could see his face. "It always has."

He stared into her eyes as the tension seemed to drain from him. "Always," he breathed. "I like the sound of that word from you." He stroked a hand down her back and then up again, fingers spread wide as if he needed to touch as much of her as possible.

"Griffin," she said softly, having the exact same need. "Tell me you love me now."

"I love you now," he said, never taking his gaze from hers, giving her a promise, a vow. Giving her everything she'd ever wanted. "I love you always."

Epilogue

One Year Later

Kate came back to Sunshine with a lot less fanfare than she'd left. She stood at the top of the dam, a light wind blowing her hair back from her face as she stared down at the lake far below.

A big, warm, callused palm slid into hers. With a smile she entwined her fingers with Griffin's. They'd just spent the past few days driving back from San Diego. Wanting one last moment to themselves before they met up with both of their families waiting for them at the ranch, they'd stopped here at Kate's place.

"You okay?" he asked.

She drew in a deep breath and smiled up into his tanned face. It had been the best year of her life. "I don't remember ever being better."

He gave her a smile. "It was a good year," he said. "But I'm thinking it's time to change things up a bit."

"We're moving back to Sunshine," she said. "I've got my

job at the school, and you were just hired on at the local ATF office. How much more can we change things up?"

He stroked the hair from her face. "Well, for starters, you could be my wife."

She went utterly still. "Are you asking me to marry you?"

"Too soon?" he asked.

The lump got bigger, and her heart swelled up against her ribcage. "No," she said, pulling his mouth to hers. "It's perfect."

Dear Reader,

Did you know Rumor Has It *isn't the only book in the Animal Magnetism series? It all started with* Animal Magnetism. *The idea for that book hit me one day when I was grocery shopping. I was trying to figure out what I wanted to write next when I ran into a guy in army gear in the cookie aisle. Be still my heart. He had on dark sunglasses, absolutely no smile, and testosterone was pouring off him.*

He ultimately chose two packages of granola bars instead of cookies, which nearly killed the fantasy, but I recovered. By the time I'd gotten to my car, I'd concocted a whole backstory for him. And just like that, Animal Magnetism *was born.*

Brady Miller doesn't smile much because he hasn't had anything to smile about in a very long time. He's an ex–army ranger, now a pilot for hire for organizations like Doctors Without Borders, back in the States at the request of his foster brothers. They run a large animal center in the middle of Nowhere, Idaho, and need his help.

He agrees to stick around for unusually complicated reasons, even though he's lived his life as purposely uncomplicated as possible. Fact is, he's not much of a family guy. He's always been a wanderer, no roots, no home base.

Maybe even a guy who can't be saved.

It takes a village to show him the truth, including one silly little puppy and one sharp-tongued, sharp-witted heroine willing to knock him flat on his ass to make sure he gets it—that he was never lost at all, and as the saying goes, home is where the heart is . . .

Turn the page to read the first chapter of Animal Magnetism. *And after Brady's story, read his foster brothers' stories in* Animal Attraction *and* Rescue My Heart. *And the series isn't over. More coming, so stay tuned. Meanwhile, I'm back in the grocery store looking for more inspiration.*

Happy reading!
Jill Shalvis

B rady Miller's ideal Saturday was pretty simple—sleep in, be woken by a hot, naked woman for sex, followed by a breakfast that he didn't have to cook.

On this particularly early June Saturday, he consoled himself with one out of the three, stopping at 7-Eleven for coffee, two egg-and-sausage breakfast wraps, and a Snickers bar.

Breakfast of champions.

Heading to the counter to check out, he nodded to the convenience store clerk.

She had her Bluetooth in her ear, presumably connected to the cell phone glowing in her pocket as she rang him up. "He can't help it, Kim," she was saying. "He's a *guy*." At this, she sent Brady a half-apologetic, half-commiserating smile. She was twentysomething, wearing spray-painted-on skinny jeans, a white wife-beater tank top revealing black lacy bra straps, and so much mascara that Brady had no idea how she kept her eyes open.

"You know what they say," she went on as she scanned his items. "A guy thinks about sex once every eight seconds.

No, it's true, I read it in *Cosmo*. Uh-huh, hang on." She glanced at Brady, pursing her glossy lips. "Hey, cutie, you're a guy."

"Last I checked."

She popped her gum and grinned at him. "Would you say you think about sex every eight seconds?"

"Nah." Every ten, tops. He fished through his pocket for cash.

"My customer says no," she said into her phone, sounding disappointed. "But *Cosmo* said a man might deny it out of self-preservation. And in any case, how can you trust a guy who has sex on the brain 24/7?"

Brady nodded to the truth of that statement and accepted his change. Gathering his breakfast, he stepped outside where he was hit by the fresh morning air of the rugged, majestic Idaho Bitterroot mountain range. Quite a change from the stifling airlessness of the Middle East or the bitter desolation and frigid temps of Afghanistan. But being back on friendly soil was new enough that his eyes still automatically swept his immediate surroundings.

Always a soldier, his last girlfriend had complained.

And that was probably true. It was who he was, the discipline and carefulness deeply engrained, and he didn't see that changing anytime soon. Noting nothing that required his immediate attention, he went back to mainlining his caffeine. Sighing in sheer pleasure, he took a big bite of the first breakfast wrap, then hissed out a sharp breath because damn. *Hot.* This didn't slow him down much. He was so hungry his legs felt hollow. In spite of the threat of scalding his tongue to the roof of his mouth, he sucked down nearly the entire thing before he began to relax.

Traffic was nonexistent, but Sunshine, Idaho, wasn't exactly hopping. It had been a damn long time since he'd been here, *years* in fact. And longer still since he'd wanted to be here. He took another drag of fresh air. Hard to believe, but he'd actually missed the good old US of A. He'd missed the sports. He'd missed the women. He'd missed the price of gas. He'd missed free will.

But mostly he'd missed the food. He tossed the wrapper from the first breakfast wrap into a trash bin and started in on his second, feeling almost . . . content. Yeah, damn it was good to be back, even if he was only here temporarily, as a favor. Hell, anything without third-world starvation, terrorists, or snipers and bombs would be a five-star vacation.

"Look out, incoming!"

At the warning, Brady deftly stepped out of the path of the bike barreling down at him.

"Sorry!" the kid yelled back.

Up until yesterday, a shout like that would have meant dropping to the ground, covering his head, and hoping for the best. Since there were no enemy insurgents, Brady merely raised the hand still gripping his coffee in a friendly salute. "No problem."

But the kid was already long gone, and Brady shook his head. The quiet was amazing, and he took in the oak tree–lined sidewalks, the clean and neat little shops, galleries and cafés—all designed to bring in some tourist money to subsidize the mining and ranching community. For someone who'd spent so much time in places where grime and suffering trumped hope and joy, it felt a little bit like landing in the Twilight Zone.

"Easy now, Duchess."

At the soft, feminine voice, Brady turned and looked into the eyes of a woman walking a . . . hell, he had no idea. The thing pranced around like it had a stick up its ass.

Okay, a dog. He was pretty sure.

The woman smiled at Brady. "Hello, how are you?"

"Fine, thanks," he responded automatically, but she hadn't slowed her pace.

Just being polite, he thought, and tried to remember the concept. Culture shock, he decided. He was suffering from a hell of a culture shock. Probably he should have given himself some time to adjust before doing this, before coming here of all places, but it was too late now.

Besides, he'd put it off long enough. He'd been asked to come, multiple times over the years. He'd employed every tactic at his disposal: avoiding, evading, ignoring, but nothing worked with the two people on the planet more stubborn than him.

His brothers.

Not blood brothers, but that didn't appear to matter to Dell or Adam. The three of them had been in the same foster home for two years about a million years ago. Twenty-four months. A blink of an eye really. But to Dell and Adam, it had been enough to bond the three of them for life.

Brady stuffed in another bite of his second breakfast wrap, added coffee, and squinted in the bright June sunshine. Jerking his chin down, the sunglasses on top of his head obligingly slipped to his nose.

Better.

He headed to his truck parked at the corner but stopped short just in time to watch a woman in an old Jeep rear-end it.

"Crap. Crap." Lilah Young stared at the truck she'd just rear-ended and gave herself exactly two seconds to have a pity party. This is what her life had come to. She had to work in increments of seconds.

A wet, warm tongue laved her hand and she looked over at the three wriggling little bodies in the box on the passenger's seat of her Jeep.

Two puppies and a potbellied pig.

As the co-owner of the sole kennel in town, she was babysitting Mrs. Swanson's "babies" again today, which included pickup and drop-off services. This was in part because Mrs. Swanson was married to the doctor who'd delivered Lilah twenty-eight years ago, but also because Mrs. Swanson was the mother of Lilah's favorite ex-boyfriend.

Not that Lilah had a lot of exes. Only two.

Okay, three. But one of them didn't count, the one who after four years she *still* hoped all of his good parts shriveled up and fell off. And he'd had good parts, too, damn him. She'd read somewhere that every woman got a freebie stupid mistake when it came to men. She liked that. She only wished it applied to everything in life.

Because driving with Mrs. Swanson's babies and—

"Quack-quack!" said the mallard duck loose in the backseat.

A mallard duck loose in the backseat had been a doozy of a mistake.

Resisting the urge to thunk her head against the steering wheel, Lilah hopped out of the Jeep to check the damage she'd caused to the truck, eyes squinted because everyone knew that helped.

The truck's bumper sported a sizable dent and crack, but thanks to the tow hitch, there was no real obvious frame damage. The realization brought a rush of relief so great her knees wobbled.

That is until she caught sight of the front of her Jeep. It was so ancient that it was hard to tell if it had ever really been red once upon a time or if it was just one big friggin' rust bucket, but that no longer seemed important given that her front end was mashed up.

"Quack-quack." In the backseat, Abigail was flapping her wings, getting enough lift to stick her head out the window.

Lilah put her hand on the duck's face and gently pressed her back inside. "Stay."

"Quack—"

"*Stay.*" Wanting to make sure the Jeep would start before she began the task of either looking for the truck's owner or leaving a note, Lilah hopped behind the wheel. She never should have turned off the engine because her starter had been trying to die for several weeks now. She'd be lucky to get it running again. Beside her, the puppies and piglet were wriggling like crazy, whimpering and panting as they scrambled to stand on each other, trying to escape their box. She took a minute to pat them all, soothing them, and then with her sole thought being *Please start*, she turned the ignition key.

And got only an ominous click.

"Come on, baby," she coaxed, trying again. "There's no New Transportation budget, so *please* come on . . ."

Nothing.

"Pretty sure you killed it."

With a gasp, she turned her head. A man stood there. Tall, broad-shouldered, with dark brown hair that was cut short and slightly spiky, like maybe he hadn't bothered to do much with it after his last shower except run his fingers through it. His clothes were simple: cargoes and a plain shirt, both emphasizing a leanly muscled body so completely devoid of body fat that it would have made any woman sigh—if she hadn't just rear-ended a truck.

Probably *his truck*.

Having clearly just come out of the convenience store, he held a large coffee and what smelled deliriously, deliciously like an egg-and-sausage-and-cheese breakfast wrap.

Be still, her hungry heart . . .

"Quack-quack."

"Hush, Abigail," Lilah murmured, flicking the duck a glance in the rearview mirror before turning back to the man.

His eyes were hidden behind reflective sunglasses, but she had no doubt they were on her. She could feel them, sharp and assessing. Everything about his carriage said military or cop. She wasn't sure if that was good or bad. He was a stranger to her, and there weren't that many of them in Sunshine. Or anywhere in Idaho for that matter. "Your truck?" she asked, fingers crossed that he'd say no.

"Yep." He popped the last of the breakfast wrap in his mouth and calmly tossed the wrapper into the trash can a good ten feet away. Chewing thoughtfully, he swallowed and then sucked down some coffee.

Just the scent of it had her sighing in jealousy. Probably, she shouldn't have skipped breakfast. And just as probably, she'd give a body part up for that coffee. Hell, she'd give up *two* for the candy bar sticking out of his shirt pocket. Just thinking about it had her stomach rumbling loud as thunder. She looked upward to see if she could blame the sound on an impending storm, but for the first time in two weeks there wasn't a cloud in the sky. "I'm sorry," she said. "About this."

He pushed the sunglasses to the top of his head, further disheveling his hair—not that he appeared to care.

"Luckily the damage seems to be mostly to my Jeep," she went on.

Sharp blue eyes held hers. "Karma?"

"Actually, I don't believe in karma." Nope, she believed in making one's own fate—which she'd done by once again studying too late into the night, not getting enough sleep, and . . . crashing into his truck.

"Hmm." He sipped some more coffee, and she told herself that leaping out of the Jeep to snatch it from his hands would be bad form.

"How about felony hit-and-run?" he asked conversationally. "You believe in that?"

"I wasn't running off."

"Because you can't," he ever so helpfully pointed out. "The Jeep's dead."

"Yes, but . . ." She broke off, realizing how it must look to him. He'd found her behind her own wheel, cursing her vehicle for not starting. He couldn't know that she'd never just leave the scene of an accident. Most likely he'd taken one look at the panic surely all over her face and assumed the worst about her.

The panic doubled. And also, her pity party was back, and for a beat, she let the despair rise from her gut and block her throat, where it threatened to choke her. With a bone-deep weary sigh, she dropped her head to the steering wheel.

"Hey. *Hey.*" Suddenly he was at her side. "Did you hit your head?"

"No, I—"

But before she could finish that sentence, he opened the Jeep door and crouched at her side, looking her over.

"I'm fine. Really," she promised when he cupped and lifted her face to his, staring into her eyes, making her squirm like the babies in the box next to her.

"How many fingers am I holding up?" A quiet demand. His hand was big, the two fingers he held up long. His eyes were calmly intense, his mouth grim. He hadn't shaved that morning she noted inanely, maybe not the day before either, but the scruff only made him seem all the more . . . male.

"Two," she whispered.

Nodding, he dropped his gaze to run over her body. She had dressed for work this morning, which included cleaning out the kennels, so she wore a denim jacket over a T-shirt, baggy Carhartts, boots, and a knit cap to cover her hair.

To say she wasn't looking ready for her close-up was the understatement of the year. "Do you think you can close the door before—"

Too late.

Sensing a means of escape, Abigail started flapping her wings, attempting to fly out past Lilah's face.

She nearly made it, too, but the man, still hunkered at Lilah's side, caught the duck.

By the neck.

"*Gak,*" said a strangled Abigail.

"Don't hurt her!" Lilah cried.

With what might have been a very small smile playing at the corners of his mouth, the man leaned past Lilah and settled the duck on the passenger floorboard.

"Stay," he said in a low-pitched, authoritative voice that brooked no argument.

Lilah opened her mouth to tell him that ducks didn't follow directions, but Abigail totally did. She not only stayed, she shut up. Probably afraid she'd be roasted duck if she didn't. Staring at the brown-headed, orange-footed duck in shock, she said, "I really am sorry about your truck. I'll give you my number so I can pay for damages."

"You could just give me your insurance info."

Her insurance. *Damn.* The rates would go up this time, for sure. Hell, they'd gone up last quarter when she'd had that little run-in with her own mailbox.

But that one hadn't been her fault. The snake she'd been transporting had gotten loose and startled her, and she'd accidentally aligned her front bumper with the mailbox.

But today, this one—definitely her fault.

"Let me guess," he said dryly when she sat there nibbling on her lip. "You don't have insurance."

"No, I do." To prove it, she reached for her wallet, which she kept between the two front seats. Except, of course, it wasn't there. "Hang on, I know I have it . . ." Twisting, she searched the floor, beneath the box of puppies and piglet, in the backseat . . .

And then she remembered.

In her hurry to pick up Mrs. Swanson's animals on time, she'd left it in her office at the kennels. "Okay, this looks bad but I left my wallet at home."

His expression was dialed into Resignation.

"I swear," she said. "I really do have insurance. I just got the new certificate and I put it in my wallet to stick in my glove box, but I hadn't gotten to that yet. I'll give you my number and you can call me for the information."

He gazed at her steadily. "You have a name?"

"Lilah." She scrounged around for a piece of paper. Nothing, of course. But she did find five bucks and the earring she'd thought that Abigail had eaten, and a pen.

Still crouched at her side, the man held out his cell phone. Impossibly aware of how big he was, how very good looking, not to mention how he surrounded her still crouched at her side balanced easily on the balls of his feet, she entered her number into his phone. When it came to keying in her name, she nearly titled herself Dumbass of the Day.

"You fake-numbering me, Lilah?" he asked softly, still close, so very close.

"No." This came out as a squeak so she cleared her throat. And, when he just looked at her, she added truthfully, "I only fake-number the jerk tourists inside Crystal's, the ones who won't take no for an answer."

"Crystal's?"

"The bar down the street. Listen, you might want to wait

awhile before you call me. It's going to take me at least an hour to get home." *Carrying the mewling, wriggling babies* and *walking a duck.*

He paused, utterly motionless in a way that she admired, since she'd never managed to sit still for longer than two minutes. Okay, thirty seconds, but who was counting. "What?" she asked.

"I'm just trying to figure out if you're for real or if you're a master bullshit specialist."

That surprised a laugh out of her. "Well, I *can* be a master bullshit specialist," she admitted. "But I'm not bullshitting you right now."

He studied her face for another long moment, then nodded. "Fine, I'll wait to call you. You going to ask my name?"

Her gaze ran over his very masculine features, then dropped traitorously to linger over his very fine body for a single beat. "I was really sort of hoping that I wasn't going to need it."

He laughed, the sound washing over her and making something low in her belly quiver again.

"Okay, yes," she said. "I want to know your name."

"Brady Miller."

A flicker of something went through her, like the name should mean something to her, but discombobulated as she was, she couldn't concentrate. "Well, Brady Miller, thanks for being patient with me." She reached for Abigail's leash, attaching it to the collar around the duck's neck.

"Quack."

"Shh." Then she grabbed the box of babies. It was damn heavy, but she had her dignity to consider so she soldiered on, turning to get out of the Jeep, bumping right into Brady's broad chest. "Excuse me."

He straightened to his full height and backed up enough to let her out, helping her support the box with an ease that had her envying his muscles now instead of drooling over them.

Actually, that was a lie. She managed both the envying and the drooling. She was an excellent multitasker.

"You're really going to walk?" he asked, rubbing his chin as he considered the box.

"Well, when I skip or run, Abigail's leash gets tangled in my legs."

"Smart-ass." Brady peered at the two puppies and pot-bellied piglet. To his credit, he didn't so much as blink. "They potty trained?"

"No."

He grimaced. "How about the duck?"

"She'd say yes, but she'd be lying."

He exhaled. "That's what I was afraid of." He took the box from her, the underside of his arms brushing the outside of hers.

He was warm. And smelled delicious. Like sexy man and something even better—breakfast wraps and coffee.

"What are you doing?"

"Giving you a ride." He narrowed his eyes at the duck on the leash. "You," he said, "behave."

"Quack."

Without another word, Brady strode to his truck and put the box inside.

Lilah looked down at Abigail. "You heard him," she whispered, having no choice but to follow. "Behave."

Photo by ZRstudios.com

New York Times bestselling author **Jill Shalvis** lives in a small town in the Sierras full of quirky characters. Any resemblance to the quirky characters in her books is, um, mostly coincidental. Look for Jill's bestselling, award-winning novels wherever books are sold and visit her website, JillShalvis.com, for a complete book list and blog detailing her city-girl-living-in-the-mountains adventures.

Ready to find
your next great read?

Let us help.

Visit prh.com/nextread